11/2 13
14 39
547992

D0483486

Dear Reader,

Bestselling author Theresa Michaels hits her stride this month with the second book in her new Western series featuring the infamous Kincaid brothers. *Once an Outlaw* is the story of a rancher who's been shot and left for dead by an outlaw gang, only to be rescued by two orphan boys who leave him on the doorstep of a young widow. Don't miss this delightful love story that *Affaire de Coeur* calls a "fast-paced, rip-roaring adventure…"

As promised, this month we are very pleased to bring you *The Welshman's Way*, award-winning author Margaret Moore's sequel to *A Warrior's Way*, which earned a 5★ rating from *Affaire de Coeur*. A Welsh rebel rescues a Norman maiden from an unwanted marriage and sets into motion a series of events that will change their lives forever in this extraordinary story!

For Love of Rory is Barbara Leigh's new medieval story of a young woman who forces a wounded Celtic warrior to help her find her kidnapped son. And from Carolyn Davidson, her first book for Harlequin Historicals, *Gerrity's Bride*, a Western marriage-of-convenience story with plenty of fireworks.

Whatever your taste in reading, we hope Harlequin Historicals will keep you coming back for more. Please keep a lookout for all four titles, available wherever books are sold.

Sincerely,

Tracy Farrell

Senior Editor

Please address questions and book requests to:
Harlequin Reader Service
U.S.: 3010 Walden Ave., P.O. Box 1325, Buffalo, NY 14269
Canadian: P.O. Box 609, Fort Erie, Ont. L2A 5X3

THERESA MICHAELS

Once an Outlaw

Harlequin Books

TORONTO • NEW YORK • LONDON
AMSTERDAM • PARIS • SYDNEY • HAMBURG
STOCKHOLM • ATHENS • TOKYO • MILAN
MADRID • WARSAW • BUDAPEST • AUCKLAND

ISBN 0-373-28896-4

ONCE AN OUTLAW

Copyright © 1995 by Theresa DiBenedetto.

Books by Theresa Michaels

Harlequin Historicals

A Corner of Heaven #104
Gifts of Love #145
Fire and Sword #243
*Once a Maverick #276
*Once an Outlaw #296

*The Kincaids

THERESA MICHAELS

is a former New Yorker who resides in South Florida with her husband and daughter—the last of eight children—and three "rescued" cats. Her avid interest in history and her belief in the power of love are combined in her writing. She has received the *Romantic Times* Reviewer's Choice Award for Best Civil War Romance, the National Readers' Choice Award for Best Series Historical and the B. Dalton Bookseller Award for Bestselling Series Historical. When not writing, she enjoys traveling, adding to her collection of Victorian perfume bottles and searching for the elf to master her computer.

To special friends who keep the faith:
Donita, Harriet, Kris, Louise, Maudeen and Shelly

Chapter One

Furious. Frustrated. Failure. These about summed up Logan Kincaid's thoughts and feelings.

It was ironic that he was helping to rob the payroll destined for the workers at the Silver Belt Mine. Ironic, because the mine numbered among his family's holdings in the Arizona Territory.

Sweat trickled down beneath his hat. The blast of the relentless sun turned the small arroyo into a furnace. He hadn't bothered to mask his face with his bandanna. Logan had been cursed with thick, fast-growing facial hair that required daily shaving. Every two days or so these past months, he'd scrape it clean with his blade. Right now the stubble itched.

Known as Lucky, to the outlaws seizing the payroll for the fourth time in as many weeks, Logan suddenly felt a tingling sensation creep up his spine. Unlike his younger brother, Tyrel, Logan didn't always sense the trouble coming his way.

A sweeping gaze up the narrow arroyo revealed scrub brush and rocks. Not a hint of life moved beyond the men grouped around the wagon.

With a jerk of his reins, Logan kept his restive horse in place. He watched as Tallyman—former slave, buffalo soldier, army deserter turned outlaw—used his massive gloved hands to shove the payroll money into two sets of saddlebags. Buckling them closed, Tallyman tossed one set to Monte Wheeler, the man who gave the orders, and the other he secured on his own horse.

The five men hired to guard the payroll were ringed by the other three outlaws. They had been stripped of their boots, guns and hats. Logan kept a sharp eye on Billy Jack Mulero, a true mixed breed of Mexican, Apache and white blood. His bloodshot eyes and fitful moves were signs that he had been chewing mescal buttons again.

Blackleg, on Billy Jack's right, caught Logan looking and high-signed him to watch the breed. No one had been killed in the four robberies in as many weeks. For some reason the outlaws wanted no murders. But no one stopped Billy Jack from taunting the five men.

Logan shut out thoughts of many descriptive ways to let a man die slowly. It had taken nearly six months to infiltrate this gang. He was furious that he had come no closer to discovering who was behind the robberies and cattle-rustling plaguing the Kincaid holdings.

Frustration ate at him. It wasn't a matter of losing silver ore, money and cattle. It was his pride that suffered from his failure to uncover their enemy.

Zach Romal's gravelly voice joined Billy Jack's. Feeling himself watched, Logan didn't dare look away from the youngest of the guards, visibly shaken by the two men's threats. He couldn't ignore the keen edge to the taunts and kept waiting for Monte to signal them to move out.

Each of the previous robberies had gone off without a hitch. Despite a varied and erratic schedule of both the payroll and ore shipments, the gang he rode with had known the exact dates and times. Their accuracy could only come from someone with knowledge of every move Conner Kincaid had planned. Someone damn close to Conner, if Logan was any judge of the way his older brother thought.

He hated the moments when he felt a reluctant admiration for whoever was behind these perfectly executed holdups.

He had a bullet earmarked for the man. Smelling the fear from the five men huddled together as Zach uncoiled his whip, Logan thought about putting a bullet to his hide. But if he made a move to protect these innocent men, he would blow his cover.

He had to do something. His back was twitching and it was more than annoyance with the sweat that rolled down his spine.

"Hey, Monte, round up these cayuses. I'm parched—"

"Who the hell you callin' a cayuse?" Billy Jack demanded.

"You, boy," Logan answered, grinning, as his fingers tightened on the leather. A cayuse was a wild horse, native bred, nondescript, runty, ill-mannered and unreliable. That about described Billy Jack Mulero and Zach Romal except for one added attribute—they were unpredictable.

Zach threw back his head and laughed, coiling his whip in quick, economical moves. "Lucky is right. We waste time."

Monte stared at the man he knew as Lucky. "Something bothering you?"

"Damn right. I've got trouble crawling up my back like a two-bit frail sister on Monday night." Since most saloons that had soiled doves plying their trade in rooms upstairs or out back hardly had business on weekdays, Monte caught his meaning. "We got what we come for, didn't we?" Logan was pushing him now, but he couldn't help it. His back felt as if someone had it in their rifle sight and was already squeezing the trigger.

In a sudden move, one of the guards made a dive for the wagon boot. Tallyman shot him before the man could grab hold of the rifle stashed beneath the seat.

Seeing his body draped over the wagon freed the others from the fear that had gripped them. With snarling rage the four of them lunged for Billy Jack. He was the one closest to them. All hell broke loose. Before Monte could shout an order to ride out, another of the guards went down. Logan was across from Blackleg, who was shooting wildly as his horse reared.

Fire slammed like a rattlesnake without warning. Fire that burned its way into Logan's shoulder. He tried to stop his forward momentum. The sandy bottom of the arroyo blurred. He caught the buckskin's mane with one hand, jerking the gelding around. He thought he heard a high-pitched scream before he dug his spurs into the horse's sides, sending him at a dead run down the narrow arroyo.

* * *

"Do ya think he's dead, Kenny?"

"I dunno. Those men took his boots an' guns. Iffen he's dead he ain't got no use for 'em."

"They took his horse, too."

"Yeah." There was a world of regret in thirteen-year-old Kenny Styles's voice. "Thing is, we can't just let him stay there. Buzzards'll come. Com'on, Marty. We'll bury him just like we did our folks."

"I'm scared. Real scared, Kenny."

"I told you, dead folks can't hurt you. And no more cryin'. Now, give me your hand." It wasn't easy for Kenny to take care of seven-year-old Marty. Not when he'd been the youngest of his family. But all they had now was each other. He'd never admit that holding hands forced him to put aside his own fear.

Climbing out of the rocks where they had hidden as soon as they'd heard the approach of horses, Kenny held tight to his rifle and Marty. They had been on their own for four months.

Down on the flat, they stood side by side and stared at the body of the man the other men had dumped and stripped before they rode away.

"He's awful big, Kenny. We'll be diggin' and diggin' all night to get him buried."

Pressing the butt of his rifle into the earth, Kenny looked around. "Dirt's soft enough. Won't take that long. We can dig around him and underneath. That way we won't have to move him."

"Kenny?"

"Yeah?"

"He's awful mean lookin'." The towheaded little boy took a step closer and squatted with his hands gripping his knees. "Do dead people bleed?"

"How should I know?" Already wielding the rifle butt as a shovel, Kenny kept his eyes on the shallow depression taking shape.

"You figure he's got money?"

"Don't know. Don't care. We ain't got use for it. Ain't nuthin' to buy 'round here. Stop gawkin' an' get to helpin' me, Marty."

"I was just asking. You sure are jumpity. An' we do so got a place to use money." Straightening, then turning to face Kenny, the boy sucked noisily on his lower lip. "We can use it for the widow woman."

"Trade her fair for everthin' we've taken, boy. Left her a mess of fish last week when I took that chicken you were cravin'." Without looking up, he added, "Now stop jawin' an' get to helpin' me."

Marty ran back toward the rocks and returned minutes later with a small flat stab of stone. He eyed the prone body and the deepening depression that Kenny steadily lengthened. The only way for him to dig was to get down on his knees. And that would bring him close to the body. Real close. Too close. He could feel his stomach churn. But he didn't want to be sick. Last time Kenny got mad at him for messing on his clothes.

"You ain't gonna get sick again?"

Marty exhaled noisily, blinking all the while. "How come you always know?"

With a sigh Kenny stopped. He braced both hands over the upright rifle barrel and leveled, on the boy, dark brown eyes too weary for a child. "You get all pasty an' sweaty, boy. I can see you shakin' in your boots from here. I ain't scared. You wanna be like me, don't you?" Marty's nod brought one of his own.

"That's right. You settle your innard's an' get to work."

Kenny started whistling and once more went back to digging. He had neared the man's feet. Anxious to get done and away, he swung the butt faster and faster. He nearly jumped out of his clothes when the foot moved. His heart pounded, and sweat popped out all over his body. It took him long moments before he realized he must have hit the foot with the rifle.

Throwing his head back, he gulped air, warning himself that he had to be the strong one. He couldn't give in to the urge to run. It was at times like this that he most resented having Marty to take care of. If he was alone, he could take off and pretend he'd never seen another dead body.

But he wasn't alone. He wasn't going to run off and leave Marty alone.

"Ken-Kenny?"

"Now what?" Scowling, he shot a look at the younger boy. Marty, ashen-faced, pointed a shaking finger at the man.

"You're lookin' dumbstruck as a turkey in a thunderstorm." Marty started shaking his head back and forth, faster and faster, his finger shaking the same way, so that Kenny was reminded of a schoolteacher scolding him for a naughty prank. But little Marty wasn't any teacher. He hadn't played a prank on anyone for far too long. Surviving was all he had time for these days.

Reluctantly, Kenny followed Marty's finger down to the body. His dark brown eyes widened. Without thought he started backing away. "Holy cow! Get back, Marty. Get away from him! He's still alive!"

Frozen where he stood, Marty couldn't move. "W-what—whata we g-gonna d-do!'

"Jeez. Oh, jeez, I don't know."

"W-we can't l-let him d-die."

The plea in Marty's voice cut through Kenny's fear. "Son of a gun!" he muttered. He didn't know nothing about the kind of wound that bled from the man's shoulder. He'd need a doctor. He'd need care and medicine. He'd need... The widow woman! He squeezed his eyes shut, trying to think of the best thing to do. He didn't want to stay here alone while Marty went to fetch her. He couldn't leave Marty here while he went for the widow woman, either. Damn!

"K-Kenny? K-Kenny. I th-think he's groan—ing!''

"If he's wakin' up, stands to reason he's hurtin'." But even as he answered Marty, Kenny shouldered the rifle in reflex. Aiming it at the man, he squinted down the long barrel. His hands were wet. He could feel sweat plastering his shoulder-length hair to his damp shirt. Jeez, but he was scared.

"You listen up, boy. There's only one thing to do. We got to take him to the widow woman. Can't leave him here alone, 'cause he might die. So you run back to the wagon an' get me Ma's quilt."

"S-supposin' she don't want him?"

"Only a wet-behind-the-ears runt like you would ask somethin' so dumb. She's a woman, ain't she? Pa always said that all a woman wants is some man to take care of her. You heard that man what's come by tryin' to coze up to her. Said she'd been without a man nigh onto a year now. Jus' listen to me. She'll be so happy to have him she'll forget all 'bout us stealin' from her.''

He met Marty's big-eyed look. "Go on with you. Time's a-wastin'. An' bring PeeWee back with you."

Jessie Winslow knew it was a waste of time to open the cash box. Money would not have magically appeared since the last time she had looked. But she opened the small metal tin anyway.

The hot afternoon sun slanted across the smooth, scrubbed wood of the pine table. She ignored the reddened state of her hands as she set aside the list she had made of bare essentials needed if she was to survive the summer and keep the small ranch.

From the box she lifted out her marriage certificate, the deed to the ranch that Harry had insisted be made over to her as a wedding gift, and an empty worn velvet bag. Her mother's silver chatelaine with its thimble holder, scissors, needle case and pincushion hanging from chains attached to the silver scroll pin had gone the way of everything of value. The velvet bag was all she had left. Her brother, Greg, would be furious with her if he knew she had sold the chatelaine and the two horses he had given her.

She glanced around the two-room cabin. The spool-turned rocker was the only furnishing she had brought with her from the hamlet of Kripplebush. Not that she missed the New York countryside. She hadn't had a home there, only a companion's place on her aunt's sufferance. There had been no reason to stay—not that she was encouraged to by her cousin—once her aunt had passed on. Greg and his wife, Livia, had welcomed her to their home, newly set up in the north territory. Jessie had no one but herself to blame that she felt uncomfortable sharing another woman's home and family. Livia would have been happy for her to continue on with them, but Jessie had hungered for a home of her own.

Her mind drifted off along that tangent for a while longer. Memories of Greg's arguments against Harry, her own stubbornness. She had believed that Harry wanted the same things she did. Hindsight had proved her wrong. He had been fixated on finding gold in the Superstition Mountains. He'd had no interest in building the ranch. No matter how she pleaded with him not to go off and leave her alone, he'd cajole and promise that it was the last time, that he was sure that big strike was waiting for him.

Perhaps he had found a gold strike. Jessie would never know. His horse had carried his fever-ridden body home, where he'd died without ever realizing she was there.

Angry, she shook herself free of her musings and returned to the problem at hand.

She was a thirty-year-old widow who owned a broken-down excuse for a ranch without a penny to her name. She had sold everything of value with the exception of Harry's shotgun.

And her wedding ring.

Sunlight glinted on the pinkish gold band as she lifted her left hand. The ring was thin and worn, having belonged to Harry's mother for almost forty years.

Jessie stared at the ring, thinking of her happiness the day Harry had placed it on her finger as they said their vows. She had never once taken it off. But this was the first time she admitted to herself that she wore it as much to protect herself as from sentiment.

Each Sunday after church services that she never attended, David Trainor, a widower and the only person from Apache Junction who did not believe that she had killed Harry, would come to call on her. They sat on the wood plank bench in front of the cabin, David on one end, she on the other, sipping lemonade she made from the lemons that David brought with him. He never came inside. As if she didn't have the most isolated ranch in the area, as if she didn't already have more gossip than anyone else whispered about.

She couldn't fault David, but his insistence on what was proper and what was not irked her at times. As long as she wore her ring, he did no more than hint of his interest in courting her. He timed his visits to last an hour and no more, checking his pocket watch from the moment he arrived to the moment he sat up on his wagon's seat to leave. His last visit had ended with his reminder that her year of mourning would be up at the end of the month.

She had no doubt that David would ask her to marry him. Marry him immediately. He was a sweet, thoughtful man, but she didn't love him. He had a family grown from his first wife, two children from the second and she had no wish to be the third Mrs. Trainor.

In her discouraged state she couldn't deny marrying David would help still the wagging tongues that gossiped she had killed Harry in order to keep for herself the gold mine he had supposedly found.

She only wished that Harry *had* discovered gold. A lot of gold. The small poké filled with tiny nuggets she had discovered hidden in his bedroll had paid for his burying costs and given rise to the whispers.

If she wasn't in such a desperate situation, she believed she would have smiled just thinking about the speculation in Silas Beeson's eyes every time she took courage in hand to go into his mercantile to trade her eggs. He kept expecting her to purchase additional foodstuffs with gold.

This time she wouldn't disappoint him. With a silent prayer asking the Lord for forgiveness, she worked her wedding band from her finger. Clutching it tightly, she closed her eyes.

If she was going to sell it, she should use the money to buy passage back to her brother. The best solution to her problem of trying to keep the ranch going.

But Jessie found she had a deep well of stubbornness. She wasn't ready to give up all she had to claim as her own.

The Lord would provide. The thought forced her eyes open. "*He* already has," she whispered, thinking of the small gifts she had been finding. True, she had also lost some items or a chicken or two, and more than a few eggs. But her unseen and unknown benefactor had provided her with fresh fish, rabbit, even venison.

The stubborn spirit that had gotten her into this brine barrel revived. Somehow she'd find a way.

Deeply engrossed in thought, Jessie jumped when she realized someone or something was thumping on the far outside wall of the cabin.

With the thought of her benefactor's gifts in mind, she wasn't unduly alarmed as she rose and went to the door. Bolting it had become habit after she'd found a rattlesnake warming itself on the hearth rug. She lifted the heavy bolt and set it aside.

Jessie caught herself pausing with her hand on the latch. Shaking off the momentary warning pang, she opened the door.

"Oh, my Lord!" The words were a whisper of sound. She sucked in a sharp, frightened breath. She pressed one hand to her chest. Instinctively her startled gaze searched the clearing in front of the cabin before coming to rest on the bundle on her doorstep.

If this was her benefactor's idea of a gift, Jessie didn't want it.

The very last thing she needed in her life was a man. A wounded man, at that!

From his vantage point on top of the shed roof, Kenny nodded with satisfaction. He slid backward and dropped to the ground.

"Tole you, Marty. She's so taken aback, the widow woman's cryin' with joy. Now she's got herself a man."

Chapter Two

Logan didn't want to open his eyes. Opening his eyes, moving, any acknowledgment that he was awake would swing wide the door to pain. More pain than the dull, throbbing ache pulsing through his body. Waking up would act as a whetstone honing an edge to pain until it was knife keen.

But there were scents that drew him. Faint, almost elusive. He thought he could smell sunshine and clean, soft linen. Damn foolish thought, but he was a man who liked his comforts and he'd been too long without them.

Tempted to discover if he was dreaming, he opened his eyes and closed them immediately. He'd been right about the pain. He waited until the edge was off, then opened his eyes cautiously this time. No unwise moves, he warned himself, that razor edge is just waiting for you.

The little he could see alerted him that he didn't know where the hell he was. The last time he remembered his eyes being open, a blazing ball of sunlight had blinded him.

Instinct that he was safe, at least for now, eased the flare of panic. He was in a clean bed, with a soft pillow beneath his drumming head.

He sure wasn't in heaven, or he wouldn't be hurting. Couldn't be in hell. Santo swore the devil would hold a fiesta for him when he arrived there. So he concluded he was alive. Alive with someone caring for him.

Who?

It was a question Logan needed answered. He knew he wasn't with the gang. Monte was the only one who knew what clean meant.

This much thought built the throbbing aches in his body and sent him close to the edge where he couldn't control the pain.

He forced himself to be calm, closing his eyes, and willed the tension to leave his body as he lay perfectly still. Struggling for answers wasn't going to do him a bit of good. Rest would help him. A simple order for him to follow.

Despite his effort, his thoughts returned to the moment he'd been shot. At his side, his hand curled tightly as if still gripping the reins and the thick, coarse mane of his gelding for a flat-out run. Behind a gauzy mind curtain, the blur of passing land and voices wavered out of reach.

Logan did remember a blow to the skull that set off a whorl of bursting colors before his eyes. And he felt again that stomach-dropping sensation of falling. He'd blacked out.

And that blackness beguiled him again.

He fought it off. He couldn't afford to rest easy, despite the pain, despite an instinctive need to heal his beaten body. He had to find out where he was, and who played Good Samaritan.

The feather tick cushioning his body bespoke softness. Anything soft brought instant association with anything female.

He should be so lucky. He denied it. He wanted to keep on denying it. After all, how could a woman move him?

He tried to gauge the size of the cabin. Wide-beam rafters laced the ceiling. Nothing strange, nothing at all unusual. Didn't tell him a damn thing. He'd have to move his head to see more. His body and will clashed over the pain that would cause.

He wrinkled his nose, sniffing the air. Sure smelled like chicken soup. Enticed, he had no choice. Eyes slowly opened, and he eased his head to the side. A burst of loud pounding came from inside his skull.

Logan blinked, looked, then blinked again. He wished for the strength to lift his hand to rub his eyes. A futile thought. Moving his head had cost him, in spades.

A blur of sunshine caught his attention. But it was the damnedest sun he'd ever seen. Sunshine didn't rise from the floor in the craziest bell-shaped curves. Sunshine—sure as he lay helpless as a pea on a hot skillet—didn't sway to and fro.

He was as parched as a dried-up mud hole and couldn't call out. The totally helpless feeling brought a rapid anger. Marshaling his formidable will, he started to sit up. An unwise move. The drum in his head was banging away and its resounding echo lanced through him to take up residence in his shoulder. The room dipped and swirled. With one foot he felt the bareness of the other. At least someone had taken off his boots before putting him to bed. Why that mattered, he didn't know.

He moaned and laid his head back on the pillow.

"Thank the Lord! You're awake!"

Sunshine had a voice. Sunshine moved toward him. Maybe he had died and gone to heaven and this was an angel of mercy coming to his side.

Her next words disabused him of that foolish notion.

"Quick, before you pass out again, tell me who you are and where you belong. I'll ride into town and get a telegram off so someone can come and get you."

Hell, he'd never expected to be welcomed to the pearly gates, but he sure hadn't figured on getting thrown out if he ever made it up that far. Some angel this was turning out to be.

"Lo—" He stopped himself, fighting against the waves of pain. He couldn't tell her who he was. He couldn't trust anyone. There wasn't a speck of moisture in his mouth. Dragging his hand up, he didn't stifle the moans, but motioned toward his mouth. He had to close his eyes against the bobbing of her head.

"Thirsty? Of course you are. Stay right there."

If he'd had the strength, Logan would have cussed her. As if he could move . . . What the hell had he gotten himself into this time? It had all the earmarks of a vinegar crock and he the one being pickled.

She was back before he formed more thoughts. He forgave her his uncharitable thought the moment cool water touched his dry lips. He swallowed every drop greedily then fell back against the pillow with a deep sigh.

"Better?" Jessie asked. "Can you talk now?"

Logan decided his charity had been misplaced. She wasn't an angel but a harpy. He kept his eyes closed. But he couldn't rid his mind of the image that she was all sunshine. It was the hair. Parted in the middle, pulled back from her face, there was just enough to show him the tawny color of a mountain lion's coat. Her bright yellow gown put sunshine in his head. The effort to think expended his strength, and left him hurting and exhausted. If he ignored her long enough maybe she'd go away.

"Don't drift off again," Jessie warned in a disgruntled voice. Her sweeping gaze over his long, supine body brought back her first thought about him. He was built like a whip, long, lean, tough and lethal.

"Surely you can manage to tell me your name? Or where you're from? What happened to you?" Thoroughly vexed when he didn't respond, she chewed her bottom lip.

She had to stop herself from reaching out to brush the damn curling strands of his dark brown, almost black hair away from his forehead. She'd done her share of petting and touching while she cleaned his wound. And she'd spent a good deal of time studying the fierce line of his nose and jaw, trying to determine why she found him attractive when those roughly cut features suggested a harsh, ruthless nature.

"It wasn't much of a guess on my part to figure out that you'd been shot and robbed." She watched him for any betraying signs. "Thing is, I've had time to wonder if you were being robbed or doing the robbing." She nearly pounced at the flicker of his eyelids.

"I see," she drawled in a honey-thick voice, "that I've finally gained your attention."

The man made a sound somewhere between a grunt and a groan. A response for sure, but not the one she had hoped for.

"You've been in my bed all night," she offered helpfully. "Don't you want to know who I am?" Her softly voiced questions elicited another flicker of his lids. "I won't hurt you. Don't be concerned that you're in any danger."

Watching him as closely as she was, Jessie saw his fingers relax. Mentally she backed off from questioning him further. She'd been harsh to push him now.

But she couldn't escape the need to have him gone.

"Would you like some chicken soup? It's almost ready."

Logan, to his mortification, suddenly discovered he had another, more pressing need to attend. One of his bleary eyes opened, squinting as he focused on the woman. Neither an angel nor a harpy, he'd decided in the past few minutes.

But how was he to convey his need to her? He just couldn't ask. He couldn't get up and he sure as hell—

"Something's wrong! Oh, dear. Is the pain worse? I only had my headache powder to give you. Would you like another? Are you thirsty again?"

No response but that one bloodshot eye staring up at her. She nibbled her lip, deep in thought.

"We must figure out a way for you to communicate with me, since you can't speak. Or won't," she added, shooting him a suspicious, narrow-eyed glare.

"If you can open and close that eye, we'll use that. Open is yes and closed means no. Think you can manage?"

Logan didn't close his eye. His head was clearing, at least to where the pounding receded to a dull ache, but his shoulder didn't bear thinking about. His Good Samaritan was rather tall for a woman. Her features were rather plain taken one by one. The apron she wore helped define her lush figure. She didn't appear to be a woman who needed headache powders...but what did he know?

And if she persisted in asking these ridiculous questions about his head hurting, or the pillow being too hard, by the time she got farther down his body she wouldn't have to ask what was wrong.

"You got a pot?"

The rusty growl startled Jessie. She was in the act of leaning closer, and straightened with a militant gleam in her eye.

"So, you can talk. Well, to answer you, of course I've got a pot. I said I was cooking, didn't I?"

"An empty one."

"An empty one," she repeated. Her gaze flew down to the crease of his thighs. She swallowed. "An empty one," she repeated again, diving beneath the bed and coming up with the chamber pot. "One empty pot."

And she fled.

"Come back here!" As a demand, Logan knew it lacked something. A little force, a whole lot of loud. She was a harpy, bent on torturing him. How the hell was he going to use the damn pot without help?

Jessie ran all the way to the corral. Embarrassed didn't begin to cover what she felt. Guilt wormed its way into her thoughts. She shouldn't have run off like a sixteen-year-old virgin who didn't know that a wounded man would use a chamber pot. He'd hurt himself. Lord!

Flinging one arm on the pole fence of the corral, Jessie buried her face in the crook of her elbow. She was not a cruel woman. She truly wasn't. But now that the first flush of embarrassment was passing, she admitted she'd been wrong to leave him alone. If she had any backbone she'd march right back into her cabin and face her unwanted boarder. She should apologize, and while she was at it, think of some reason beyond impropriety that had sent her fleeing like a ninny.

Feeling a nudge against her arm, Jessie reached out with her free hand. "Oh, Adorabelle, I've made a muddle of this."

The swaybacked mare's thick lips and velvet-soft muzzle pressed against her arm.

"I know you're not concerned. But I am. I'm the one who has to go back inside and face him." A gentle nip of teeth forced Jessie to look up. Stroking the mare's white-blazed face, she shook her head. "I'm sorry, darling, there's no sugar left."

The decrepit old mare greeted this news with a snort, her ears flicking back and forth. Jessie smiled. Her horse almost appeared to be waiting for confirmation of what was said.

"We are in poor straits, Adorabelle." A glance behind her reminded Jessie that a decent amount of time had passed. Sooner or later, she had to go back inside the cabin.

After wiping her hands on her apron, Jessie patted the mare once more, then executed a sharp turn on her heels.

"This is my cabin. I have nothing to apologize for. He is here on my sufferance. And I am an independent woman who no longer accounts to anyone for my behavior."

She repeated her reminders all the way inside.

Finding her unwanted houseguest facedown on the floor next to her bed sent a sharp pang of guilt through her.

Jessie ran to his side and dropped to the floor. Smoothing his hair away from his face, she pleaded with him to speak to her.

He was clammy to her touch and white about the mouth. Guilt pangs drove deeper. "Forgive me. Please forgive me. I'm going to help you back to bed," she murmured, heartsick that her embarrassment had caused him additional pain.

She was almost afraid to touch the bandage she had made for his shoulder. The only other place for her hand was his bare skin. Jessie had avoided looking at the dark, curling hair on his chest earlier. But she couldn't avoid looking and touching him now.

"Be brave," she muttered, unsure if she meant it for him or herself.

Logan gave a brief thought to pretending that he'd blacked out again. But her contrite tone, combined with the gentle stroking of her hand and the fact that he'd attempted to struggle back to bed alone, forced his eyes open.

"I'm alive. It was touch and go—"

"Mister!" Jessie snatched her hand away from him.

He ignored her even as he realized how she had taken his words. "I survived."

"I may not."

Logan peered up at the tart-as-green-berries pursed lips. Now he understood.

"You're one of those."

"One of what?" she demanded.

"Ain't had much truck with men."

"If you are implying that I'm a dour spinster, mister, you're wrong. I'm a missus. See?" Jessie stuck her left hand in his face. "That ring is a symbol that a man found me worthy of marriage, mister. And since you find yourself in the position of being dependent upon my good graces, best be careful of what you say to me."

"Right, ma'am. Your husband...er...is he around?"

"No. That should be obvious. And having this conversation on the floor is ridiculous. Up you go."

For all that she spoke with a tart tongue, her hands were very gentle as she slid one of his arms over her shoulder, and wrapped her own arm around his narrow waist.

Logan managed to grunt his way to his knees. She seemed to understand what the effort cost him, for she made no move to push him.

He breathed deeply, gathering up the last reserves of his strength. Once again, without speaking, she appeared to know that he was ready for the final move.

Jessie's hands slid on his sweat-damp skin. His chest labored with every breath he drew and her own was none too steady. She braced her legs to make the last move to get him into bed. He was heavy despite his whipcord-lean appearance.

She realized that she was still leaning over him, and slowly straightened. Arching her back, she rubbed the small of her back, feeling the pull of muscles.

"We made it."

Logan, feeling like a fish that had been tossed from a stream and flopped about without oxygen for too long, merely moved one finger. It was all he was capable of doing at the moment.

Shoving the loose tendrils of hair that had come free from her coil, Jessie realized the damp spots beneath her arms showed. Mortified, although she didn't understand why since his eyes were closed, she locked her arms down at her sides to hide the dampness.

Her position was awkward as she leaned over and studied his bandaged shoulder. "Thank goodness you didn't cause it to bleed again. Though," she mused, more to herself, "I put enough pine tar—"

"Pine tar? You put pine tar *on me?*" Logan's teeth came together with a snap. "Lady," he went on without opening his eyes, "I'm not some damn tree you're getting ready to graft. I'm a damn man." *Jeez, was she blind?*

"You sure are a damn man," she muttered. "I can see perfectly well that you're an ornery male who wouldn't know what was good for you if it sat up and bit you on the...the...well, somewhere! Not only are you male, but you're wounded. I hate to remind you, but you're rather quick to jump to conclusions for *a man* who is dependent upon me for care. It's obvious to me, *as a woman,* that you, *being a damn man—*

your words, not mine—wouldn't know the many uses for pine tar from green apples.''

Oh, Lord! Button up, Logan. She has a testy tone in that vinegary mouth. Pine tar, for Pete's sake? Where the hell had she come from? Likely he was on the road to dying with her supposed care of his wound.

Nodding to herself as she straightened, Jessie was satisfied that he was going to heed her reprimand, and so continued to explain what she had done to his wound.

"After I dragged your quilt-wrapped body from my doorstep—"

"What?" Logan's eyes snapped open. Despite his helpless state, he managed to target her face with all the pent-up anger and frustration inside him.

"I...said," she repeated slowly and testily, "that...I dragged . . . your quilt-wrapped body—"

"I heard that part, lady." Damn! Confusion held sway over his thoughts. He remembered the blow to his head. Remembered waking dazed to that blazing sun overhead, but he was as sure as the Lord made this woman to vex man that no one had wrapped him in a quilt.

That was an act of kindness. Kindness was not a word familiar to the outlaws he'd ridden with. Just witness the way they'd dumped him once he was wounded.

Or had that been the only reason that they'd gotten rid of him? The ache in his head intensified with the sudden forced concentration of his thoughts.

Had they somehow discovered his real name?

No. He dismissed it. If they knew who he was, they would have killed him, not just left him for dead.

Tapping her high-buttoned shoe with impatience, Jessie said, "Do I take your silence as a wish for me to continue?"

"Yeah. Go ahead, lady, and tell me."

Jessie couldn't help it. She glanced heavenward and rolled her eyes. Not the most gracious person she had ever come across. Instantly she chided herself for the uncharitable thought. Putting herself in his place, she knew how anxious she would be. With a heartfelt sigh she strove to make allowances for his display of temper due to his wounds and the poor man's obvious confusion as to how he had arrived on her doorstep.

As if he had read her thoughts, Logan asked, "Did your husband find me?"

"No." As an answer it left something to be desired. Jessie studied the rough, beamed ceiling, the chinked, logged walls, even the wide-planked floor. She stared blankly at the nicks and scratches in the bureau. She avoided the mirror.

In those few minutes she discovered that her guest had a great deal of patience. He waited. True, he was watching her the whole time, but he didn't say a word.

She warned herself to answer him carefully. Pointing out her wedding ring had been an act of protection and, she admitted, feminine pique. Her vanity, the little she had, had taken enough woundings in years past. She knew how plain she was, how her ripe figure did not meet fashion's dictates. She'd heard as much and more from the few men who deemed her suitable to court when she had lived with her aunt. Harry, bless his departed soul, had never once made a disparaging remark about her looks.

Her chin lifted. Her mouth firmed with the reminder that she didn't have to tolerate anything from this man.

"So," Logan said when her gaze returned to his, "you're the one who found me, lady?"

"My name is Mrs. Winslow. And I already said that I found you on my doorstep."

"Little early for Christmas."

"I don't consider you a gift, mister."

Jessie fought the temptation to explain at length about her unknown and unseen benefactor. Although her wounded, unwanted houseguest carried no gun, he was a stranger who had revealed a tendency toward a surly nature. Like a man who was used to giving orders. The stray thought distracted her.

Logan, still watching her, became fascinated with the way she nibbled her lower lip. First she licked the spot, then drew it between small, even teeth. He had just realized that she tended to do this a lot. A nervous habit that gave a little away about Mrs. Winslow. She wasn't as calm as she appeared. Her remark about him not being considered a gift rankled. Since he was in no position to argue, he was forced to wait patiently until he had her focused attention once more.

Jessie glared at him. Her unknown benefactor had been goodness itself until yesterday. She wasn't in a mood to extend forgiveness to whoever it was. Any more of this man's scowls and she might never be ready to forgive.

Sensing he was fast losing ground with her, Logan strove for a hopeful expression. He had a feeling that if he pushed too much, Mrs. Winslow might toss him back outside.

"So, uh, ma'am—"

"Yes?"

"Tell me what your husband thinks of you taking me in?"

Jessie's gaze turned thoughtful. She didn't trust his grin. She couldn't lie to him. She hated lies and the people who told them. Harry had been an accomplished liar. Always promising her it was the last time he'd spend money to buy some phony map. Promising it was the last time he'd go prospecting for gold. That he'd always be around to take care of her. Ha! So much for men and their lies!

"We'll have to wait to find out what my husband thinks." *A long wait. Longer than either of us will live.*

Uncomfortable with his omissions of who he was and that she had nothing to fear from him, Logan nonetheless couldn't abide someone lying to his face.

"Oh, lady, you're good, but not good enough. So we're gonna wait to find out what your husband thinks? There ain't been a man around here in a long time."

If his head hadn't hurt so much Logan would have laughed. Her mouth dropped open to a soundless O.

Gotcha, lady!

Chapter Three

Jessie rolled over for the third time. Double thick quilts cushioned her body from the hard floor where she made her bed. She still fumed over her inept handling of her guest. She spoke only when necessary, although treating him to a silent study lacked a certain flair. She had refused to admit the truth. Not that it seemed to matter to him.

The man intimidated her.

A ridiculous thought when she considered that he was helpless and wounded, but it was nonetheless true. She didn't like feeling intimidated. All her life she had been dominated by strong-willed people. Now that she was free, or had been until he showed up, she had believed that no one could do that to her again.

Resentment flared that *he* had proved her wrong.

He had told her his name was Logan.

Right after he thanked her for the soup, her care and giving him her bed.

He had even sounded sincere.

No softening, Jessie.

I am not softening, she argued with herself, I am simply making an observation. He has a very nice smile, too. If there had been any softening going on, the smile had accomplished it. His harsh features appeared a great deal softer, almost handsome. Certainly attractive...

You're softening, Jessie, the little nag warned.

Go to sleep and then maybe I can, too. With that said, she rolled over once again.

How was a man supposed to get any sleep with her twisting and turning and thumping about on the floor? Those weren't the only reasons Logan lay awake, but they were the ones he concentrated on. Anything to distract himself from the pain in his shoulder.

His prissy Samaritan claimed there was no bullet lodged there. Said the wound had bled profusely. Even showed him his bloodstained shirt, which she'd then washed and mended. She hadn't had much more to say to him after he'd caught her in her lie.

He didn't understand why he was still thinking about her. He had more pressing matters that demanded his attention.

There was something about the way her gaze met his, something about the way she lifted her rounded chin when she challenged him.

She didn't lack spirit.

Spirit was a good thing to have...in a horse. His women he liked accommodating. And she was on the plump side. There again, he usually liked a woman the way he liked his steaks, on the lean side and a little raw. She had an easterner's bite on her words. Rawness might shock her. Didn't appear to have a dependent bone in her lush body.

Quit thinking about her body.

Guess I'm on the mend.

Well, remember that her tongue would spur any man who called himself one to move on.

Is that what had happened to Mr. Winslow?

If there had been a Mr. Winslow.

He could still envision her mouth falling open. A rather nice mouth, he recalled. Wide and generous, the type given to easy laughter.

Dumb, fanciful thought!

From what he had seen of her cabin, it hadn't taken much to determine that a man hadn't been around—if ever—in a long time. The pegs on the wall revealed a woman's trappings—shawl, gown and a floppy felt hat. There was a small wooden chest beneath the window, carved with pretty birds and flowers. A woman's possession, for sure.

He hadn't spotted a razor strop hanging on the wall.

No, he decided, there wasn't a man living here with her.

Logan lifted his hand and rubbed his bearded face. He felt stronger after two bowls of her chicken soup.

"Mr. Logan?"

Her voice flowed out of the dark and startled him.

"Told you, it's just Logan."

"Logan, then. If you can't sleep, I could mix one of my headache powders for you."

"Didn't realize I was making so much noise that I woke you."

"Oh, you didn't. I haven't been asleep. I've been thinking."

Logan didn't like the sound of that.

Jessie ignored his silence and continued. "You never said what you were doing in these parts. You never mentioned how you were shot. Don't you think you owe me some answers?"

"I'm not real sure where it is I am exactly." Keep calm and do a little thinking of your own. Preferably fast.

"Outside of Apache Junction," she offered helpfully.

A ways north of the mine. Logan blocked out the sound of her voice. He couldn't remember the outlaws ever heading this far north before. Were they going to a new hideout? Or finally meeting with the man behind the robberies? Damn! That he should lie here helpless as a babe when these were the answers he sought.

Even deep in his own thoughts, Logan became instantly aware that tension rolled across the cabin. Since Mrs. Winslow was the only other occupant, he figured that it came from her.

"What's wrong?" he whispered, wishing he had his gun.

"Didn't you hear it?"

"What?"

"The noises coming from outside. I bet it's the henhouse again."

He could barely make out her shadow, up and moving. Sounds of shells being rammed home alerted him to her intent.

"You're going out there?"

"I don't see anyone else around here willing to protect my property. I need those laying hens."

"But—" She had the door unbolted and herself on the other side of it before he struggled to sit up. "Damn! And double damn!"

Cursing relieved some tension. Every move proved a struggle for him. He couldn't stop thinking about who might be out there. There was no time to waste. He wouldn't put it past Monte Wheeler to come back or send someone back to make sure he was dead.

And she was out there alone.

His bare foot slammed into a bench near the door. Swearing up a silent storm, he shoved the bench out of his way just as a blast rocked the night.

"Damn that woman! She's likely to get herself killed!"

Head pounding, shoulder throbbing and his foot sending shooting pains up his leg, Logan scrambled to yank the door open.

Jessie flung herself inside.

They hit the floor in a tangled heap. Logan lost his breath for a few moments, then his renewed cursing melded with her mutterings.

The second she attempted to untangle herself he bellowed with pain. The hot shotgun barrel pressed against the bare skin of his arm.

"Oh, I'm sorry. I didn't mean..." Jessie tossed the gun across the floor, where it landed with a clatter.

"Here, let me, ah, let me..." Her voice trailed away.

With a great deal of gulping, Jessie took stock of the exact position of each body part that belonged to her, and where its counterpart—his bodily counterpart— met hers.

Her bare feet inched along the inside of his legs. Her knees were cradled between his spread thighs. Their position had gone beyond impropriety to indecent. Her nose pressed against his chest. Hot, damp skin wet her nightgown.

"Lord," she muttered, "this is as sticky as divinity fudge."

That's one way of putting it, lady.

Jessie strained to make sense of his noises. She wasn't sure where to brace herself so she could get off him. His grumbling held a desperate note. Maybe she was hurting him.

A year of handling all the chores and repairs on her own had strengthened her muscles. Jessie blessed that strength as she spread her hands on either side of his shoulders and managed to lift herself a bit.

"Th-thank God. You...were smothering me."

Well, it was all fine and dandy for him. But now she could feel herself pressing from the waist down against his body.

"Look, lady, you need to move."

"I know! I'll go to the right and you move to the left. Ready?"

"Yeah."

Jessie inched her upper body to the right. And froze. Something very warm touched her breast through her nightgown. It was too soft to be his nose, although she felt his breath real close by. That left his mouth dampening the cotton, heating the skin beneath.

"Tart berries," Logan muttered under his breath.

"What?"

"Start moving, I said."

"Yes. I am. Right now." She flung herself to the side and lay on her back. It had been his mouth, and she forced herself not to reach up and touch the place he had kissed. *Kissed? You're imagining things.*

Oh, no, I'm not. She eyed his sprawled figure next to her in the dark. Tart berries, indeed!

"What were you shooting at?"

"The henhouse." *Had he really kissed* . . .

"That doesn't make any sense," Logan prompted. He knew he shouldn't have taken advantage—no, that wasn't right. He didn't take advantage. Her nipple was just *there*. But she'd known. He still heard that funny sound she'd made. Startled, almost. As if she couldn't believe he'd done that.

Should she say something? Jessie shook her head. She couldn't. She simply could not say a word.

"Are you all right? You didn't get hurt rushing out there, did you?"

"No." That much was true. Jessie had been so mad that she'd hardly felt the stones beneath her bare feet. A strangely warm feeling unfurled inside at the thought that he had cared to ask. She didn't remember anyone but her brother or his wife expressing concern about her.

Somehow, she wasn't surprised when he enfolded her hand in his. She was calmer now, her thinking clear. She knew she should be the one to make a move to get up. His silent comfort, his being someone to share with after being alone for so long, filled a need she wasn't aware of having until this moment.

Logan fought a silent battle with himself. His body demanded rest, his mind insisted that he try questioning her. The need to know ruled him.

"This ever happen before?"

"A few times. It started a few months ago." There was something else she should be remembering, but couldn't seem to focus on what it was.

Tension seeped out of Logan. It wasn't Monte, or any of the others, come back for him. He wished he had the strength to move. The floor was hard and he was hurting. The door remained open. And he couldn't forget the lush weight of her pressed against him.

Lured by the dark intimacy, Jessie whispered a confession. "The other times I wasn't frightened, but tonight I could swear that something growled at me. That never happened before."

"Growled?" Logan struggled to angle his head to the side so he could see her. Worry was evident in her voice. "You mean the way a dog growls?"

"I couldn't be sure. It all happened so fast. When I hear the hens squawk I usually go outside and shoot the gun in the air. It seems to chase off whoever or whatever is out there. The hens get upset. That means no eggs tomorrow. I just hope I won't find another of the hens gone."

"If you're still worried, I'll take a look outside." Logan knew his offer was ridiculous. If he couldn't move from the floor, he'd be in no condition to go roaming around outside.

Jessie was having the same thoughts. Wisely she held her tongue. There was no sense pointing out the obvious to him.

"I think the best place for you is in bed. Whatever disturbed the hens is gone, or you'd hear my rooster."

"You know, I don't feel comfortable with the idea of you sleeping on the floor. You take the bed and I'll bunk down—"

"You can't. I mean, I won't let you risk catching a chill. In your weakened state that could bring on a fever."

Jessie freed her hand from his. She scrambled to her feet and hoped his night vision wasn't good. It was silly to worry now, but her nightgown was worn from washing. She felt exposed standing while he lay there, but she couldn't avoid offering him a hand to get up.

Logan eyed her extended hand. He wanted to refuse her help. He had thought she was softening a little toward him, but her last words were lightly coated with tartness again. And it went against his grain to need a woman to help him stand. But refusing would only spite himself.

He drew a deep breath and braced himself for the pain. Catching hold of her hand, he lunged upward.

Jessie caught him as he stood swaying, wrapping her arms around his narrow waist. She took the weight of the arm he slung over her shoulders. She could almost feel his resistance to leaning on her as she led him toward the bed.

Despite the cool night air, his body was warm. She hadn't thought much about touching his bare skin before, but noticed the play of muscles beneath her palms. He was lean and hard. She felt the dampness of her palms slide over his waist and belly as he moved to lower himself to the bed. Her heart was pounding and she knew better than to fool herself that it was helping him that caused it. Harry had always been covered up, either with a shirt or his nightshirt. She couldn't remember him ever encouraging her to touch his body.

Instinct warned that Logan would not only encourage a woman to touch him, he'd like and expect it.

Jessie, don't go off on a tangent and start getting ideas about him. He's a moving-on kind of man. He'll be ready to go in a few days. Keep that in mind.

She backed away from the bed and barred the door before finding her way to her own bed.

Logan heard the rustling of the quilts as she settled down to sleep. "You're a brave woman, Mrs. Winslow. Guess I got lucky after all."

The last made no sense to her, so she ignored it. "Good night, Logan. And it's Jessie. Somehow Mrs. Winslow sounds too formal now."

"Jessie, then." Logan found himself smiling. *Jessie.* The name suited her. A foolish notion to have when he had to grit his teeth as the throbbing in his arm renewed itself.

He had to keep in mind that his job wasn't finished.

She had trembled as she held him.

The thought surfaced and stayed.

This is crazy, he told himself. He felt the subtle changes in his body, the sexual tightening that a desirable, available woman often brought him. He had no right to feel like this. As if to reinforce his conclusion, he broke out in a stomach-churning cold sweat. The moment of sexual awareness that Jessie had caused disappeared.

Wouldn't have done him a lick of good to let things progress on their natural course. He was weak as a newly hatched chick, helpless as a freshly dropped calf, and she'd helped him to bed. If he'd started anything, Jessie would have had to help him all the way.

Tantalizing as the thought was, Logan couldn't avoid figuring what he was going to do once he'd recovered and could travel.

He had an added score to settle with Monte and the others for stealing his horse, his gun and rifle, and his belt buckle. He was right partial to his horse and weapons. A man broke those to the feel of his own hand.

A stay-around kind of man had the pleasure of knowing his woman was partial to the touch of his hand.

Logan frowned in the dark. Where had that stray thought come from? Surely he wasn't still thinking about Jessie?

He couldn't be. He wouldn't allow thoughts of her to interfere.

An attempt to shift position ended in frustration. He hated sleeping on his back. His brothers teased him that his belly-down position, arms and legs flung to the four corners, made him look like a splayed frog that hogged the bed. But that teasing had happened in the days before little brother Ty had had a bellyful of Conner's orders and had lit out for parts unknown.

It was a major source of friction between him and Conner. His older brother had never indulged in the horseplay with him and Ty, never got rip-roaring drunk on Saturday night. But Conner was steady as a rock. And Conner held people to their promises.

He would be going crazy if Logan didn't get in touch with him soon. Conner wasn't going to be happy to learn that he'd got himself shot and lost his gear.

He could still hear Conner's warning the day he had left the ranch. *Get what you're going after, but don't get killed.*

Well, he hadn't gotten himself killed, thanks to Jessie Winslow. But he sure as hell hadn't got what he'd been after.

One more mess-up for Conner to shake his head over. But only if he went home with his tail between his legs.

He'd find a way. Somehow, he would.

"What happened, Kenny? You said she'd be so happy having a man. Didn't you? How come she shot at you? How come, huh?"

"Jeez, you an' your questions. Don't you ever stop with 'em?" Kenny, more frightened than he cared to admit to Marty, nursed his swollen thumb. He'd figured that widow woman would be so busy taking care of the wounded man that he could steal some eggs or a hen. She'd scared the dickens out of him when she'd come out and let that big shotgun of hers go off. He'd slammed the henhouse door on his thumb, dropped the two eggs he had managed to find and got pecked on the cheek by the rooster.

It appeared that she got madder than one of her hens when it got wet.

Climbing into the wagon that was their home, Kenny knew he wasn't going to tell Marty about the man he'd seen nosing around the widow's shed. No sense in both of them worrying. And he didn't want more questions that he couldn't answer.

Could be, he thought as he blew out the lantern and stretched out on his bed, that they had brought the widow woman more than a man. They might have given her a passel of trouble.

Chapter Four

Logan, Jessie decided two days later, led a charmed life. And a dangerous one, she reminded herself as she recalled the smaller, old scars on his body. He hadn't regained anywhere near the full use of his arm, but his wound was healing at a rapid pace. After she had cleaned and bandaged it this morning, she had told him she wouldn't use any more of the pine tar salve.

Thankful that there had been no more attempts to steal her hens or their eggs, Jessie scattered feed to them. She couldn't stop thinking how little she had learned about Logan beyond a few personal likes and dislikes.

He wasn't a fussy eater. He was polite, always offering some compliment about a meal, or her gentle touch. Sincere compliments, too. Someone had taken time to teach him manners. He took his coffee black with lots of sugar, and when she informed him there wasn't any, he apologized for asking.

He was a man used to doing things for himself. Accepting her help for the simplest tasks bothered him. His total lack of expecting her to wait on him forced her to see Logan in another light. Her brother was the only other man like this that she knew.

Jessie threw another handful of seed to the hens, checked to make sure the gate was securely latched and headed back to the shed.

Admonishing herself not to be so curious about Logan didn't do a bit of good.

Setting the feed bucket down, she eyed the few bales of hay left for Adorabelle. She couldn't put off going to town to sell her ring. Just as she couldn't put off riding out to see her small herd of cattle. Taking the halter down from its peg, Jessie went back outside to the corral.

A quick look showed that the cabin door was open, but there was no sign of Logan. She had made a spur-of-the-moment decision last night and hauled out the trunk of Harry's possessions she had stored away. Logan now had a few shirts and pants to wear, ill fitting unfortunately, since Harry was shorter and heavier. But Logan had a pair of boots to wear. Harry was buried in all new clothing. Upon reflection she wondered if it had been a foolish, empty gesture to use all his gold on a burial.

The one item in the trunk that she hadn't been able to bring herself to give Logan was Harry's gun. Something held her back.

Adorabelle, bless her, stood placidly awaiting Jessie's attention.

Logan called her.

"Water's boiling."

"Be right there," she answered. How could she forget that she had promised to shave him? Once she had hidden the gun in the shed and dragged the trunk outside, Logan had pounced on the strop and razor lying on top of the folded clothes.

Walking back to the cabin, Jessie added cleanliness to the list she mentally kept about him.

She spared him a glance where he sat at the table, the basin, strop, towel and razor laid out neatly in front of him.

"It's real kind of you to take the time to do this for me, Jessie. I tried to strop the razor but that's a two-handed job."

"I don't mind. If I did, I wouldn't have offered." *Please, Lord, guide my hand. Don't let him know I've never shaved a man before now.*

The whistling kettle warned that she had no time left to dither about it. Logan didn't hide his anticipation as she poured the boiling water into the basin.

One look at Jessie's trembling mouth as she began to strop the razor, and Logan promptly forgot about his shave.

The more time he spent with Jessie, the less control he had over his response to her. Even something as simple as watching her graceful moves around the table was enough to distract him from whatever he was thinking or doing.

The reaction was unaccountable. She didn't flirt with him. Logan wondered if she even knew how to. But he'd caught her sneaking looks at him, and more than once he was surprised to see a sensual curiosity in her gaze.

When she gave him the trunk belonging to her deceased husband he no longer questioned that she'd been married. But the longer he was around her, the more it bewildered him that she revealed a certain discomfort with their enforced intimacy. It didn't make sense. Just some tantalizing, vague feeling that he had about her.

He thought of his parents, and of Santo and Sofia, who had come with his mother when she married. There were always whispers and looks shared between husband and wife, hinting of secrets shared. Not that he expected Jessie to share secrets or special looks with him. But she didn't seem to know how to respond to simple compliments about her cooking or the little things that she did to make him comfortable.

Since he'd never courted a woman, and wasn't about to begin, Logan knew he should keep his own curiosity under wraps. A week or so and he'd be ready to leave.

Jessie, he had learned, wasn't a woman to bed and then walk away from.

Besides, she'd let drop enough hints that she wasn't in the market for another husband or a man in her life.

If the need to get on with what he'd set out to do hadn't been pressing, Logan would have taken up that challenge and seen where it led.

He looked up to find her staring down at him, the towel held in her hands.

"Are you ready, or have you changed your mind?"

"Ready." Surely he was mistaken that he heard a wishful note in her voice that he had indeed changed his mind. "You're sure you know how to shave a man, Jessie?"

"Sure. You just lather up some soap and cut real carefully."

As she wet his heavy beard stubble and began to work the soap into it, Logan closed his eyes. He didn't like thinking about how many times Jessie must have done this for her husband. The thought was so strange. Why the hell should he care? It would be different if she was his woman....

Jessie gazed down at Logan's closed eyes and knew her touch pleased him. There was a hint of a frown that disappeared as she worked the soap into the beard. Standing behind him, she tried to avoid pressing her breasts against the back of his head, but she quickly saw the position as awkward.

"You won't move or anything, will you?" she asked, reaching for the razor. *Please, Lord, keep my hand nice and steady.*

Squinting up at her, Logan shook his head.

"That's good. Real good. Just close your eyes and leave it all to me."

Mentally, Jessie reviewed the moves she had seen her brother and Harry make when shaving. Scrape up the throat and down the cheek was all she could remember. Releasing a deep breath, she set to work.

Using a light touch, she began on his left side, her motions neat, only a slight betraying tremble giving away how nervous she was. She had never thought of all the small intimacies that a woman shared with a man who lived with her. Not that she thought of Logan as exactly living with her, but it seemed that way.

She lifted his chin and began on his throat with light, even strokes. Rinsing the blade and wiping it on the towel as she went along, Jessie became more confident. True to his word, Logan hadn't moved. All she had to ignore was the warmth of his breath on her hands, and the brush of his head against her breasts.

"I need you to turn a little so I can shave your upper lip. That is, if you don't want that mustache."

"No, it goes, too." But Logan opened his eyes to see her frowning. "What's wrong?"

"You're not sitting right. Maybe if you faced me."

Jessie backed up as he swung his legs over the bench and faced her. "Better?"

She nodded, but it was anything but better. She would have to stand between his legs to shave that small spot. Well, if he didn't see anything wrong with it, she wouldn't, either.

The moment she stepped up close, Logan raised his hands to her hips.

"Whatever are you doing?"

"Just keeping you steady, Jessie. That razor's so sharp I wouldn't know that you cut my throat until I saw the blood drop."

"I didn't cut you!"

"No. But I aim to keep it that way."

"If you were so worried, Logan, that I would slice your throat," she said testily, "then why did you agree to have me shave you in the first place?"

"'Cause my beard itched and I couldn't do it for myself."

"Then let me finish." Jessie took hold of his chin with one hand to steady herself. Without asking, Logan rolled his upper lip over his teeth to make it easier for her. Her breaths reflected the tension that built inside her as she scraped away at the small area. When done, she wiped it clean with the towel.

His mouth was firm and sensual. The thought startled Jessie. She wasn't a woman given to inspecting men's mouths. There were tiny lines fanning from the corners of his as if Logan smiled and laughed a great deal.

"Miss a spot?"

"What?" Her gaze clashed with his. She would have jumped back, but he held her firmly in place.

"You're staring so hard at my mouth I thought you'd missed a spot."

"No. No, I wasn't." But she didn't attempt to move.

And Logan found himself drawn to her eyes, as if he could probe their depths to find all her secrets.

Jessie closed them. "I think you'd better let me go."

"And if I didn't want to?"

"You don't mean that."

"We've been living together for almost a week—"

"Four days. It's just four days, Logan."

"Right. Close enough. Aren't you the least bit curious about kissing me?"

Jessie went still. *How could he know the curiosity kept her awake at night? Lie, Jessie. Lie like crazy.*

She was so quiet that Logan thought about letting her go. If she had asked, he was ready to tell her that the curiosity drove him crazy. But Jessie wasn't asking. Jessie was tense and, he thought, a little afraid of him.

"I wouldn't hurt you, Jessie. I've never hurt a woman."

His deep, slightly rough voice ruffled her nerve ends. Her hands slid down, one touching his unbandaged shoulder, the other falling to her side. Why didn't he just take a kiss if that's what he wanted? Why did he have to ask? *Because asking makes you a willing party,* a little imp's voice whispered.

And you are willing, aren't you, Jessie? Almost eager?

Yes. Oh, Lord, yes.

But it wasn't right.

"Jessie?"

She didn't answer him. Didn't want to. Keeping her eyes closed was a coward's way of dealing with him. An unsettling warmth unfurled inside her. The same warmth she'd begun feeling since he'd come into her life. His skin felt warm beneath her hand and she just knew that his lips would be warm and maybe gentle if she let him kiss her.

"Jessie, listen to me." Logan wished she would open her eyes. His mother always said they were the windows to a person's soul. But he didn't push her. "Tell me if I'm wrong. I didn't get the feeling that you're still in mourning for your husband. I'm not asking you to tell me about him and your marriage. But I think I've got the right to know if you still care deeply for him."

Jessie couldn't hide any longer. Gazing down into his dark blue eyes that held untold secrets, she summoned her courage.

"Why do you want to know? You're not courting me. You're not asking me to marry you. All you wanted was a kiss. That doesn't give you any rights at all." This time when she moved, he let her go. "I have cattle to check."

Grabbing the floppy felt hat from the peg near the door, Jessie paused. Without looking back at him, she said, "I'm not mourning Harry."

Wrapped in a silent blistering for his clumsy handling of her, Logan took a few moments before he understood. When he did, Jessie was gone.

He could have gone after her. But his instincts warned that Jessie needed time alone. It was little enough to give her after the way she had taken care of him.

Logan didn't want to start questioning himself about why he'd been tempted to kiss her. Trouble was, he was bored with having nothing to do. Glancing around the cabin, he knew that wasn't true. There was enough work to keep a man busy through to winter around the whole place.

Taking stock of her poorly supplied pantry confirmed what he suspected. Jessie was in dire straits. And he was helpless as teats on a boar to aid her. Having him to feed had depleted what little food she had. It added to the score he had to settle with the men who had left him to die.

From the high branches of an aged cottonwood tree, Kenny and Marty watched Jessie ride out at a walk on her old mare.

When she was far enough away that she couldn't hear them, Kenny signaled Marty to climb down.

"Now, you stay here and keep watch."

"But the man is still at her place, Kenny. He could shoot at you, the same as she did."

"You saw same as me. He ain't walkin' around. I know I'll get us a hen this time. Hang on to PeeWee and wait for me." Kenny started to walk off, then turned. "If she comes back, you whistle like I taught you, okay?"

"Okay."

For all the brave words, Kenny still approached the henhouse with caution. There hadn't been any rain in weeks and his boots kicked up tiny puffs of dust as he darted from tree to tree, and when they disappeared, he crawled from bush to rock. His gaze split between the henhouse and the cabin. But he didn't see anyone moving around.

Still, he waited. Something didn't feel right to him. He wiped the sweat from his brow with the back of his hand and crept closer to the pen. From his pocket he took out a few of the worms he dug for fishing and began tossing them to the rooster.

Black-and-green feathers gleaming under the hot sun, the big bird attacked the worms and Kenny slipped around back of the small wooden house. There was a board he had worked loose that the widow woman had not discovered. It was just big enough for him to squeeze through and get inside.

He had just gotten busy digging the loosely piled dirt away from the bottom when he heard a noise. It sounded like rock hitting rock. Just his luck that Marty had forgotten how to whistle.

Kenny slowly turned around, then froze. A horseman was stopped not ten feet from him. With the sun behind the man, Kenny couldn't see his face. But he was one of the biggest men he'd come across.

"You, boy, your folks around?"

Kenny swallowed a few times. His throat and mouth were so dry he couldn't manage to spit dust.

"Something wrong with you, boy?"

Kenny shook his head. He prayed that the man in the cabin wouldn't be able to see him. If he didn't answer, this stranger would go to the cabin and be sure to say something about him. Then someone would come and take him and Marty away. He had to risk it. Kenny stepped out of the shadows cast by the hen-house.

"Folks ain't here now. They, er, went to town. You want to water your horse or something, mister?"

"Just want a little information."

Wiping his damp palms on his grubby pants, Kenny wondered again why Marty hadn't warned him. He offered a lopsided smile and took another step closer.

"I'll sure try to help if I can."

"I'm looking for a man, boy."

Kenny pressed his knees together. They were shaking so badly he swore he'd fall in another minute. "My pa—"

"Don't think so. This man's name is Lucky. Last I saw of him he was near dead, but he ain't where I left him."

"Oh, Jeez!"

"You seen him, boy?"

Kenny shook his head. He eyed the way the big man controlled the moves of his horse, then stared at the whip coiled around the saddle horn and knew he should run like the devil was chasing him. *God, help me out here and I'll never steal from the widow woman again!*

"Ain't seen no strangers around here, mister. And my ma don't like me talking to strangers. I got chores to do."

Zach Romal touched his heels to his horse and moved it closer to the boy. "You wouldn't lie to me?"

"Ain't got no reason to, mister. You said he was near dead. Maybe the buzzards got him or a mountain cat. Could be," he added with a shrug of his thin shoulders, "that he made it down to the Junction."

Kenny kept looking up at the deeply shadowed face. He was too scared to do anything else. But he was going to whup Marty's butt good for not warning him.

Without another word Zach turned his horse and left.

Kenny fought the urge to run. He didn't think his legs would let him run far. And he was panting as if he'd already run hard. He didn't know how long he stood there with the sun beating down on him. He didn't know what made him turn around.

But he sure understood in a hurry what his pa meant by saying a man could get caught between a rock and a hard place.

Just beyond the gate to the hen yard stood the man whose life he and Marty had saved. The man the stranger was asking about.

Chapter Five

"Who the hell are you, boy?"

Not again. Remembering too well the whippings his ma had given for lying, Kenny started to back away. Despite his ma being dead, he believed that he'd be punished for all the lies he'd told so far. He wasn't going to make it worse for himself by telling more.

"Answer me," Logan demanded. "You the one that's been stealing Jessie's chickens and eggs?"

"Ain't stole them. Traded her fair. Ask her. You go ask the widow woman if I didn't."

"We both know that she isn't here, boy. I heard what you said to the rider. Mighty obliged. You the one who found me and brought me up to Jessie?" Even as Logan asked, he studied the slight body and knew it was impossible.

"Maybe." Kenny turned and ran.

"Wait! Don't run off, boy. I won't hurt you." Logan stumbled, but went after him. He was still reeling from the shock of looking out the cabin's window to see Zach there. Why the devil had he come back?

Kenny glanced over his shoulder. Despite the man's faltering walk, he was coming after him. He ran faster, his gaze pinned on the big cottonwood tree where he'd left Marty. Damn! Where was he?

"Marty, we gotta run. Where are you?" he asked in a furious whisper.

"Up h-here."

"Jeez!" Kenny leapt for the lower branch and quickly climbed into the concealing boughs. "Why didn't you whistle to me? I almost got caught."

"Th-the man on the h-horse. He w-was one of th-them. S-scared me."

"Okay. Okay. Just be quiet. Real quiet."

Kenny peered between the smaller limbs and saw that the man had paused. He tried holding his breath, afraid that he was breathing hard enough to be heard.

Logan paused near a small rise and scanned the scrub brush, rocks and a few ancient cottonwoods that offered plenty of concealment to a boy. He didn't want to frighten the child. Harry's boots fit a mite on the tight side, and he was still weak, so the best he'd managed was a slow walk.

Not fast enough to catch the boy. He looked like a half-wild critter, all big dark eyes and long hair.

Wild or not, the skinny kid was sharp.

"If you're listening, boy, I'm beholden to you for saving my life. You got trouble, you come see me. I'll be obliged if you come tell me if that man comes nosing around again."

Logan waited, but not even a breeze stirred in answer. Just as well if he headed back to the cabin. He felt as if he'd been wrestling steers all day. And he'd thought he was almost ready to move on. Like it or not, he was stuck here.

Halfway back, Logan stopped cold. Jessie rode out and Zach showed up. He was crazy to think... but there had been talk about a place in the mountains, a safe place, isolated, too, where no questions were asked of the men who hid out there.

Jessie involved with outlaws? If he had the strength he would laugh. If his life wasn't on the line...if Zach hadn't suddenly shown up. What could he be looking for? Unless Jessie had lied to him when she'd said that he'd been stripped of all but his clothes? Or that boy? He could have stolen the horse, rifle and gun. And that silver buckle. Damned if he didn't regret the loss of that buckle. He'd had one made specially for Ty's birthday, liked it so much that he'd gone back and gotten one for Conner and himself.

With a rough shake of his head, Logan continued walking back to the cabin. That blow to his head had given him more than headaches, it had affected his thinking. How could he worry about a lost belt buckle?

Because an object keeps you from thinking about Jessie and her possible involvement.

Jessie puzzled over the reinforced brush fence at the end of the small valley where she kept her cattle.

For the past few months she hadn't been frightened by the missing eggs or hens, or the blankets stolen from her wash line. She had appreciated the gifts of food left in their place, and accepted the unasked-for trade.

But seeing the newer brush tightly interwoven with the older, dried fence made her question if her benefactor had discovered the valley. The thought sent a chill of foreboding through her. Why?

The large, heavy-bodied cattle with their short, curved horns had been inbred with the Texas long-horns. Harry had started the herd, and lost interest when he realized how long he would have to wait for his profit. Jessie didn't mind waiting. She found pleasure in watching the calves fatten on the lush grasses in this blind valley. A stream ran through it year-round, and she had thought them safe with the brush fence she had erected.

Knowing that someone had stumbled upon her small herd left her feeling violated. As if her dream could be snatched away at a whim. Someone else's whim.

She recounted the cattle again to make sure that none were missing. Eggs she could lose, hens, too, but not her dream of having a thriving herd to build her ranch. Perhaps she stubbornly clung to the idea that she could do this on her own, but she had to try. If she didn't, she would have to admit defeat, sell out and go back to living with Greg and Livia. Not that they wouldn't welcome her, but Jessie knew she wasn't ready to give up yet.

First she would have to stop being so trusting. Just look at the way she had taken Logan in and let him get away without answering her questions of where he had come from or what he'd been doing to get shot.

It didn't take the brains of one of her hens to figure that one out for herself. People got shot all the time. There wasn't much law in the territory. The last time David had come calling, he had left a four-month-old copy of the *Arizona Star*. Bank holdups, train robberies in the north, raiding Apaches, cattle rustling, news item after news item reported the violence in the land.

She had no one but herself to blame for shying away from pushing Logan for answers. The admission came hard, but Jessie made it now. She was afraid of what he would tell her.

She didn't want Logan to matter, she certainly didn't want to care about him, but she had been alone so long that it would be a lie to say there weren't any feelings stirring for him.

A darn foolish notion, but a real one. Did Logan think she was gullible?

Maybe she was....

And maybe her unknown benefactor had done more than secure the brush fence. Maybe by trying to protect her cattle someone got shot. Someone like Logan.

But if that was true, she argued with herself, then why had Logan been brought to her?

"Why?" she whispered, glancing around at the craggy, sloped walls of the valley. "Who are you? Where do you hide? And why, oh, why did you pick me?"

The mare's nicker drew Jessie's gaze to her. "I might as well ask you the questions. I'll get the same nothing for answers."

Heading back through the boot-high grass to where she had left Adorabelle tied, Jessie remembered some of the stories that Harry had told her of the men he occasionally met on his prospecting trips.

Sometimes he would share a campfire with one, at other times merely nod in passing. Names, Harry had said, if exchanged at all, told little about a man or his past.

Like Logan. If Logan was really his name.

But not all men wandered the Superstitions in a search for gold like Harry. Some men ran from a tragedy, the law or to simply ease an inborn wanderlust.

Just as all men were not bred to violent acts. One of the attractions that Harry had had for her was his gentle nature. Her brother was a hard but fair man, unashamed to reveal a tender side.

And Logan . . .

No, she must not allow herself to be distracted by the secret feelings that Logan effortlessly encouraged to surface. Or was that part of his game?

Jessie took the brush fence in a rush, snagging her hem and tearing it free. She hurried to untie the mare and swung herself into the saddle.

Putting thoughts of Logan aside, she spurred Adorabelle toward home. Whoever watched her, or whatever it was he did, may have shot at Logan to warn him. The bullet could have ricocheted and hit him. Jessie knew all about ricocheting bullets. She had almost hit her horse one night, which was why she now aimed the shotgun in the air.

The closer she got to home, the greater her suspicions grew that what she had figured out about Logan's wound was all too possibly true. She worked herself up to confront him as she dismounted near the corral. She had started to loosen the cinch when Logan came to the door of the cabin.

Jessie paused and looked at him. A clean-shaven face should have softened the fierce line of his nose and jaw. Should have, but didn't. If anything, with his narrow-eyed gaze pinned on her and the way he hung back in the doorway so that the late-afternoon sun and shadow played equally over him, Logan appeared dangerous.

And Jessie weighed his appearance and her suspicions carefully. Perhaps confrontation wasn't the path she would take after all.

"Mighty sorry-lookin' excuse for a horse."

"Adorabelle gets me where I need to go. I don't see you with better. I see you with nothing at all."

It had been the wrong thing to say to her. Now she had her back up and that vinegar-mouth primed and aimed at him. He hated having to watch her yank the saddle off that swaybacked mare and sling it over the pole fence. It just went against the grain to stand there useless.

"I managed to put on beans," he said by way of a peace offering, thinking of how difficult it had been to perform each task with the use of only one hand.

Jessie, stripping off her worn leather riding gloves with jerky moves, wasn't interested in food.

"I'm glad you found something useful to do."

"Well, hell!" It wasn't just her mouth then, the edge of her voice said Jessie had loaded a verbal shotgun and was gunning for big game . . . Logan size.

"Don't curse." She turned her attention back to the mare, scratching her behind the ears before she removed the halter. Adorabelle had such a placid nature that she remained as she was, waiting for what came next.

Jessie went into the shed and came out carrying a curry brush. Tossing her floppy felt hat on top of the pole, she found herself drawn to look at Logan again.

He had taken off Harry's toe-pinching boots and stood barefoot, dressed in too-short black twill pants held up by a tightly belted strip of leather. The old bib-front chambray shirt, reduced to the faded color of smoke, should have added no appeal to a woman's eye. But despite the ill-fitting clothes, she felt a prickle of sensual awareness for Logan as a man.

Adorabelle's nudge served to draw her back to the chore at hand. She swung open the pole gate of the corral and, without urging, the mare stepped inside. Jessie followed her. "Don't mind him none, sweetheart," she stated loudly as she began brushing. "He wouldn't know what to do with a kind-natured lady like you."

"Well, double hell!" Logan deliberately raised his voice. "What's got into you, lady?" Even with the distance separating them, he felt the impact of Jessie's golden brown eyes glaring at him. But he was mad now. "Don't tell me that someone stole your damn cow?"

"No one stole my cows. No thanks to you."

When a man has had enough, he's had enough. With complete disregard for his bare feet, Logan stomped across the yard and stopped just outside the corral.

"What the devil was that supposed to mean?"

"I'd say if the shoe fits, wear it, but you don't have any shoes, or boots, of your own. You don't have anything that could prove who you are, what you are or how you came to be here."

The attack was so unexpected that Logan couldn't answer her. He ran his hand through his hair. What had happened to her while she'd been gone? She ducked beneath the mare's neck and began brushing again. He could see the way she nibbled her lower lip. So, she'd blown up at him, but she wasn't at all sure of herself.

"Jessie, why are you suddenly angry with me?"

"I did a lot of thinking while I was gone. I didn't wrap you in a quilt—"

"Are we back to that again?"

"Yes." She stood and looked at him. The mare swished her tail, and when Jessie paid no attention, walked off to the water trough. "It's important for me to know who brought you to me. I have a right to know how you got shot."

There was a wealth of demand in her voice, and a wealth of confusion in her eyes. And she had asked him for the one thing he couldn't tell her—the truth about himself. All the earlier suspicions surfaced, even though he had dismissed the idea of Jessie being involved with any outlaws. They'd pay for a safe place, and pay dearly. Jessie had an abundance of questions, but he'd bet his gear—if he had any—that she didn't have money.

"Have I hurt you, Jessie?"

"No." There wasn't any hesitation. Logan had awakened feelings, but they were hers to deal with. He wasn't even aware of the temptation he presented to her. And Jessie vowed to keep it that way.

"No," she repeated. "You haven't hurt me. But you ask me to take you on blind faith. I'm having a difficult time doing that. See," she said with a shrug, walking toward the gate, "I'm being honest. Try it. I promise the ground won't shake and the sky won't fall."

He closed his eyes briefly against the plea he saw in hers. She said she'd done a lot of thinking, and she'd come up with the worst conclusions about him. With the added problem of Zach nosing around, Logan didn't want to put her in any danger. And, he admitted to himself, he had to protect himself, too. Zach's appearance also cut off his thought of leaving immediately. Jessie wasn't about to give him a gun and her horse, sorry critter that she was. Jeez, who the hell named a swayback Adorabelle?

The fierce, frowning look of concentration on Logan's face alarmed Jessie. She started toward him and stopped. If she softened, gave him one more excuse not to tell her the truth, she would have only herself to blame if she got hurt.

"Logan?"

His eyes targeted her with a bleak expression. "Do you want me to leave?"

"Do you have somewhere to go?" she countered.

"Another dead-end question, Jessie. Either you let me stay awhile longer or I'll leave."

She chewed her bottom lip, tearing off a piece of skin. "You are making me responsible for your well-being." Coming out of the gate and latching it, Jessie picked up her hat and her gloves. She knew he was waiting for her to finish. There seemed to be no other choice. As she entered the cooler shadowed shed to replace the brush, Jessie made up her mind.

"Let's go taste these beans you cooked."

Logan turned to follow her, but at a slower pace. He eyed the loose-fitting faded blue shirt she wore and his gaze traveled over the sway of her rounded hips.

"Why, Jessie?"

She stopped but didn't turn around. "Does it matter? I made a decision. Until you give me reason to change my mind, you can stay."

When she started into the cabin, Logan saw the rip near the hem of her tobacco-colored skirt. While the shirt was worn and thin looking, the skirt was of a heavier fabric. Where had Jessie been that she'd ripped the cloth?

Once more Jessie paused. She felt his heated gaze on her and fought the need to turn around. "Are you coming?"

"I really want to know why you're letting me stay despite whatever suspicions are churning in your mind. And how did you rip your skirt?"

"Caught it on the brush fence. I wasn't meeting anyone, Logan. Not that you have the right to ask."

"No, I don't have any rights, Jessie. But I still want an answer."

"I spent a lot of time worrying about your wound. Be foolish to throw it all away by chasing you off now." *You'll go soon enough.* Jessie folded her gloves into her hat and put it up on its peg. Smoothing back her hair, she turned.

"You set the table!"

"Usual when you're gonna eat."

"Of course." But it meant more to her. And he'd found flowers. She reached out to touch the petals of a wild buttercup. How could she have suspected him of trying to steal her cattle?

"I don't want you to think—" Logan began.

"No one ever— I'm sorry. Please, finish what you were about to say."

Logan kept his distance; not that he wanted to. The slanting sun from the window caught in Jessie's hair, shading the coil at the back of her neck with gold. She appeared fragile, leaning over the taller spikes of pale blue flowers. He had been tempted by the thought of kissing her, but now temptation turned to desire.

She glanced at him, slowly straightening. "Logan?"

"Yeah. I just saw them and thought you'd like some. I didn't mean anything by it. Woman like you should have pretty things around her."

Her smile was radiant. "Thank you," she whispered. "No one ever picked flowers for me before. These are larkspurs?" she asked, once more touching the taller spikes in the canning jar.

"Mouse tails," he corrected, then grinned. Logan heaved an inner sigh of relief that Jessie had put aside her quest for answers that he couldn't give her.

"Mouse tails, Logan?"

"Why not? Names are no more than what a body sees. A man finds water, he looks around to find a way to mark the place. A jagged rock that's sprinkled with mica sparkles in the sunlight. Next thing you know, he's passing along word that there's water at Sparkling Rock or Silver Rock, or some such name."

"I never thought of it that way. But mouse tails," she said, then laughed when he shook his head.

"I truly don't know why they're called that. Santo—"

"Santo?"

"Someone I know. He taught me how to find wild greens that are safe to eat." Frowning, he tugged his earlobe. "Don't you know? Didn't anyone teach you—"

"I was born and raised in New York, Logan. After my aunt died I came out here to live with my brother, then married Harry. Livia had just given birth, so there wasn't time for her to show me much. There were three other children to take care of."

"And Harry? Didn't he show you—"

"Harry, I'm afraid, was more interested in what the rocks held than in what grew near them."

"I'm sorry, Jessie. Look over on the cupboard. You've got a whole garden on the other side of the well. Hog onions, Indian lettuce and red maids. The maids are a mite salty, but taste good. If I have time... Lord," he said with a rough shake of his head, "that's all I do have. I'll scout around and see if I can find some seeds to make you desert tea."

"I'm not sure I like the sound of that. But you be careful. The area behind the well is rocky. Until that shoulder heals you shouldn't climb over there, you could hurt yourself. And no food is worth that."

Her concern touched him. True, he'd rather have Jessie physically do a little touching, but a man took what he could get. Rubbing the back of his neck, Logan decided he would tell her the truth.

"I wasn't exactly looking for food, Jessie. We had a visitor while you were gone."

"A visitor? Here?"

"That's what I said. I—"

"But who?" Truly puzzled, Jessie frowned. No one ever came to visit her...unless it was... "David? David was here?"

"David? Who the devil is he?"

Chapter Six

"David Trainor is a widower who has been calling on me. Usually he confines his visits to Sunday afternoons." One of the hardest things for Jessie was to turn around and face Logan. She lifted her chin and leveled a direct look at him. "David is the only one in Apache Junction who doesn't believe that I killed my husband."

She gripped the overhanging edge of the cupboard, refusing to look away from him. It was somewhat startling to find Logan's expression incredulous.

"No way you killed him or anyone, Jessie."

"What? How can you say that? You don't know what happened or why anyone would make the accusation."

"Are you trying to convince me that you did kill him? It won't work. You haven't got that killer instinct."

"How would you know, Logan?" Jessie fairly bristled. Her tone had been resentful, which she realized was ridiculous. But she didn't like his assumption that he knew her so well.

"I just know. Jessie, I've got your back up saying that, but now I don't know why. If you could kill, why the hell did you—"

"Don't curse."

"Like I was saying, why did you take me in? Why do you shoot in the air when someone or some animal steals your eggs? If you did kill anyone, it would be sheer accident. Even then I wouldn't believe you did—"

"That's enough. You've made your point. Logan, I do thank you. You can't know the gift you've given me with your belief."

Logan eyed the distance between them. As a measure of space it wasn't all that much. But if he gave in to the desire to go to her and take her into his arms, it would be a step from which there'd be no retreat. If he kept his distance from her until he left, there would be few regrets. If he... Cutting off his thoughts, Logan moved.

Jessie watched him skirt the table and come toward her. In some dim corner of her mind she knew if he touched her, he would kiss her. She wanted him to kiss her. She had been dreaming of it, tempted and taunted by turns. And at this moment she needed to be held. He stood before her, his dark hair tumbling over his forehead, and she fought the urge to reach up and touch it. Needs swept through her, combining with a desire that allowed no pretense. She felt compelled to lift her face to his.

"Jessie." Logan touched her cheek with a gentle stroke that she turned to follow. His thumb brushed across her bottom lip. That poor abused lip she constantly bit. "You should let someone have care of this," he murmured, brushing her lips again, "who won't hurt it so."

"I don't—"

"Hush. You do." His lips touched lightly on her hair, skimmed across her temple, then Logan covered her mouth with his. He expected to taste sweet softness, not the sharp tang of passion.

He knew he shouldn't give in to the desire to taste her lips once more, but his resolve faltered. Jessie felt perfect in his arms, those wide eyes gazing up at him, watching, and filling with unnamed needs. But learning the shape and temper of her kiss forced him to hold back a hunger that flared to life.

Jessie liked kissing. She had been kissed by three men and all left her wanting something more. But none had brought their whole body into play. She gave herself easily into Logan's care, enjoying the tease of his mouth brushing against hers. She liked the gentle touch of his callused hand cupping her cheek and the way the warmth of his body sheltered hers.

And then she lost herself in his kiss, her own lips as feverish as his, discovering that she could follow his seductive, coaxing moves as the shifting pressure of his mouth set her on a path of longing.

There was untold pleasure for her in the caressing ply of his hand sliding down from her shoulder to the curve of her waist. Their lips parted for a moment so that they could draw breath, then he slid his hand around to the small of her back, urging her closer to his aroused body.

Jessie's arm was caged by the embrace, but she raised the other to hold the back of his head as she fed dreamily on the rich taste of the passion building between them.

A faint warning attempted to make itself heard, but she refused to listen. All her curiosity was being slaked, and, at the same time, newer temptations beckoned her to explore the desire that encompassed her.

Logan eased his mouth from hers. He tasted longings in her lips that he couldn't give her, wouldn't. He'd tell her no lies and Jessie kissed like a woman looking for promises.

Logan pulled back a little to gaze down at her face. Her light-tipped lashes, fluttering like skittish butterflies afraid to settle, made shadowed crescents on her cheeks. Reaching up, he used one finger to trace the slightly reddened shape of her generous mouth, more aroused than he could say when she parted her lips and kissed his finger.

A tremor passed over her body, one that he felt as if it were his own. Caution whispered a warning to him that he should move away from her, now, while he still could. But need was stronger. He angled his head to take her mouth once more.

Jessie understood how dangerous Logan could be to her. He touched a depth of passion inside her that made her feel threatened by its powerful force. But she had been alone for so long that she couldn't find the needed strength to pull away.

But when she felt the heated tip of his tongue seek to part her lips, she twisted her head away. "No. Don't kiss me...like that." She tucked her cheek against his chest, wondering why all the gentle things had to end so quickly for a man.

"Jessie? Jessie, tell me what I did wrong?"

Tell him? She wished she could burrow right through him and escape. How could she tell him? How could any woman discuss such a thing with a man?

"This was a mistake, Logan." But when she tried to slip by him, he blocked her way.

"Maybe it was, but it sure answered a lot of questions." Logan braced one hand on the edge of the cupboard and, although it hurt him to put pressure on his wounded shoulder, he did the same on the other side to cage her in front of him.

She wouldn't look up at him, and he didn't push her to. "How long were you married, Jessie?"

"A year." She didn't hesitate to answer him. At least he wasn't trying to kiss her again.

"And you said Harry's been dead nearly as long?"

"Yes, but—"

"And there hasn't been anyone else, has there, Jessie? David hasn't... I mean—"

Her head snapped up and slammed into his jaw.

"Ouch! Damn it, Jessie! I only asked you a damn—"

"Don't curse, Logan. I keep telling you that, but you don't listen very well."

"Answer my question, sunshine. I promise I'll listen very well to your answer. There hasn't been—"

"I heard you the first time. No," she stated, feeling heat rise in her cheeks, "there hasn't been anyone else. Not that I see what business it is of yours."

He kissed the tip of her nose. "Thank you for telling me, Jessie. I just wanted to be sure—"

"Of what?"

"Woman, you have the damn—" The militant gleam in her eyes made him heave a sigh. "All right, you have the *darnedest* habit of interrupting me when I'm trying to talk to you. Please let me finish?"

She almost blurted out no, afraid of what he was going to tell her. She'd guessed Logan's age to be close to thirty, and from the first sensed that he'd had more than one woman losing her heart over him. He was no stranger to sharing a home with a woman, either. And she didn't think she wanted to be told that she lacked whatever it was that men looked for in a woman.

But Logan watched her with those dark eyes still shimmering with need. And she'd have to be carved from wood, like Miss Millicent's fashion doll, not to feel that he was still aroused.

"All I want to tell you, Jessie, is that when it comes to experience I'm probably your grandfather. I didn't mean to let things go so far."

Was he sorry that he'd kissed her? *Remember you are an independent woman,* a little imp's voice whispered. *Are you going to let him imply that you don't know how to kiss?* She searched his features, wishing the little nagging voice was wrong, hoping to find some sign that he didn't find her lacking.

Logan turned away before she had an answer. Lifting her hand to her lips, Jessie knew it was for the best. No sense in starting something with a man who had traveling on his mind. But the taste of him lingered on her mouth and she wondered if it was already too late.

He stood by the doorway, his good arm braced above him, staring outside. She gazed at the lean, hard body, feeling again its press against her own, and she was tempted to call him. Jessie bit her lip. It was just

as she had told him—a mistake. One worth forget-
ting.

Looking away from him, her gaze lit on the stove
and the pot of beans that he had cooked. Bacon and
biscuits would have been nice to add, but the flour was
gone and she didn't remember when she'd used the last
of the bacon.

If Logan was well enough to go walking around, she
could leave him and make her trip to town. It was time
to sell her ring. If she knew more about the right time
to sell cattle... She cast a speculative look over her
shoulder at Logan. He might know. But how to find
out without revealing her dire straits? She knew he
didn't have any money. When she'd found him, she
had searched his pockets for clues about him and
hadn't found any.

Searching... Rubbing her forehead, Jessie tried to
remember what he had said about searching for
someone. The visitor!

"Logan?"

"Yeah?" He didn't turn around to her. He didn't
like making mistakes, and kissing Jessie had been a
major one.

"You said someone came to visit?"

"That's right."

"But I don't have any neighbors. I told you what
people think about me. So, who came to call?"

"Wasn't exactly a social call, Jessie."

She ignored how distracted he sounded. Setting
aside the wooden spoon she'd been stirring the beans
with, Jessie turned around.

"Who was it?"

"I think I found your egg thief."

"My egg thief," she repeated. *Oh, dear, my silent protector likely came around to check on him.*

"You're real sure," he said, making an abrupt turn and coming back into the cabin, "that you have no one living close by?"

"I told you so. I've had time this past year to ride Adorabelle over the land within a few hours' ride. The only thing I found was a deserted shack back in the mountains."

"No signs that someone was living in the shack?"

Jessie planted her hands on her ample hips and blew heavenward. "Logan, it was months ago that I was up there. For all I know there's a renegade band of Apache camped up there now. What's more, I don't care who's up there. I've had no reason to go back. I don't even think the shack is on my land."

"I just wanted to make sure—"

"The heck with making sure! You talk about me having a habit of interrupting—take a look at your own annoying habit of secrets and dragging things out till a body's ready to give up the ghost awaitin' on you."

"Now, Jessie, there's no need to get all fired—"

"Just tell me! Now," she demanded, rounding the table and going toward him.

"I'm not trying to keep it secret. I'm really puzzled about this. The thief's a boy, Jessie. No more than chest high." He had the satisfaction of watching her stop short, surprise bright in her eyes.

"A boy? But that can't be."

"Hard to figure how old he is. Never had much truck with young'uns."

Shaking her head, Jessie backed up and pulled out the bench. She sat down abruptly. "A boy," she repeated, unable to believe it. "How could a child survive alone?"

"Who said he's alone?"

She looked up at him. "What are you saying? That someone taught a child to steal? Well," she quickly amended, "not exactly steal, more of an unasked-for trading arrangement. I've always found fresh-caught fish or a skinned rabbit, even a haunch of venison when one of the hens or eggs go missing."

"Didn't you ever think to find out who was doing it?"

"Don't take that tone with me like I did something stupid. Of course I wondered. No real harm was done. If you are asking if I set a trap, obviously not. If I had, I wouldn't be sitting here, with you ready to strip my hide over this."

"Jeez, Jessie, that's a hell of a thing to say! Take my word for it, I don't need you putting images in my mind."

For a few moments she stared blankly at him, then color tinted her cheeks. She squeezed her eyes shut, lowered her head and released a moaning sound.

"Leave it to a man," she mumbled, "to twist an innocent remark."

"You're right. It would be innocent if minutes ago you weren't running like hot honey all over me."

"Running like hot honey...." Jessie raised her head. "Why, you overblown tommy noddy!"

"My name's Logan!"

"Is it?" She eyed him with every ounce of suspicion that she harbored about him.

"Sure as hell is. Has been from the day I was born."

"Stop cursing in my home." Since she felt at a decided disadvantage sitting, Jessie rose, but she didn't trust herself to go near him. Grabbing hold of her skirt with both hands, she squeezed tight, wishing it was his thick head she held.

"Jessie—"

"No. I'm not finished. I'm mighty happy to know that you were born. 'Course, you can't prove that, can you? But I was beginning to think you dropped from the sky and landed on your head. It's the only way to explain," she added with an overabundance of sugar drawling in her voice, "why you're so puffed up over a kiss."

"It was more than *a kiss* and—"

"And I was not," she interrupted, "repeat, not running like hot honey all over you. That blow on your head must have done something to your memory. You kissed me, mister."

"Ain't likely to forget it." Mentally, Logan took a few steps back. In seconds he understood where the flare of temper had come from. He'd left Jessie wanting more. Hell, he wanted more. Trouble was, he knew what would happen if he let himself get tangled up with range calico that was likely as innocent as that dumb remark that had started all this fuss.

And if he was being honest with himself, he *was* feeling a little puffed up that—regardless of what Jessie said—she'd run warm and sweet in his arms, just like honey.

But if he said two words about how easily they could get rid of the frustrating tension, Jessie'd be dodging him like a mossback. Lord knew he'd done his share of trying to catch old longhorns that were skilled in hiding from a rope.

"Jessie, I—"

"Enough said. Your beans are burning."

Chapter Seven

A raw wood shanty stood beside a newly erected pole fence in which six horses were standing. Inside the low-ceilinged room, the air was hot and laden with the odors of bacon grease, sweat and horse manure.

Dusky shadows mixed with the glow from a single lantern that lit the room where four men sat around a rickety table on kegs and crates.

Monte Wheeler held a match to the smoke he had built from his makings and hunched forward. "If you didn't find Lucky breathin', an' you didn't find his bones picked clean, Zach, then where the hell is he?"

"I told you twice now, ain't hide or hair of him around. All I saw was that kid. He didn't know nuthin' 'bout a stranger. Didn't figure it smart to keep pushin'."

"You don't get paid to think."

"Shut up, Billy Jack. Don't see you findin' him. If you hadn't had a hankerin' for his fancy gear, we wouldn't be worryin' where in the hell is he." Zach sent a scowl the half-breed's way.

"Who stopped me from finishin' the hombre?"

Billy Jack's fingers curled over the edge of the table as if he was more than ready to spring at Zach.

From across the room, Tallyman threw his knife. The blade quivered in the center of the table, adding another scar to its already cracked surface.

"What'd ya do that for?" Zach demanded.

"I'm tired of listening to you two. You ain't been cooped up here for five days. Still can't understand why Monte only sent you to look for him."

"Then ask me." Monte blew smoke toward the ceiling. "Boss didn't like us leaving him where his body could be found. Boss wasn't happy that two guards got killed and we lost a man. If we lost him. He doesn't like loose ends. Till I know what happened to him, Lucky's a loose end. My back gets ridden with spurs, you can bet I'm setting my rowels on someone else's back."

"You shoulda let us all go search," Tallyman insisted.

"Nope. One man asking around won't raise a fuss when folks gets to talking. An' look at the lot of you. You'd scare the pants offen some poor sodbuster."

"Ain't got no sodbusters 'round here. Ain't nuthin' but lizards, snakes an' rock." Blackleg poured the last of the coffee into his tin cup and strolled back over to the table. "Maybe the 'Pache got him. Buzzards could've cleaned his bones in five days. Man's bones could be scattered from here to the border by now."

Monte listened to them argue, blaming himself for no' making sure that Lucky was dead, and then burying him. Old Charlie had sure poured damning down on his head. He'd tried to warn him that after all this time odds were he wouldn't find him. If the boss didn't insist that they keep their distance from him, Monte knew it wouldn't have taken him two days to ride to meet him, then two days back. he just never figured that Zach wouldn't find the body, or what was left of it. Damn!

"You sure that kid didn't follow you, Zach?" Monte asked.

"Couldn't. Weren't no horses around. Wild little thing, too. Kinda reminded me of when I was a kid." His gap-toothed grin didn't find any answering ones on the faces of the men staring at him. "You want I should go back there, Monte? Ain't another homestead around."

Monte didn't answer him immediately. He gazed up at the ceiling. Taking another deep drag of his cigarette, he blew smoke rings while he thought over his problem.

The boss wanted him to hit the Kincaids harder. Despite the repeated losses of money, silver and cattle, they weren't ready to knuckle under and sell out. With old Charlie setting his sights on a governor's seat when Arizona became a state, Monte knew he'd have work for years to come. Thing was, he knew he couldn't afford to make mistakes. What old Charlie wanted cost money, lots of it. The land he'd been buying, or stealing, if Monte knew his boss, was only the start. The cattle herd made him respectable to the other landowners. But old Charlie never let on why the Kincaids had been made the main target of his vendetta.

The boss always played his hand close to the vest. Monte knew he'd hired other men to do other jobs for him around the territory. He knew better than to ask questions. He had always followed orders and made sure his jobs had no loose ends. But that didn't let him escape from the way old Charlie had been proddy as a locoed steer over him letting the men dump Lucky's body.

He could've kept his mouth shut. It was the damn divvy that had caused the problem. He'd stupidly pointed out that he needed only five shares this time, not six, and the boss had bellowed like a newly made steer.

Lowering his gaze and searching the faces of the men who watched him, Monte knew they'd likely think he was loco for being honest about the shares. But he knew the boss and they didn't. Old Charlie had ways of finding out when a man lied to him. Man told him the job was done, it had better be so, or the boss'd hire someone else to clean up the mess and shoot the liar. Monte was fond of his skin and he aimed to keep breathing in it.

"Monte?" Zach prodded.

"Yeah, I heard you. I'm still thinking."

"Think too damn much, if you ask me," Billy Jack asked.

"He's been coiled and spittin' like a caged rattler while you were gone," Tallyman observed.

"Can't blame him none. My share's burning a hole in my pocket." As if to prove it, Blackleg slapped his hip. "Can just taste me some whiskey. You can't keep a man workin' dry, Monte."

Billy Jack threw his cup at a rat scurrying across the floor. "Soon, amigo. We go very soon."

"You threatening me, boy? We go when I say so. Anybody gonna argue that?"

"Ain't no one arguing, Monte," Tallyman assured him. "But Billy Jack an' Blackleg got a point. We can't spend our shares in this hole. We've been on the prod for nearly a month. Come to think on it, we ain't seen whiskey or a female since the night Lucky joined us. Just can't see what harm'll come if we go down to the Junction for a night."

"Ain't had nuthin' but scanty fare to fill our bellies for weeks now. Who the hell's gonna know?"

"I'd know," Monte answered. But he knew when he had pushed them as far as he could, and with an abrupt nod he gave his consent.

"You're all right. And maybe at the Junction we'll pick up some word about Lucky. Sack out, and come first light we'll ride."

Scraping the burned beans from the bottom of the cast-iron pot, Jessie vowed that come first light she would go to Apache Junction. The supplies were needed, but that was just an excuse, even if a truthful one. She needed time away from Logan.

It had come as a shock to her to find out that she had a temper. Part of it came from the feeling that things were moving too fast between them. She couldn't believe the way she had sassed him, yelling and shouting right back in his face. Added to that shock was the fact that she was pleased with herself. She had held her own with Logan, even to having the last word.

She was getting the hang of this independent role. She could say what she wanted, do what she wanted, and no one could hold her accountable.

True, with her morals and values firmly in place, she wouldn't think of doing anything wrong. The only unpleasant result was Logan taking himself off in a brooding sulk.

Jessie paused in her scrubbing and thought about that. She was in fine fettle. Logan wasn't going to be allowed to spoil that.

Working on one last stubborn spot, Jessie was glad when the last bit of burned crust came free from the bottom of the pot. She pumped clean water into the kettle and rinsed it a few times. Once she dried the pot with a linen cloth, she placed it on the still-warm stove. Scooping out a bit of bacon grease from the crock, she put it in the kettle, waited a few minutes, then wiped the pot again. Livia had taught her to do this to prevent rusting.

With her hands at the small of her back, she arched and stretched to get rid of the ache in her back. Harry had always promised he would raise the level of the dry sink for her, but had never gotten around to doing the job.

A glance at the open doorway revealed a pool of light spilling from the lantern that Logan had taken outside. He'd been sitting on the bench since their silent supper had ended. She hadn't been aware that she had listened to his low-voiced swearing and mumbling, but now that it had stopped, Jessie wondered what he was doing out there.

As if thinking about him suddenly conjured him up, Logan appeared in the doorway. He held the lantern in one hand, with a pair of pants tossed over his arm.

Jessie would have looked a little like a startled deer but for the way her hands slid forward to rest on her hips, giving her a disgruntled appearance. He glanced down to make sure he hadn't dragged any dirt inside with him.

"You wash away all that sass along with the leavings from supper?"

As the first words he had spoken to her since their heated argument, Jessie thought they lacked a certain something—like apology.

"And if I didn't?" she asked with challenge flaring in her eyes.

Coming forward to set the lantern on the table, Logan thought of several ways to rid Jessie of that sassy tongue. Since all of them involved putting his hands on her again, he kept quiet. Honesty demanded that he admit he liked the way she stood up to him. He'd always had a liking for a woman who could hold her own. With his own mother an example of a female with a formidable strength of will, Logan had no trouble with Jessie exhibiting the same.

Jessie's unfortunate curiosity got the better of her. "What were you doing with your pants?"

"Digging for gold."

"Pardon?"

"I said I was digging for gold." Logan tossed his pants onto the table. With them fell a kitchen knife.

"I heard what you said. I didn't understand how you dug for gold in those," she said, waving one hand at the pants. Stepping closer to the table, Jessie bent over to examine the pants. "You've torn off the buttons and the...the..." Unable to finish saying that the placket of material where the buttons were sewn to close his pants was now ripped out, she stared at him.

"I suppose you intend to share the joke with me. Or did you intend for me to mend these? I can't see where you'd be digging for gold . . . uh, well, there."

Grinning at the way she fumbled over the words, Logan held up a fist. He liked Jessie with a tint of pink in her cheeks and that endearing bright-eyed look as she waited for him to finish revealing what he'd done.

He opened his hand and the contents plunked down on the table. "Five bone buttons, five double eagles."

She rapidly looked from his face to the table. She knew she could trust what she saw for herself, but she reached down and picked up one of the twenty-dollar gold pieces.

"It's real," he assured her.

"And very clever," she returned, wondering what he intended to do. She replaced the coin near the others on the table. Her gaze lingered on the play of the light over the bright gold coins and the softer pink gold of her wedding ring.

Before she could move, Logan covered her hand with his. "Are you angry that I didn't tell you about the money?"

"Why would I be angry?" A small tug failed to release her hand. She leveled a direct gaze at him. "It's your money, Logan. You do as you wish with it." Once again Jessie tried to free her hand. He exerted a light pressure to keep her in place. She had the oddest desire to smooth the errant lock of hair from his forehead, but such a move would lead to trouble.

"Truth is, I forgot about the money."

"As I said, it was quite clever. I don't believe I've ever heard of anyone hiding gold in...in cloth that way."

"Good thing, too."

Jessie yanked her hand out from under his. "I am not a thief. I admit I searched your clothes for a clue to who you were. I can assure you that had I found anything in your pockets, which I might add were nearly ripped off before I mended them, you would have found the contents the minute you were awake."

"Don't take on so, Jessie. I didn't mean that you'd steal from me. I was thinking about everything else of mine being stolen, so it was best that I didn't have this money hidden in my belt."

"Oh."

"Yeah," he agreed, then grinned. "Oh."

"It's a great deal of money," she murmured, wishing the suspicions about him wouldn't come rushing back. But she might as well have wished away the night for all the good it did to stop thoughts of where he had gotten a hundred dollars. Money he obviously didn't need if he could sew it up and forget about it.

Logan watched her face. He could feel her withdrawing from him, but he didn't understand why. She lifted her lashes and glanced at him. A fine tension coiled through his body as he gazed into her tawny eyes. For a moment there was fear within them. Fear that he would stay, or fear that he would go? She looked away before he decided.

"You're afraid of me again."

Jessie felt trapped by the intent look in his eyes. He wasn't asking, but she answered him anyway. "This," she said, pointing to the money, "raises more questions about you. I don't know anyone who can afford to hide a hundred dollars away so that they could just forget about it."

"You're a mighty suspicious woman, Jessie."

"Wouldn't you be in my shoes?"

To her surprise, Logan straightened and appeared to give her question serious thought.

"I don't know," he said after a few moments. He studied the light playing over her upswept hair, making it appear varying shades of spices. He wanted to take the pins from the thick coil and see her hair loose. Shaking his head to rid himself of the distraction she presented, Logan finished.

"I can't picture what it's like to be in your shoes, Jessie. I can sure imagine how attracted I am to you, but I can't imagine being you. I always figured a man's and woman's ways of thinking about things were at odds with each other. Women tend to complicate matters and a man's real straightforward in his thoughts."

Jessie felt the increased racing of her pulse. She knew she shouldn't push this, but couldn't seem to help herself.

"Are you?"

"Am I what?"

"Attracted to me?"

The moment the words were said, Jessie clamped her hand over her mouth. Mortified that she had been so bold, she started to back away from him. *What was wrong with her?*

Logan caught hold of her wrist in a gentle grip, stopping her flight. "Jessie," he said solemnly, his lips twitching, "if you're still asking, I'm sorry. Guess I'll have to rectify that fault at the earliest opportunity."

He drew her hand from her mouth and brought it up to his own.

"Don't," she whispered, knowing the condition of her work-roughened hands.

He met her protest with a brief shake of his head and turned her hand palm side up, then lightly kissed it. Still holding her gaze with his, he bit the fleshy pad below her thumb.

"And now," he murmured, drawing her closer, "seems like a mighty fine opportunity."

A shiver ran through her, then another when he repeated the small bite. She searched his hooded eyes, her gaze lowering to the flush mantling the golden darkness of his face. She stood so close to him now that their breaths mingled. A part of her reveled in his open desire for her, a part remained worried that he slipped so easily past her guard.

"You are the devil's own temptation, Logan."

The breathless way she spoke deepened his smile. "The only one I'm interested in tempting is you." Still holding her hand, he rubbed it against his cheek. "Be honest with me, Jessie. Am I succeeding?"

She glanced away a moment, then faced him. "Far too well, but I suspect you know that." She pressed her fingers to his cheek. Regret filled her eyes as well as her voice as she disengaged her hand from his and let it fall to her side. "You already explained that I don't have your experience. I—"

"Jessie—"

"No, please. Let me finish." She stepped back a bit, needing the distance. "I've been very bold with you.

I've said things to you I've never spoken to another man. Honesty is called for, Logan. I'm very tempted to give in to these feelings you cause inside me. Tempted, but I remind myself that it would be foolish.

"The money you suddenly remembered," she said, looking at the coins on the table. "It's your means to leave here."

"Jessie, I didn't mean to hurt you in any way."

A bittersweet smile creased her lips as she slanted a look at him. "I believe you. But that doesn't change the way I feel."

Logan watched her looking at the money. The thought that formed had to be voiced. "Jessie, you didn't think I meant to pay you like some nickle-a-ride daughter of joy?"

"No! The thought never crossed my mind." She spoke with such conviction he had no choice but to believe her.

"I didn't want any misunderstanding. I do intend for you to have part of the money. No, wait," he demanded when she rounded on him. "I need a horse, boots and a gun. I can't go into town and buy them for myself. You need to do that for me. Whatever is left is yours."

As much as she had dreaded hearing the announcement of his intent to leave, Jessie knew it was for the best. But she wasn't about to do it his way.

"Logan, I trust you to bring Adorabelle back to me despite what you think about her. Take her and buy your gear tomorrow—"

"I can't ride your horse into town, Jessie. Think for a minute. Your reputation will be in shreds if folks learn you've had a man staying with you. For your own protection, you do the buying."

She had the strangest feeling that while he spoke the truth, there was a lie buried within the words. And he had forgotten what she had told him about her reputation.

"If I take your money it will raise questions about where I got it. Buying a horse wouldn't be a problem. I'll just look for one that won't remind you of Adorabelle. But buying a gun, oh, Logan," she said with a laugh, "what I know about guns would fill a teacup. And boots—what reason would I have to buy men's boots if I'm protecting my reputation? End of the matter. You'll have to go yourself."

Have to go. Saying the words brought home the fact that by this time tomorrow night he would be gone. The need to be off by herself so he would never know how painful it was for her to turn away from him and the chance to discover passion in his arms grew powerful. Jessie knew she had to get away from him now.

Logan gripped her upper arm and stopped her. "I can't go."

"Can't go?" she repeated, slowly raising her head to look at him.

It pained him to crush the hope he saw flaring in her eyes. "To town, Jessie. There are... Damn, I didn't want to get into this with you."

"Tell me. I know there's more to it.'

"You're a woman made for sharing with a man, Jessie. I had forgotten how soft a woman could be and—"

"I'm not soft. I'm strong. So just tell me why."

"There are men looking for me."

"The men who shot you?"

"Yeah, those men. I can't let you get tangled in the mess I'm in. That's why I need to pull out fast."

"You think they know you're here with me?"

Another omission to expose. Logan rubbed the back of his neck with his injured arm, needing the pain's distraction from the cold knot forming inside him for hurting her.

"The kid wasn't the only one around. A man caught him. A man asking questions about me. I don't know why the boy lied to him. Said his folks weren't here and he'd seen no strangers around." His gaze was bleak as he searched her face for understanding. "What if he'd found you alone? I don't want to think about it, but I do. I can't risk having something happen to you, Jessie."

"You're so sure—"

"Hell, yes, I'm sure. They'd rape and kill you and never give you a second thought."

She reached up and covered his hand still gripping her arm. "You're not like that. I don't understand why you'd be in the company of such men."

"Don't ask. I can't, no, I won't tell you. The less you know the safer you'll be. I'm a danger to you. Now will you agree to go to town and buy what I need?"

"All right. I don't have a choice." She glanced away. "I'll do whatever I can to help you. I can't seem to do anything else."

She tugged her arm and after a few seconds Logan let her go. He found the act of releasing her difficult. He wanted to sweep her up into his arms, despite the dull ache in his shoulder, and not let her go until the sun rose. He'd asked her about temptation, but wondered why Jessie didn't see how tempting she was. If he had time... But he didn't. Unless he found a way to get the man behind the stealing, he never would. Who had reason to want revenge against his family?

And when he left, who was going to protect Jessie?

Chapter Eight

Logan woke late to find a gun and holster beside him in the bed and no sign of Jessie in the cabin. The day was overcast, as gloomy with the threat of rain as he'd seen, and suited his mood.

Once more he'd lost the argument with Jessie about sleeping in her bed. She had reminded him that it might be a long time before he slept in one again. Regret that he couldn't tell her the truth added to his dark mood.

He examined the gun, an old Remington army pistol, with its plain handgrip and well-oiled barrel. This, too, must have belonged to Harry.

He wondered what Harry would have made of all this. Logan was living in his cabin, sleeping in his bed, wore his clothes and boots, and now had his gun. The only thing he hadn't done was sleep with Harry's wife.

His mood changed from dark to foul in a moment. He rose from the bed and found his mended shirt and newly repaired pants folded on the table next to a box of cartridges. The money was gone. Raking back his hair, he knew it was a waste of time to go outside to look for Jessie, but he did it anyway.

The corral was as empty as the cabin. He couldn't blame her for wanting to get rid of him as quickly as possible.

But there was something he intended to do for her before he left there. Returning inside, he eyed the departed Harry's narrow-toed boots as if they were filled with scorpions. The way they pinched his toes, they might as well have been home to the stinging critters. As he struggled to pull them on, he cheered himself with the thought that the pinch of the boots didn't have any venom.

Fire streaked out from the wound in his shoulder. Logan ignored it. When a man lived with a brother like Conner, who could roust you from bed after a night of drinking left you feeling as if the entire Apache nation had set up camp and played their war drums in your head, you had to learn to work through any pain.

Outside he doused himself with water from the bucket, shaking it off like a hound after a rain, grabbed one of Harry's shirts and headed out. He was going to find that boy.

A fine dust rose from Adorabelle's hooves. Jessie believed she had swallowed every particle. Early as it was, she felt the humidity of the summer's oppressive heat. As the horse plodded up the street, Jessie wiped the sweat from her forehead. She'd forgotten how much cooler her cabin high in the mountains was, compared to town. With her felt hat pulled low, Jessie didn't look at the clustered, weather-beaten shacks lining the street.

She stopped outside Beeson's, dismounted and tied Adorabelle's reins to the hitching rail. A few months ago the sign above the old trading post had been painted over with Silas's last name in large red letters that covered the faded words Trade Goods, Livery and Saloon. Silas had never announced that he served as undertaker, too.

Sliding her canvas sacks from the saddle horn, she admonished herself to overcome her reluctance to go inside. The upturned keg where Silas usually sat in the morning was empty. Only a customer would make him leave his place.

The door stood open, and she stepped up to the wooden sidewalk, then to the doorway. Even if the sun had been shining, it couldn't help dispel the darkness of the interior. Two walls were lined with shelves, crowded and cobwebbed with unwanted goods. Silas had told her that most of the items had been taken in trade by the previous owner.

Peering inside, Jessie, overcome by the smells, wrinkled her nose. The odors of brine, oil and leather were rank. Like Silas himself. He never cleaned, and reasoned that sooner or later someone would buy his stock if for no other reason than his was the only store within a day's ride. Crates and barrels were stacked in a haphazard manner wherever there was room, and, working her way to the counter, Jessie feared one of the piles would topple.

Jessie didn't know the man purchasing a tin of tobacco. She waited until he walked away from the counter before she approached Silas. Balding, squint-eyed, sober as a hanging judge and miserly, Silas brought with his attention a feeling of revulsion. His pasty skin and yellowed teeth turned the smile he offered into a leer.

"Miz Winslow, ain't seen you in a time. Bet you're runnin' low on supplies."

"Good morning to you, Silas." Determined to remain cheerful, Jessie forced a smile to her lips. "I do need supplies. Here is my list. I would also like to buy a horse."

"Well, now, a horse, you said?"

"That's right. Do you have any?"

"I might. Ain't gonna take no trade. Hard cash only. Or gold? You got gold, Miz Winslow?"

"I can pay for whatever I buy, Silas."

"That so?"

Jessie knew he wouldn't fill her order or show her the horses unless he was assured that she did have money. Stripping off one of her leather riding gloves, she reached for the small sack tied to her belt and tugged it open far enough to allow two fingers to slide inside and remove one coin. Holding the twenty-dollar gold piece in front of the man, Jessie gritted her teeth for the time he took to study it.

Impatient now, she asked, "Satisfied, Silas?"

His gaze went from the coin she held to the small sack. "You got more. Horses don't come cheap."

"From you, I wouldn't expect anything cheap. But tell me how much you're charging for a horse these days?"

Stroking his pointed chin, he took his time answering her. Jessie resisted the urge to tap her foot, just as she resisted the urge to look away from the greedy, speculative gaze in his eyes.

"Twenty dollars for a horse, ten for a saddle."

Now it was her turn to mull over what he named. It was a pity that Logan had never bothered to tell her how much to spend. Well, she had tried to tell him.

"You still interested, Miz Winslow?"

"I might be. But the price seems steep. Now, if you were including a bridle, canteen and saddlebags, Silas, I would be inclined to think we struck a fair bargain. Providing," she added, sliding the coin back into the sack, "that the horse isn't as old as I am."

"Miz Winslow, you wound me sayin' such a thing. I wouldn't try to cheat you. That stock is young an' sound. Was thinkin' of keepin' one for myself. But I can't see my way to agreein'. Now, if you was offerin' forty—"

"No. I can't pay that much."

"Thirty-five dollars an' not a penny less."

Jessie eyed the bony hand he held out, palm up and waiting for the money. "I want to see the horse first."

"Sure thing. Help yourself. There's two out back in the corral. You go on, an' I'll jus' fill your order. When you're ready, you com'on in."

He waved her toward the narrow pathway between goods that led to the rear door. Jessie shook her head. Silas had attempted to corner her once, and only the appearance of his Indian woman had sent him scurrying back to the counter. Jessie chose to go out the front and walk around to the corral.

Heavy as the air was, Jessie took a deep, cleansing breath the moment she was outside. Sweat pooled between her breasts and rolled down her back. She plucked up the shirt and camisole that were stuck to her skin. Untying the reins, she led Adorabelle around to the back.

There was a film of dust on the water in the horse trough. Jessie labored with the squeaking pump until a thin stream of water overflowed the wooden sides of the trough. Leaving her horse to drink, she walked closer to the corral. Two horses stood beneath a slanted roof. It was the only form of shelter the animals had.

"At least Silas wasn't lying about the horses," she muttered. "They're not as old as me." Shooting a look over her shoulder at her horse, she added, "No offense, girl. But you're near a grandma to those two."

The sound of her voice brought a white-and-black paint trotting over to the pole fence. Large irregular black patches mixed with smaller ones of brown across the back and rump of the horse. The horse's clear eyes and friendly manner piqued Jessie's interest. But she had to remember that the horse was for Logan, not herself.

The other horse, brown with black tail and mane, stood quietly watching her from the shelter. Jessie had the funny feeling that she was being studied in return.

Even as she patted the paint's muzzle, Jessie kept her gaze on the brown horse. The longer she looked, the more certain she became that that was the one to buy for Logan. She knew there was more to buying a horse. She should be examining their teeth to make sure that her eyes and Silas's claims weren't lying about the horses' ages.

She reminded herself that she didn't have more places to go, not if Logan was to leave today. She had the foolish thought that the brown horse's quiet manner was a clue to the animal being stable. Jessie laughed to rid herself of the strange thoughts. For all she knew, the brown's quietness might mean the animal was ill.

The paint was showy, and very determined to have Jessie stop ignoring her. She tossed her head and bared her teeth. Jessie withdrew her hand.

"That does it. I'm afraid you're likely to nip my sweetheart on her rump. Your friend over there is a lady all the way."

At least, she thought they were both mares. Just as she turned away the air was filled with yells and whoops. Jessie ran a little way and saw the flash of horses go by. There was only one place they'd be going, and that was into a saloon attached to the store. It was too early for decent men to be in town drinking. Forewarned, she chose to use the rear door this time. She wouldn't have to see or be seen by anyone inside.

Before she stepped into the shadowed store, Jessie removed three of the double eagles from her sack. No doubt Silas had heard the jingle of coins when she had taken the one out to prove that she could pay him, but she didn't want him to know exactly how much she had after paying for the horse, gear and supplies. She knew the man too well. Silas would raise his prices the next time she came in, and Jessie had no intention of keeping any of Logan's money. Most of the supplies that she had ordered were items that she would split with Logan, at his insistence—coffee, flour, beans, bacon and a piece of sugar loaf. Jessie had taken it upon herself to add the last, remembering that he had a sweet tooth.

Still, Jessie found herself hesitating by the door. Part of her was in a hurry to get back and spend

whatever time was left with Logan. The other half—
the foolish, lonely woman she'd been trying to hide—
wished to delay his leaving.

No matter how many times she had told herself, as
the long hours of the night passed in restless tossing,
that she didn't want Logan, she had come to the conclusion that she was lying to herself.

And to him.

She regretted those moments when he had held her,
teasing and tempting by turn, and she had refused
him. Regretted, but not enough to overcome a life-
long belief that it was wrong to sleep with a man
without the blessing of marriage. Logan had traveling on his mind, not settling down.

What she couldn't understand was why this decision plagued her. Never before had it been difficult to
make a moral choice, the right one for herself, and
have the matter ended.

But you've never met a man like Logan before.

Shouts and howls of male laughter from inside the
saloon snapped her from her thoughts. A shiver of
distaste raced through her and she had to force herself to go inside.

Silas wasn't at the counter. His Indian woman was.

"You pay. Go quick."

Her voice, like her dark eyes, held no emotion.

Jessie, despite her discomfort, carefully checked to
see that her list had been filled. She loaded foodstuffs
into the large canvas sack she'd left on the counter. A
glance showed that Silas had circled the total due on
the bottom of her list.

Always unsure of how much the woman understood, Jessie pointed to the amount and revealed the

three twenty-dollar gold pieces on her palm. "I will need change. Please tell Silas that I want the brown horse. He promised me a saddle, bridle and saddlebags, too."

Another loud burst of laughter made Jessie glance over her shoulder, then back at the woman. If she had been a cat her tail would have been twitching nervously. She wished she knew the woman's name, but she had asked her once and received no answer. Silas told her all he ever called her was woman.

"And tell Silas that I'm in a hurry, please." Jessie shoved the canteen into the sack. For a few moments more the woman stood there, dark eyes staring at her. The woman's skin was the color of desert mallow, deep, rich and warmly hued against the greased blackness of her long, braided hair. Looped around her ear were pretty colored beads, and in the open V of her red shirt Jessie saw a large, bright blue stone set in silver hanging from a strand of smaller beads. When the woman finally moved, her broad hips sent the yellow-and-red-striped skirt swaying as she went to fetch Silas from the saloon.

Sliding the wrapped coffee beans into her sack, Jessie felt the bulky shape of the sugar cone, but she suddenly realized that Logan would need a coffeepot. Harry's old battered one counted among the items that had disappeared from the shed. She wasn't going to think about that boy now. Once Logan was gone, she'd have time enough to find him.

Leaving the counter, Jessie paused, then slowly walked down the aisle looking at the crowded shelves. As she drew nearer to the arched opening that led to the saloon, she was appalled to hear the coarse remarks directed at Silas's woman. She found herself waiting to hear Silas silence those men. Moments passed, but she didn't hear his voice raised in protest. How could he let them argue about who would bed her first?

She knew Silas wouldn't appreciate her interference. If anything, he'd be likely to yell at her. She spotted the coffeepot and brushed aside a small cobweb to take it from the shelf, still bothered by what she was hearing.

Just as her hand closed over the enamel handle, she grew aware of the silence. At the same time a creeping sensation shivered up her spine. The air she breathed was filled with the foul odor of an unwashed body. She knew the smell from all the times Harry had come home from one of his long treks into the mountains.

Every womanly instinct came alive in alarm and urged her to run. Jessie felt her insides turn to mush. Mush that seeped right through her legs. She trembled where she stood and swore to herself that her boots were all that kept her standing. The next breath she drew added the reek of whiskey to the overpowering smell.

A hand touched her shoulder. She hunched over, trying to make herself smaller, wishing she had more courage, and the strength to move away.

"Ain't gonna hurt you none, little lady. Jus' wanna have some fun. Turn so's I can see what I got for myself."

The man had a gravelly voice, slightly slurred. Jessie thought of all that bold sass she had when faced with Logan. She could use a little of it now. But Logan had never truly made her afraid of him. This man, briefly touching her shoulder again, did.

Cowering would only make him take a firm hold of her. She would do almost anything to avoid that. Jessie turned around.

Eyes the color of sage and as lifeless met her gaze. The corner of the man's mouth lifted in a lopsided smile.

Jessie shivered and pressed back against the shelves. When he shoved a ragged army hat back on his head, he revealed a narrow scar that ran from his hairline down across his eyebrow. His face was rough with a thick growth of dark whiskers that added to his unsavory appearance. He was taller than Logan, broad through the chest and shoulders, and filled her immediate vision.

"Silas?" Jessie called.

"He's busy, little lady."

Jessie couldn't respond.

"Zach? Where'd ya go?"

Jessie tried to peer over his shoulder to see who spoke, but her legs were shaking so badly she couldn't stand on tiptoe.

"Look what I found us, Billy Jack."

"No. You haven't found anything, mister. Step aside." Jessie attempted to infuse the words with force, but her mouth was so dry they came out a whisper.

The front door was only a few feet away. Jessie glanced from the door to the man and saw that the second one had rested his chin on his friend's shoulder and was grinning at her.

"*Ai, caramba,* a woman worth having."

Heat stole into Jessie's cheeks, not a blush of temper but one of shame. No man had ever looked at her with lust shining in his eyes. She tried to inch her way past them.

Zach moved to block her, leaving the other man swaying on his feet.

"Ah, Zach, you're a true amigo to share such bounty with me. I drink to you." Billy Jack lifted the bottle he held and drank deeply.

Jessie's eyes grew wide and round as he swallowed what appeared to her to be an enormous amount of liquor until the whiskey ran down his chin. A backhanded swipe sent drops flying.

Nausea churned in her stomach. The swarthy skin of his neck was ringed with dirt, like the ragged edges of the nails on his blunt fingers.

Where was Silas? Surely he was aware of what these men were doing? She wished she could believe they only meant to taunt her, but there was that look in the second man's dark eyes, the one called Billy Jack, that twisted her belly into a cold knot of fear.

With one in front of her and the other man at her side, Jessie didn't know which one to watch. Zach reached out to touch her again and she batted his hand away, only to have her hat snatched by Billy Jack.

"Never have I seen such hair. Take it down for me, *señorita*. Take it down now."

Jessie lunged for the hat. Too late she understood the gleam of laughter in Billy Jack's eyes. Taking her hat was a ploy that brought her out of the corner where she had the shelves at her back.

Billy Jack dared her to try for the hat with a look from his bloodshot eyes. Jessie couldn't meet his gaze.

Her fear increased the more she looked at his face. Lowering her gaze beyond the fancy worked-silver conchas on his open vest, she saw that he wore a tarnished silver belt buckle. His taunt to come and get her hat distracted her.

Laughing, Billy Jack sidestepped another attempt to grab the hat. He held it high and out of her reach. "Ah, such a brave *señorita!*" Making a mocking bow, he added, "I salute your bravery!" Once more he raised the bottle to his lips, but his eyes never left her.

Jessie sensed more than felt Zach slip behind her. She realized that she still clutched the coffeepot and acted without thinking. She swung it backward in a wide arc. Zach's grunt added courage to her depleted store.

She kicked back and knew by his bellow that her boot heel had found its mark. Zach grabbed her hair, yanking her head back, and Jessie screamed. The coffeepot fell from her hand and landed with a solid thunk on the floor. Her second scream died before she gave it voice. Billy Jack loomed close, so near that she squeezed her eyes shut and held her breath as the fumes of liquor and his foul breath flowed over her face.

"Open your eyes, *señorita.* We will drink a little an' my friend, he will play music for us. You will dance for me, no?"

Jessie set her lips, gritting her teeth behind them. Tears burned behind her closed lids, but she fought not to cry. Pain lanced her scalp from Zach's grip on her hair, and fear had turned her bone marrow to water.

Billy Jack caught hold of her chin. "Open your eyes." When she didn't obey him, he put the bottle to her lips, tilting it so the liquor ran over her mouth.

Jessie felt his thumb pressing the corner of her mouth, forcing her lower lip open. She tried struggling, but stopped the moment she felt their bodies press even tighter against hers. Their laughter changed, turning darker, more threatening. The bite of whiskey made her eyes water and she gagged when it trickled into her mouth. She managed to twist her head to the side, taking the bottle from her lips. The jerky motion sent liquor spraying over her before Billy Jack yanked the bottle upright.

Whether he staggered or suddenly lost his balance, Jessie felt the press of Billy Jack's body ease away, and in an unexpected move she brought up her hand and slammed the bottle from his.

The air turned blue with his swearing. Zach slung his arm around her, locking her arms to her sides, his grip beneath her breasts so tight her rib cage felt bruised. Her hair came loose, but couldn't shield her from the sound of Zach's heavy breathing filling her ear. Inwardly she cringed to feel Billy Jack's fingers toying with the top button of her shirt. Jessie's eyes flew open. It was worse to imagine those dirty fingers touching her skin.

Two buttons went flying with a quick, hard pull, and only Zach's arm stopped Billy Jack from ripping more from her shirt.

She was dizzy and faint with the fumes of liquor rising from the floor, her clothes and their breath.

"Blackleg!" Billy Jack yelled. "Play for us. The lovely *señorita* has agreed to dance for me." Touching a handful of her hair, he jerked his head toward the arched opening where the sounds of a harmonica filled the air. "*Vamos*, amigo. I grow tired of this playing." He spun on his boot heel and disappeared into the saloon.

Jessie dreaded going in there. She no longer hoped that Silas would do something to stop them. If only someone would come into the store. The pressure from Zach's arm eased and for a moment hope flared that he was going to let her go. In the next moment she felt his open hand cup her breast. Her cry was cut off. Zach slid his other hand into her hair, twisting her head to the side, and kissed her.

Shuddering with revulsion, Jessie kept her lips sealed against the pressure of his tongue seeking entrance. Bile burned her throat. She tried to get her arm free, her fingers curling into claws, ready to defend the second she had the chance. Abruptly, Zach let her go but shoved her toward the opening. Jessie caught hold of the rough brick edge to keep her balance. The few moments' respite showed her the other three men sprawled in chairs around one table. Behind the bar, no more than roughly cut planks set on overturned barrels, stood a watchful Silas.

The man playing the harmonica changed to a lively tune. The Indian woman, sitting on another's lap, never once turned to look at her. Jessie felt the nudge that Zach gave her, but she couldn't make herself take a step.

"If you let them get away with this, Silas, I'll rouse every law-abiding person in town to run you out."

"If you're still alive to talk," Zach whispered from behind her.

Billy Jack started for her. A man kicked his chair back and rose. The stub of a cigar hung from his mouth. Jessie didn't know why her gaze fastened on him, but it did. He moved quickly to intercept Billy Jack, speaking to him in what she thought was Spanish, and when talking didn't work, he sent him staggering toward the bar with a hard shove. Then he turned on Zach.

"Get the hell in here. Alone." Monte didn't worry that Zach wouldn't obey, so he didn't bother to look at him.

The music stopped. Jessie kept staring at the man with the cigar.

Monte avoided the woman's eyes. He didn't spare more than a glance at the way she clutched her shirt together. Shaking his head, he knew he had no choice. He didn't want to kill her, and he knew it would come to that to keep her quiet. Having questions raised, or some do-gooder out hunting them, would have the boss tearing strips out of his hide. On the other hand, denying Billy Jack what he wanted could be worse than stepping into a nest of riled rattlers.

Taking the cigar out of his mouth, Monte made up his mind. He walked over to her. "Ma'am, I'm real sorry this happened. My boys got carried away havin' a little fun."

"Boys," Jessie hissed. Free of the fear that had gripped her, she lit into him. "They're not boys. They're animals. They belong locked up and—"

"Now, you're just a mite upset—"

"I'm not a *mite upset,* mister. I'm furious. Those men attacked me."

"Now, now, Miz Winslow," Silas said, hurrying toward her. "Don't carry on so. You ain't been hurt none."

Jessie looked at the Indian woman, thinking that she saw resignation in her dark eyes, but then the woman looked away. She focused on Silas. "You wouldn't know what hurts a woman, you miserable excuse for a man."

"Now, you hold on. You ain't got no cause to talk to me like that. Mr. Wheeler here stopped them before any harm was done."

Trembling, Jessie refused to back down. She wasn't going to let Silas or this man get away so easily. "No harm was done? I beg to differ. My shirt's ripped. I smell like a brewery. I've been mauled and spoken to in language that shamed me and you think no harm's been done. Let me tell you something, Silas, folks around here won't take kindly to hearing that I was attacked in your store."

Monte stepped closer and grabbed her upper arm with a sharp biting grip that forced her hand to release the torn edges of her shirt. Giving her a little shake, he spoke softly. "You listen and listen good. You're gonna get paid for your clothes, an' whatever the hell else you came in here to buy, then you're gonna leave and keep your mouth shut or I'll turn Billy Jack loose on you. Understand?"

Before Jessie could form an answer, a man called out for Silas. Jessie sagged against the wall. It was David.

"Over here," Silas called out, shooting her a spiteful smile.

Jessie had wished for a rescue. She ignored Monte pressing closer and taking hold of her other arm as she turned to look at David. His normally pleasant features wore a horrified expression as he took in her disheveled state. She knew before he spoke that there would be no help coming from him. And who could blame David? He wasn't a match for these men. He didn't even wear a gun.

"Jessie? What's going on here? What are you doing with these men?" Clutching a split ax handle, he came closer. "My God, you've been drinking!"

"This your husband?" Monte asked.

Jessie barely shook her head. She felt so ashamed when David burst out in loud denial. And she wouldn't worry over making the decision about marrying him now. David likely wouldn't have her to wife.

"Mister," Monte said, holding Jessie tight in warning, "you got business with Silas, then tend to it an' leave the little lady to me an' my friends."

"But, Jessie—"

"Come along, David," Silas urged, taking hold of his arm.

For a few moments more, Jessie held David's gaze and her silence. She didn't want to see him hurt, and these men would do that. But it pained her that, while he appeared confused, he demanded nothing more by way of explanation. Could he truly think so little of her that he believed she was willingly in the company of men like this? If it had been Logan coming through that door, Jessie had no doubt what his reaction would have been. Logan would not have bothered to ask her questions. He wouldn't believe what surface appearances revealed. Monte would be flat on his back, while the others—*Oh, stop it!* she admonished herself. *Wishing and hoping isn't getting you out of this.*

She hung her head as Monte stepped back but didn't release her. Silas hurried to usher David to the other side of the store.

"You didn't answer me, lady."

"I just want to get out of here."

"Not good enough," Monte stated. "I want your word you ain't gonna make any trouble. Although," he said, glancing at the floor where he picked out gold coins and a coffeepot, "if that fella's what you got around here calling themselves men, I ain't got much to worry about."

She didn't bother to answer. Any threats she made would be empty ones.

"If you're smart, lady, you won't get folks riled over a little fun. They've been hard up for liquor and a pretty woman. Can't blame them none."

The tone of his voice warned Jessie she faced a new threat. Much as it galled her to beg, she did so. "Please, mister, all I want to do is collect what I came for and get out. Just keep those men away from me."

She heard approaching footsteps and looked to see David. Whatever conclusion he'd come to, whatever Silas had told him, he didn't hesitate, but left the store without looking at her.

It was only then that Monte stepped away from her to allow her passage to the store. "Silas, you give the woman whatever she wants an' I'll settle up with you."

Jessie held tight to the counter. She couldn't stop shaking. The music started up again and she blocked out the sound and Silas's insistence that she was a fool not to take the man's offer. Staring straight ahead, but unable to focus, Jessie found herself thinking that the man called Billy Jack wore a large tarnished silver belt buckle, but the initial *L* was engraved over a coil of rope. The initial could be the man's last name, but it could be Logan's buckle. Logan said men were looking for him. These had to be the same ones. They had shot him, robbed him and left him for dead. They had attacked her.

And there was no law to call upon.

With a rough shake of her head, she set aside her thoughts. She had to get out of there and quickly. But Silas was right. She was being a fool to refuse to let them pay for everything.

"You've made your point and convinced me, Silas. I need a coffeepot, a rope and—" she paused, scanning the shelves behind him "—that hat. I want the black one, too."

"You already got a hat, Miz—"

"I want a new one."

Taking it down, he said, "It's too big for you."

Jessie snatched it from his hand. "I'll take it anyway. Two new shirts, and a red bandanna." Pursing her lips while Silas scurried to get them for her, she tried to keep calm. If she didn't think about what had happened, she wouldn't be sick.

When Silas returned and set the shirts with the folded bandanna on top of her sack, Jessie leaned closer. "And I want two bottles of whiskey."

"Whiskey? You want—"

"For medicinal purposes, Silas." Holding her hand out, Jessie had no need to fake the trembling.

The hat was too large for her—it covered her brows—but Jessie left it on. Carrying the two bottles, she followed Silas out of the store and waited for him to saddle the brown horse. She kept promising herself that she wouldn't cry. And she vowed to find a way not to tell Logan what had happened.

Silas led the horse to where she stood. "You know this ain't happened before. You musta done something to get that man all het up about you."

Eyeing him as if he was an ant she'd enjoy stepping on, Jessie set aside her feelings to latch on to what he said about those men.

"They've come here before?"

"A time or two. Womenfolk don't come in the store when they see their horses out front. Smart women, that is. Decent ones that ain't looking to hook onto a man any way they can."

"Smart women, Silas? Or women that know their men haven't got any backbone?"

"Ain't gonna jaw with you over this. You want I should thank Mr. Wheeler for you?"

"Tell him to go to hell. And tell him there are plenty of woodsheds around here if he wants to teach his *boys* some manners."

Stepping up into the saddle, Jessie knew that Silas wouldn't repeat a word that she said. Taking hold of the spare horse's reins, she rode out.

She managed to keep her brave front almost halfway home. She couldn't stand the way her skin felt as if things were crawling over it. She pulled rein and slid from Adorabelle's back. The nausea rose and Jessie fell to her knees. She remained there until the heaving stopped.

How was she going to face Logan?

Taking the top from her canteen, she rinsed her mouth. She slid the strap over the saddle horn and looked down at herself. Her shirt gaped open. Dirt smudges showed on her white camisole. She couldn't stand having the whiskey-soaked clothes on for one more moment. Grabbing one of the new shirts, she cast a hurried look around. A lizard watched from the top of a small pile of boulders. Stripping off her shirt and camisole, Jessie bundled them and shoved them into a crevice of the rock. The new shirt was a coarse weave but it didn't smell.

Tucking the tails into her skirt, she eyed the top of the whiskey bottle poking out from her saddlebag.

"Medicinal purposes, hell," she muttered, taking hold of the bottle. Someone had told her that men got a false sense of courage from whiskey. Jessie didn't care what kind of courage it was. She needed something to help her face Logan and lie to him.

Chapter Nine

❦

Logan used the simple law of survival to locate the boy. Every living creature depended upon three things. Water, food and shelter from predators.

It was midmorning before he found the trickle of a stream and followed its course back to where it widened. Churned-up dried mud drew him to hunker down and study the spot. The soft sounds of water rushing over the rocky streambed soothed him. He let himself be distracted by thoughts of Jessie. If old Santo, more father than guardian of all that bore the Kincaid name, could meet Jessie, he would say she was a lot of woman. Logan would agree. It went beyond her lush body to a strong will and stubborn mind. He wished there was time to explore the feelings stirring for her.

He wasn't a man given to wishing for what he couldn't have. Bringing his thoughts back to the problem at hand, he studied the ground. More than one set of bare feet had churned the mud. Rising, he scanned the bank with its low-growing brush. A few yellow-and-black dog-face butterflies hovered over the scattered wildflowers. Two hawks circled above, and he heard the incredible rapid whir of a humming-bird's wings but couldn't spot the tiny bird.

There were plenty of places that would offer concealment. Logan began to quarter the area, looking for clues. Upstream he found a deeper pool, a place where the grasses had been crushed often and a small pile of flat smooth stones such as a boy might collect for skimming the water. He knew he wasn't mistaken about the last. He and his brothers had often held contests to see who could send a stone skipping the farthest.

Ty, the youngest, was an impatient cuss, he not much better, but Conner would have them hopping from one foot to the other waiting for him to select the perfect stone, the right spot to stand, even wetting one finger and holding it up to test the wind before he'd finally make his throw. Conner usually won, too.

As he worked his way back from the stream, Logan thought of how sure Jessie was that no one had staked a claim on land near her. When he caught the smell of frying fish, Logan knew Jessie was wrong but he was on the right path.

Concealed in a thicket, he carefully parted the brush and nearly gave away his hiding place. Two wagons—prairie schooners, for they were smaller than the larger and cumbersome Conestogas—canvas tops intact but wagon tongue empty of oxen or the draft horses needed to pull the sixteen-foot-long wagon, rested beneath a half circle of cottonwoods. In the center a small fire burned, and Logan saw two trout frying in the black pan. His mouth watered. It had been a long time since he'd fished and fried his catch. Too long.

The campsite wasn't new. Deadfall was piled high, an ax protruded from a stump, signs of the clearing being enlarged showed in dried clump grasses that had been pulled from the earth. Two rocking chairs sat off to one side. Between two trees a line was strung with a few pieces of clothing hanging over the rope.

What Logan didn't see was the boy, or anyone else moving around. Those fish sure smelled ready to come off the fire. Anyone leaving them to burn had to do so for a good reason. He knew before he heard the snap of a twig behind him that he'd been caught.

"Come up slow and easy, mister."

Poked with a rifle barrel, Logan didn't have any choice. "I didn't come looking to hurt you. I just wanted—"

"Makes no never mind. You toss that gun aside. An' jus' remember that I'm watchin'."

"Boy, when a man comes friendly-like to your camp you don't hold a gun on him."

"Didn't see no sign of you being friendly, mister. You're creepin' 'round back here, watchin' us."

"Us?" *So there was someone else taking care of the boy.*

"That's what I said. An' I'm still waitin' on you."

Logan tossed the gun aside. He could have gotten the drop on the boy, but he wanted to prove he meant no harm.

"Now what?"

"Now you mosey into camp. An' remember I'm right behind you." Kenny swiped at the sweat dripping into his eyes. It was a good thing the man didn't turn, or he'd see how scared he was. Marty was hiding, and not likely to come out.

Standing in the clearing, Logan glanced around. The delicious smell of the frying fish made his belly rumble. "Your fish are gonna burn if you don't turn them, boy. And since I've done what you asked, why don't you tell me your name?"

"What's yours?"

"Logan. You can't think I'd hurt you after you saved my life?"

"Can't be too careful, mister. 'Sides, I seen the men you were with. I wouldn't trust one of 'em iffen I was paid to."

"I ain't asking you to trust anyone but me. And Miz Winslow. Jessie, that's her name, Jessie Winslow, is the widow you've been . . . er . . . trading with."

"What'd ya come lookin' for?"

"You and whoever you're with. I need to leave Jessie, and I'd feel a mite better if you'd keep an eye on her. You say you saw those men that left me for dead. Then you can understand why I'd be worried about her being down there alone without a man to watch over her."

"I ain't no man."

"Maybe not in size or years, boy, but I'd be proud to call you a friend. It was a mighty fine thing you did, taking care of me and getting me up to Jessie's place."

"Yeah, well, jus' so's you know. We were buryin' you when you started moaning. Like to scared me spitless, too."

"You were burying me!" Logan exclaimed. By almighty heaven, he'd had a closer brush with death than he had known. Buried? Lord!

"That's what I said. Couldn't leave you for buzzard bait. Ain't fittin' for folks to be a meal for 'em."

"Then I'll double my thanks. I'd still like to know your name. Can't thank you properly unless I do. You can't be running from the law?"

"Like you, mister? Naw. We ain't running from anyone. Guess I can tell you. It's Kenny."

"Pleased to meet you, Kenny. Now that we've exchanged names, do you think I could sit down? It was a trek from the cabin and I'm mighty thirsty. Standing here and smelling that fish is making my innards grumble something fierce. Will your daddy mind if I join you?"

"My pa's dead."

"Sorry, boy. Mine is, too." The question had been a wild shot, but Logan had no idea why he told the boy about his father.

"Guess it'd be all right for you to sit over there against that big cottonwood. I can keep an eye on you."

"Trusting young'un," Logan muttered beneath his breath as he settled himself on the ground. He hadn't lied about his belly rumbling from the delicious smell of the fish, but he had a feeling that the wiry boy holding the shotgun on him wasn't going to be won over easily. He'd never met such a distrusting kid. But it was that very trait that made Kenny perfect to look after Jessie. Not that he didn't think Jessie wasn't smart enough to take care of herself. She was. She had been doing fine until he'd come along. But he couldn't forget seeing Zach nosing around. There was no question that he couldn't stay, so Kenny was his next choice. If he could convince the boy and whoever was with him to do it.

"I'm not going anywhere, Kenny. You can put that shotgun away. Maybe you should fetch your ma?"

"She's dead, too. I ain't got no folks, no family but for my cousin."

"Then you got more than Jessie. She's alone but for that swayback mare of hers and her chickens." Once more Logan looked around, trying to find some clue if the cousin was near, was male or female.

Kenny saw that the edges of the fish were browned and ready to come off. He grabbed a rag and took hold of the frying pan's long handle, sliding it from the grate over the fire to a flat slab. His own mouth was watering to taste the fish he and Marty had caught. Marty wouldn't come out unless he called him and told him it was safe. This Logan didn't talk down to him, and there was something about the man's eyes, the way he looked right at a person when he talked, like he didn't have anything to hide. His ma sure set store by a person doing that.

Logan sat very still, sensing that Kenny was studying him and making up his mind if he would trust him or not. It made Logan lean toward thinking that the other half of the "we" Kenny had mentioned was a female. That only sent his curiosity flaring. Why would they be living here?

"You know, Kenny, you really are a very brave boy. Not many would have gone through the trouble you did for me. I'd like..." Logan said, lifting his hip to get into his pocket, then remembered that he had given all his money to Jessie. "Damn! Listen, when Jessie gets back, I'll have a little something to thank you with. But I promise you, Kenny, I'll reward you for what you did."

"Don't want nuthin'. I got all I need right here."

Logan stared at the boy. His wheat-colored hair hung to his shoulders, there was a rip on one shirt-sleeve and his pants had been clumsily patched. His brown eyes, dark and shadowed too deeply for a boy his age, never left Logan. He was, to Logan's mind, as patient as a peach ripening. Most disconcerting to have that direct gaze focused on you, making him feel as exposed as a chicken in a stewpot.

"Do I get to meet your... er... cousin, was it?"

"Yeah. My cousin. Don't know if the feeling's the same. Figure you're a right sort of man judging by things my ma tol' me. Marty!" he yelled. "Com'on out. He ain't gonna hurt us."

"Thank you, Kenny," Logan said with every bit of sincerity he could muster.

"You're welcome, mister. Com'on, Marty. Bring PeeWee with you."

"PeeWee?" Logan turned at a sound from the far wagon where a smaller boy was climbing down. Wrapped around his neck was a long thick fur. When he turned, blue eyes dancing with inquisitiveness, Logan smiled.

"So this is your cousin?" The import of that hit him. Logan looked at Kenny, then the younger boy. These two... that thin-limbed little boy and Kenny...

"Lord, I was figuring you were talking about a man-size cousin, boy."

"Me and Marty get by jus' fine. I take good care of him. And we got PeeWee."

"Ah, yes, PeeWee. Just what is—"

"Show him, Marty. Go on, get closer and let him see." To Logan he said, "If you're real gentle you can pet him."

Logan judged the smaller Marty to be about five or six. Like Kenny, the boy was fair skinned, but his hair, while as long, was straight corn-silk blond. He almost looked too pretty to be a boy, but Logan wisely kept his thoughts to himself. Kenny still had that shotgun within easy reach.

"It's all right, Marty. You can come closer to me. I promised Kenny I didn't come here to hurt either one of you. And I'd sure like to get a better look at PeeWee."

Marty tilted his head to the side and rubbed his chin against the soft caramel-furred animal. Logan saw the inquisitive nose twitch, and he smiled, for it reminded him of the boy who held him.

"PeeWee's a ferret," Kenny informed Logan. "He can climb trees and run so fast he's a blur goin' by. We got a muzzle for him to help us hunt rabbit. PeeWee goes down into their burrows an' drives the rabbits out. Long as we keep him clean and warm, he's happy to stay with us."

Logan reached out and stroked lightly over the ferret's back. He was almost three feet long, with a black mask and black feet and resembled a small weasel. "Bet he likes to fish and hunt mice."

"An' s-squirrels, too," Marty added.

"Don't mind Marty's stutterin'. He does that when he's real excited or 'fraid of something."

The longer Logan spent with Kenny, the more he was coming to admire the boy.

"I'm g-glad you're all b-better, uh—" Marty broke off and glanced at Kenny. "What's his name?"

"My name is Logan, Marty. And I offer you the same thanks I gave Kenny for saving my life."

Digging one toe into the ground, Marty swayed back and forth. "Shucks, couldn't do nuthin' else. It shore was a sight to see the widow woman so happy when she found you that she was cryin'."

The last was said so fast that Logan found it hard to make out what he said. Jessie so happy that she was crying? Not likely. Not the Jessie he knew. She had probably cried out of frustration for finding him in her doorway. But they had gone on long enough about him. It was time that he got some answers.

"You'd best go put PeeWee back in his cage 'fore we eat. He had his share, Marty, so don't be lookin' at me like that."

To Logan's surprise, Marty obeyed him. And his fear grew that the boys were well and truly on their own.

"Kenny, I think you should tell me what happened to your folks."

"Tol' you, they's dead."

"But when did they die? You and Marty didn't haul those wagons here by yourselves.'

Kenny hunkered by the frying pan and carefully divvied up the fish into three tin plates. He heard Logan repeat his question. Finished with the preparation, he rose and brought a plate to Logan.

"All we got is water to drink."

"That'll be fine." Logan hated pushing the boy, but time was short and he refused to leave without the answers and the promises he had come for. "How long have you and Marty been here?"

"I don't reckon the days so good. Maybe three or four months. Know we set out in March, 'cause Pa was all het up 'bout that Hayes fella gettin' elected." Marty picked up a plate with two hands and carefully carried it to Kenny.

"Can I sit with you?"

"Be my pleasure to have your company. Both of you," Logan added. He poked through the flaky fish and picked out some bones, then, following his young host's lead, ate with his fingers.

"Where'd you set out from, Kenny?"

"You sure do ask a lot of questions. Guess there ain't harm in sayin'. We're from Kansas. Ain't that right, Marty?"

The boy was ravenously attacking his fish, and barely nodded.

"Maybe it's painful for you to tell me, but I'd like to know how the two of you ended up here alone. Don't you have kinfolk back home? I could send a telegram to them so they could come and get you."

It was only because he was watching them so closely that Logan noticed Marty paused in shoveling fish into his mouth, and Kenny shot him a narrow-eyed look.

"Marty and me ain't got no kinfolk back home. Jus' him and me. Ain't no one gonna separate us."

"Whoa, Kenny. I'm not looking to do any such thing. No need to get surly with me, either. I'm asking 'cause I want to help."

"We ain't asked for any."

"Boy, I can tell you haven't had anyone put a muzzle on your mouth for some time. I'm here. I'm gonna help, and in return, so it's fair, you'll help me." He glanced at Marty and saw the boy blinking rapidly, sucking noisily on his bottom lip. "I shouldn't have yelled."

"That's right. You shouldn't." Finished, Kenny rose and went by Marty. He placed his hand on the little boy's shoulder. "Marty here gets real upset with yelling. So don't do it again or you'll have to leave."

"Best watch out the 'Pache don't get hold of you, Kenny. They'll make a warrior out of you."

"Already had a run-in with 'em when they stole our stock. Took the oxen teams, three horses, our milk cow, chickens and pigs. They ain't been back, though. Guess they don't figure same as you." He walked over near the wagon, then carried a bucket and dipper to Logan, who helped himself to a drink of water. Next he took the bucket over to Marty and made sure he drank before he took a dipper for himself.

All Logan could think at that moment was how much Kenny reminded him of his older brother, Conner. Conner the Caretaker was what he and Tyrel had called him behind his back, and never in kindly terms. But seeing Kenny care for the younger boy, cousin or not—Logan had not made up his mind if he believed that—made him understand something that both Sofia and Santo often said about Conner. He'd been a man before he ever had a chance to be a boy. The elderly couple had come with his mother upon her marriage to claim the land grant that had belonged to her family in this new territory. They had helped hold the Kincaid family together when his father died. Logan knew he'd been rich with more than the family wealth;

it was the family itself, including those like Santo and Sofia, that gave him more than these two boys had.

And there rose within him a craving to be home, to be surrounded by people he trusted, by those he loved. But he wasn't going anywhere without having finished what he started out today to do.

"You finished, Logan?"

He started, so deep were his thoughts, and found Kenny standing in front of him. "Sure, boy. I'm done. Best I've tasted in a long time."

Kenny nodded, but before he turned away, Logan caught the hint of a smile on his thin lips. He went to Marty, scraped the plates and reminded him it was his turn to wash the dishes, then bury the remains of the fish.

"And dig the hole deep this time, Marty. We don't want animals nosin' around camp again."

The moment Marty headed off in the direction of the stream, Kenny came to sit alongside Logan. "I been doin' some thinkin'. Iffen you ain't stayin', who's gonna take care of the widow woman? Marty an' me sorta figured that you an' her—"

"Hold up, Kenny. Let's get finished with you and then we'll discuss Jessie. You are going to tell me what happened here, aren't you?"

"Ain't no reason not to. Couldn't say much in front of Marty. He still gets real bad dreams. Sometimes he cries."

"Then he's mighty lucky to have you." *But who holds you when the bad dreams come, boy?* The question was not one he'd ask.

"We come up on this place an' Pa figured it was a good spot for us to stay for a few days. He was thinkin' 'bout filin' on a piece since they passed a...a...some kind of act.''

"The Desert Land Act. It brought lots of settlers out to the territory to file a twenty-five-cent-an-acre claim on six hundred and forty acres. What no one tells folks is that the Apache have hunted this land for longer than white men have lived in this country an' they ain't about to give it over without a fight.''

"Pa didn't know that. Marty's pa knew less. We were here maybe three or four days when Pa found color up in a blind canyon a ways back. They all went lookin' for gold. Marty an' me took PeeWee downstream. This storm come up. Ain't seen nuthin' like it. We got real scared an' hid under a rock shelf. That rain an' thunder jus' kept comin'. The sky got all black then lit up jus' like back home when they got fireworks.''

Shaking his head, Kenny repeated, "Ain't seen nuthin' like it. We stayed hid for hours. I dunno. Sudden as it come it was gone, but it was real dark by then. No one come callin' us so we stayed where we was till mornin'.''

Logan gave in to the impulse and took hold of Kenny's hand. "You don't need to say more. Your folks were caught in that blind canyon when the water rose, and they couldn't get out.''

Kenny left his hand within Logan's larger and stronger one. He looked away. "Weren't easy to bury 'em.'' He sniffed and wiped the back of his hand back and forth under his nose, grateful that Logan didn't say anything about his sniffling.

A few minutes later Logan murmured, "A man who can't feel sorrow when he loses those he loves ain't much of a man to my way of thinking. Nothing at all to be ashamed of. I wasn't much older than you when my pa died. I was lucky to still have my mother, folks so close they could have been family. There we were, my brothers and me, all sneaking off to grieve on our own, crying, too. Till one time we come upon Santo— he was real close to my pa—and there he was brushing down Pa's horse, talkin' and cryin' over how much he missed him.

"Learned a lesson that day from a man I respected. We all did, come to think about it. Santo wasn't any less of a man in our eyes for having such deep feelings and not being afraid to show them. But I'll bet it's a hard thing to do when you're trying to be strong for someone else. Someone little, who needs so much."

"'Tain't fair," Kenny mumbled, enticed to confide his feelings by the soft, understanding way that Logan spoke.

"Life ain't fair, son. A hard lesson to learn and one that stays with a man. But my problem and your troubles could have a way of working themselves out together. All I need is your word that you'll try."

Kenny pulled his hand free of Logan's. He turned to look at him, then, still holding Logan's gaze, yelled, "Marty, stop hangin' back! You come sit an' hear this. Ain't doin' no decidin' without you."

"Aw, Kenny, how'd you know I was there? I was trying so hard to do like you said and be real quiet and all. How'd you know?"

"I jus' got this sense, that's all, Marty. You'll get it, too. Soon as you get bigger. Com'on an' sit."

Logan turned his head to hide his smile. He would bet that Kenny had finely honed senses. The boy was going to be a hell of a man when he was full grown. Logan wasn't a man to waste time cursing what fate set before him, but he made an exception this time. Here he was, with Jessie, a woman made for a man to share with, and these two boys in need of a home, and he couldn't make promises to any of them.

"So," Kenny said, slinging an arm around Marty's bony shoulders, "tell us what you got in mind."

"Kenny, you promised you'd ask him first."

"Ask me what?" Logan glanced from Marty to Kenny. "Speak up. If I can answer you, I will."

Marty, squirming around, started elbowing Kenny in the ribs. "Do it. Go on. Ask."

Kenny spoke, but he wouldn't look at Logan. "Those men that left you for dead, they're outlaws, ain't they? An' I figured if they are, that makes you one of 'em."

"Are you asking me or telling me, Kenny?"

"A little of both, I guess. I sorta trust you, but I gotta know. On account of Marty. I'm big enough to take care of myself but he's little. I can't let him get hurt none."

Logan wished some of the men he knew could lay things open as well as this young boy. Hard times and a land he sometimes believed was belched up from hell could do a job of aging that no amount of years made up for. But the boy's question left him in a quandary. If he lied, he risked Kenny knowing and deciding not to help him. But to tell him the truth risked the boy if Monte or any of the others got hold of him.

"What's the matter, Logan? Got you between a rock an' a hard place?"

"Don't you just know it. I'll tell you what I can and hope that you'll trust me. If that's good enough, say it now."

"An' if it ain't?"

"Then I'll be mighty disappointed and be on my way."

"Marty, you want we should listen to him?"

Drawing his lower lip into his mouth, Marty started sucking. Rocking back and forth, he finally nodded.

"So talk to us."

Logan put his simple but mutually beneficial proposition to them. Kenny, with the instincts of a wary animal and the natural inquisitiveness of a boy being included in grown-up plans, questioned Logan at every turn. When he was finished speaking, Logan didn't say a word when Kenny hauled Marty to his feet and walked off a little way with him to talk things over.

And talk is what Kenny did. He listened, too, to Marty's questions, farfetched as some were, never getting angry, just answering until Marty seemed to be reassured.

Watching them, Logan found his liking and respect for Kenny and his pity for little Marty turned to a desire to take them home to the Rocking K. His mother would be in her glory to have young boys around the house again. Maybe with them to distract her, she'd stop haunting him and his brother—for Ty hadn't been back long enough these past few years for her to catch hold of him—about getting married and giving her grandchildren before she was too old to enjoy them.

Shaking his head with regret, Logan knew it was impossible now. He'd be riding hard with no time to watch or worry over two boys. He still had a promise to keep to Conner. And a score to settle with Monte and the others.

He looked up to find the boys holding hands as they came toward him.

"We decided. But we can't come with you now. My ma taught me proper that to go callin' means we got to wear Sunday-go-to-meeting clothes."

Logan opened his mouth to protest that it wasn't necessary, but Kenny had such a look of pride about him that he agreed.

"I'll look for you near supper." He rose, then stood a moment scratching the back of his neck. "You wouldn't mind if I borrowed your part of the stream to take a bath, would you?"

"Not me." Marty stuck his bottom lip out in a pout.

"Not you. Do I make you take baths? But I bet you'd like to go swimmin' again?"

"That's fun, Kenny."

"Only did it once," Kenny explained to Logan. "I had to keep watch an' I worried 'cause he don't swim so good."

"Tell you what. I'll keep first watch and you two go swimming, then I'll take a bath. Jessie, Lord love her, will be grateful to us for the consideration."

Chapter Ten

The thick band of clouds still hovered as Logan approached the cabin cautiously. He scanned the immediate area, puzzled when he spotted the two saddled horses loose in the corral.

Jessie was back and she'd found him a horse. His gut gave a something's-wrong twist and he started running. Jessie would never leave the horses unattended unless she was sick . . . or hurt.

"Jessie!" He rounded the corner of the cabin in a skid, saw no sign of her and headed for the door. When he grabbed the iron latch and it didn't give way, fear seeped into his voice.

"Jessie!" he yelled again, pounding on the bolted door. "Jessie, open the door!" Logan tried to be calm. He pressed his ear to the door, but heard no answer.

Inside the cabin, Jessie hid in the corner near the cupboard, ignoring Logan's shouted demands that she open the door to him.

All the way home she'd wanted a bath, but her need had grown so strong to feel clean again that she'd impatiently settled for a basin of hot water. The cabin was filled with shadows—she hadn't bothered to light a lamp—and the gloom suited her dark mood.

Stripped to the waist, she had scrubbed her skin until she realized it was useless. She'd never feel clean again. Eyes open or closed, she couldn't wipe away the image of leering eyes in a merciless face looming over her. No matter how hard she rubbed her skin, the crawling sensation of being touched by those dirty hands remained on her flesh.

Telling herself that she had not been hurt made no difference. She was ashamed. There wasn't enough hot water or talking that could take away the feeling.

Not even the copious amounts of whiskey she forced herself to drink, until her stomach heaved in rebellion, stopped her from reliving the terrible scene of helplessness.

And she cried for the unseen but wrenching robbery those men had committed—they had stolen her belief that she could live here alone and protect herself.

She refused to think about David at all.

But Logan, whose voice now coaxed through the door, was not David. Logan wasn't a man to run from trouble.

The thought settled in her mind as unshakable truth. Logan wouldn't run, even if the trouble wasn't his.

"Jess, please, just answer me," Logan pleaded. His hand closed over the butt of his gun, the gun Jessie had given him, and the one he was about to use if he had to. He was getting desperate to break the wall of silence from the cabin. The bolted door proved she was inside.

But didn't prove that she was alone.

The thought erupted from his mind and sent him staggering back away from the door.

What if Zach had come back? What if he had been waiting inside? Jessie, sweet, trusting Jessie at the mercy of him.... *Stupid, blind fool!* He called himself that and worse. He'd never thought to search the area beyond the cabin. The blow to his head had done damage. He'd lost his edge, to be so careless and put Jessie in danger.

If Zach or one of the others was inside, he couldn't retreat. They'd only hurt Jessie if they couldn't find him. If they hadn't done that already...if that wasn't the reason she didn't answer him. Too many ifs....

And his going off half-cocked with worry over Jessie handed anyone inside the cabin with her one hell of a weapon.

He hadn't known how deep his feelings were for her until this moment. He'd do anything to keep her safe. Logan didn't put any qualifiers on that. Whatever it took, whatever it cost, he was willing to pay the price.

A rock and a hard place.... His mind went blank. He'd been in tough situations, made lightning-swift decisions, but now all he could think about was Jessie, not what he should do.

The silence, the utter absolute silence from the cabin sent him back to pounding on the door. He resumed calling out to her, knowing he couldn't let his voice or his actions give away what he suspected.

Hearing Logan's fist drumming on the door again, Jessie covered her ears, but she couldn't shut out the sound of his pleading demand that she answer him.

She knew she couldn't hide forever, not from him and certainly not from herself.

Dragging her hands down, she bit her bottom lip, not noticing that she tasted blood. Wide and blank, her eyes targeted the door. With a shaking hand she reached out for an old wool shirt that had belonged to her brother.

She needed the shirt's warmth as much as she needed its comfort.

"A minute. Just a minute more," she pleaded, then repeated it like a litany as she hurried to button up the shirt. A trembling seized her. She took hold of the basin and water sloshed over the edges, dripping down the front of her dark brown skirt. Tears burned her eyes and she blinked them back. How could she have any tears left?

You are strong, Jessie. You survived a sham of a marriage. You made a new life for yourself. You can face Logan and lie.

The basin fell into the dry sink with a clatter. She stared at the mess she'd made, clinging to the edge of the wood frame.

"Jessie! If you don't open this door I'll tear it apart!"

Roused by the fury in Logan's voice, she answered him, "I'm coming!" Anger for his presence when all she wanted to do was hide fueled her rapid move to the door. Anger that built to rage lent her strength to throw off the bolt and fling the door open.

For a moment there was a glint of ruthlessness so savage in his eyes that it caused a shiver to run through her and forced her rage to retreat.

Just as she physically retreated a few steps into the cabin. Then she saw the drawn gun he held.

Like those of a hunter who'd run his quarry to ground, his instincts flared toward the chase when she backed away from him. A small voice of reason ordered him to take a moment before he spoke, before he dared move inside with Jessie.

The surge of need to have him hold her staggered Jessie. And it frightened her that she had come to depend upon him, anyone, so much. Fear couldn't make the need go away.

Logan holstered the gun, knowing without needing to look or ask that Jessie was alone. But his eyes met hers and within those wide golden brown eyes were the shattered dreams of a child and the needs of a woman. The tightening in his gut was unexpected—raw and purely sexual. His mind was wiped clean. He fought against the power, releasing a breath he hadn't realized he was holding.

"What the hell happened?"

Her head moved slowly from side to side, the shaking becoming faster as she once again backed away from him.

"Don't, Jessie," he snapped, frustration lighting the fuse on an already short temper. The silence that followed was thick with tension.

His gaze took in the spill of her hair on one side, the overlarge man's shirt, the wide damp spot on her skirt. His gut twisted to see her lower lip swollen where she had bitten it, and the faint mark at the corner of her mouth. His gaze moved beyond her to the bottle of whiskey on the table. It appeared almost empty.

Suddenly he felt as if he were walking around quicksand. He lifted his hand toward her, waiting agonizing seconds while she stared at him, then his outthrust hand, before she turned away.

"Jessie?"

"Did you ever think I'd like some privacy after having you underfoot for almost a week?"

Her voice was hoarse as if she'd been yelling . . . or crying. Logan couldn't shake the feeling that something was very wrong. Annoyed that he couldn't figure out what it was, he raked his hand through his still-damp hair, never taking his eyes from her back.

Push her. The thought came quickly, but Logan was slow to obey it. "If you wanted me gone, Jessie, all you had to do was say so."

"I guess I just did."

"The hell you say!" He went after her, catching her shoulder and spinning her around to face him. "I asked you a question an' don't put me off. You wouldn't leave that swayback nag you're so fond of saddled. You wouldn't have taken so long to answer me or open the door if it was just a matter of privacy."

She twisted out from under his hold, but the table halted her retreat. Her eyes searched the cabin, looking for escape. This was a Logan she had not seen. The faint dark stubble on his face reinforced the relentless gaze that pinned her in place. Without realizing what she was doing, Jessie raised her hands before her.

"Stop it! Put your hands down, Jessie. I'm not gonna hit you. I'm not going to hurt you. I've never raised my hand to a woman in my life and I won't start now no matter how much you push me." He stepped closer, bracing his hands on the table's edge, caging her hips between them, just as his body caged her against the table itself. "And you are pushing me, lady."

"I wanted to wash. I couldn't very well do that with you here."

"And the whiskey? What was that for? Some new scent I've never heard of."

With her head lowered, he could barely hear her mumbled reply.

"I don't owe you anything. It's none of your business. You've got your horse. There's supplies in the sack tied to my horse. Take it all and go."

"I can't hear you. And I want to see you face-to-face when you say it, Jessie."

He didn't know what made him look around. She said she wanted a bath, but all he saw was the basin tossed in the dry sink. A washcloth hung over the edge, dripping water on the floor. And nowhere he looked was the shirt she'd been wearing when she left for town. Alarm shot through him.

Logan kept one hand on the table, the other he slid beneath her chin to gently urge her to look at him.

Using every ounce of his control, he spoke softly. "I know that something happened. I'd sell my soul to see you smile right now, pretty lady. I'd sell everything I own if you'd trust me enough to tell me what's wrong. And don't close your eyes against me, Jess. Trouble shared is trouble halved."

She searched his features, settling on his mouth, fighting the panic taking hold of her. He wouldn't like being compared to her deceased aunt's little dog, but right now Logan reminded her of Ulysses—named for the general and previous president. Like his name-sake, the dog would not be deterred when he went af-ter what he wanted. A trait that Logan shared.

Trouble shared is trouble halved. The words re-played in her mind. But she would double his trouble, not halve it, if she told him the truth.

"Jess, I'm a real patient man—"

"Who asked you to be? It wasn't me. I haven't asked you for anything."

"No?"

Confused by the challenge in his voice, she looked up at him. Two seconds later Logan took her by the arm and marched her to stand in front of the bureau. The mirror hanging above was not of the best quality. Wavy ripples played in the reflections of their bodies.

"Take a good look at yourself, Jessie. Go on, look. Then see what I've been seeing. Especially your eyes. They're asking all kinds of things from me. Trouble is, I'm not sure you know what you want."

Logan was caught by the way she closed her eyes as if the image was painful to her. His grip on her upper arms pulled the shirt taut over her breasts. One of the spaces between the horn buttons gaped open. His gaze targeted that bit of bare flesh. He ached to touch her with the intimacy of a lover, but Jessie had denied him that place in her life. Yet there remained the desire to offer her some small comfort. He thought about tak-ing her head between his hands and covering her in-credibly sad face with kisses. He couldn't do it. He wouldn't stop with soft, gentle kisses. If he ever kissed her again, he wouldn't stop at all.

And he envied the man whose ring she still wore. Jessie wouldn't be erecting any barriers with him. Logan found himself experiencing jealousy. A new emotion, one whose fangs sank deep. He didn't want Jessie turning to another man when he was gone. He wanted to be the one who filled her thoughts, and her body.

"Jessie, let me help you. Let me make what's hurting you go away."

Her head drooped to the side as if she no longer had the strength to hold it upright. Two hairpins slipped to the floor and her loosened burnished hair covered his hand.

Caught in the grip of emotions too tangled to name, Logan lifted his hand from her arm and gathered her hair as he leaned forward to trail kisses along the arch of her bare neck.

"Jess, oh, Jess," he whispered, "why can't you trust me?" He took her earlobe between his lips, gently scraping the sensitive flesh with his teeth. The faint trembling of her body acted as a caress to his.

"Logan? Hold me. Please just hold me."

She twisted around, locking her arms around his waist. Her mouth blindly sought his. It was an act of desperation to silence him, it was a need to replace one memory with another. A memory that wouldn't hurt. She knew she would be safe with Logan. She had to be. Jessie leaned into him, feeling the captivating heat of his body that warmed her own chilled flesh. The pressure of his lips against her mouth was deep and persuasive and undeniably enticing. When his thumb touched the corner of her lips, she didn't understand at first what he wanted. The gentle ply of his tongue skimming the seam of her mouth urged a response, and she moaned softly. Her hands grabbed his shirt, and she braced herself for the invasion of his tongue.

But Logan was subtle. He didn't want to frighten her. There was no storming of the faintly whiskey-scented delicate skin, but a careful, coaxing foray that left her shivering.

It was only as he slowly filled her mouth, tasting her intimately, that Jessie realized what she had started. This was how gentle and thorough his ultimate possession would be of her. If she allowed it...if she wanted...

She held on tighter, burrowing her body against his. All the masculine strength and heat that had been unsettling her for the past days swamped her now. His touch was, she thought, exactly as she had dreamed it would be, rioting her senses, luring her deeper into passion's web.

Jessie wasn't short or petite, but she felt so frail to Logan beneath his hands. He stroked her arms, her back, puzzled over the chill of her flesh beneath the wool shirt, wanting to dispel it. When his fingers brushed the underside of her breast, he felt a womanly fullness that made him ache. He couldn't stop himself from touching her.

He heard the catch in her breathing and thought she would push him away. To his pleasure and surprise, Jessie clenched her hands more tightly around his shoulders. Reluctantly he broke free of her mouth and trailed questing, tormenting little kisses along the line of her jaw and up to her earlobe.

He covered the unfettered fullness of her breast. The kisses grew more frantic. The tips of her fingers bit into his shoulders. He answered the hungry little sound she made with a groan of yearning.

"Jessie," he whispered hoarsely.

God, this was good. So damn good. More than he had dreamed of. He was so hard, he had to bare his teeth against the pleasurable pain of it. She needed him. Not the ghost of a dead man. Not the suitor who hadn't touched her. It was real and it was honest. And her quiet desperation made him want to please her.

"Jess. I want you so much. My sweet, pretty lady... tell me what pleasures you."

"You. You do, Logan." Her soft murmur became a moan as she closed her eyes against the feel of his delicate bite to her earlobe. This is what you wanted, she told herself. And what he wanted, too. He was fully aroused, rocking his hips against hers, and she could feel the softening of her body to fit the harder contours of his.

But this was all happening too fast. She knew so little about him. *Yet you'll trust him with your body when you can't trust him enough to tell him what happened to you.*

Jessie ignored the nagging little voice. Never in her life had she needed and wanted a man the way she wanted Logan. Denying it would be forever denying herself a chance to know what it meant to be swept by a desire that burned inside her.

He kissed her lightly, feeling the coolness of her lips, but inside her mouth was hot. He rubbed his lips against hers, drinking the small, hungry sounds she made. Their tongues touched, and she moved against him restlessly. Her hands climbed the back of his neck, sliding into his hair to grip his head. Jessie became the aggressor and ignited a powder keg of sensation.

Heat suffused his chest and spilled down into his belly and thighs. The strong, primitive feelings that made his arousal almost painful strengthened. He touched her nipples and she tore her mouth from his to utter a soft cry.

"Jess, tell me you're not afraid of me." His hands slid down her back, forcing her gently against the length of him. When his palms reached her rounded buttocks he cupped her and lifted her up into the heat of his thighs.

"No. Yes. I don't know." The fear was buried beneath need and desire. A desire that was mutual. She could feel the rigid shape of him pushing against her.

He brought his hands around to stroke up her sides, cupping her breasts and tugging gently on her nipples. He whispered dark words, praise, sounds of need as he felt the passion come to life in Jessie. She covered his throat with random kisses and tiny bites she instantly soothed with her tongue.

Logan longed to feel her skin against his, to take her nipples into his mouth, to bathe them with his tongue for a long time and feel them flushed and hard, while she cried out his name.

"You can't be afraid of me when you can tell so easily how much I want you?" His voice lowered to a husky groan as he pressed her tight against him.

"Logan, please..."

"I want to. I want to pleasure you like no one else has, or ever will again."

There was a raw, primitive sound to his voice that should have alarmed her. It didn't. Jessie felt her blood sizzling inside her body. She started to trail kisses over the hard line of his jaw, but he turned her within the gentle cage of his arms until she stood with her back against his chest. Swaying slightly, she attempted to turn around again.

Logan held her still. "Stay, Jess. Open your eyes. I want you to see us. Together."

She lifted heavy-lidded eyes and watched them widen with shock. She didn't know the woman reflected in the mirror. With her lips swollen, parted, and her hair tumbling down to her waist, there appeared a wanton, not the Jessie she knew. She leaned back against Logan and saw only half of his body showing behind hers. He looked lean and spare, a flush mantling his cheeks, like the heat that tinted her own. His eyes were hooded, watching her, his facial muscles tight, and she wanted to reach back to touch the errant lock of dark hair that fell across his forehead. She didn't move. She couldn't. Her breathing grew shallow as her body tensed with waiting.

There was a strength and male beauty about him that stirred fear and heightened her desire at once, but she never averted her eyes.

"Do you see yourself as I do?" he whispered, opening the top button of her shirt. He slid his hand over her neck, stroking her, taking the tension with him.

"Desire," she murmured, surprised that she said it aloud, surprised that she saw what he asked. There was a languid heaviness to her gaze, a silent pleading invitation within the depths. She wanted to close her eyes against the sight, but the glitter in Logan's eyes stopped her. A delicious shiver began inside, turning her knees to jelly, sending a flood of heat that rose tremoring through her thighs to settle low in the pit of her stomach.

Jessie studied the woman in the mirror and knew, impossible as it seemed, that she would be safe with Logan. The very gentleness of his touch allowed her to be vulnerable with him.

"What?" he questioned with a slow, sensual smile spreading across his lips. "I can see you want to ask me something." Softer then, "Ask me." His tongue rimmed the shape of her ear and his smile deepened when a languid sigh drifted forth. "Ask me, Jess. Anything."

Chapter Eleven

She moistened her lips. No words came. She closed her eyes, thinking it would somehow be easier to ask that he touch her again, that he ease the ache that seemed to swell her breasts. But all she thought of was the feel of his hand stroking her throat. She didn't want to lose the gentle, tender touches.

So she remained silent, wishing she could ask him not to stop the sweet caress, but only to slide his hand lower.

Without ceasing the ply of his hand on her throat, Logan slid his other hand around her waist and spanned the curve of her belly. She arched into this new touch, but he pressed her tight against him, slowly rocking her to and fro, needing to ease his aching flesh as much as he needed to heighten the passion that Jessie still guarded.

Jessie felt the whisper of his fingers moving up the front of her clothes, and the cooler air against her skin warned that he had unbuttoned her shirt. The tease of his hand moving like a shadow over the land sent a flood of sensations over her skin. And Jessie was tempted to allow herself one bold action.

She caught hold of his hands.

"Yes, Jessie, yes. Show me," he murmured encouragingly.

A dreamy smile tilted her mouth, for there had been a smile in his voice. The sense of being safe spread throughout her as she drew his hands to cover her breasts.

She had wanted, but Jessie wasn't prepared for the wealth of desire that streaked out from his rough, callused palms as they met her bare flesh.

"Don't be afraid, Jess. I won't hurt you. I'd never hurt you."

An overpowering urge flooded her to see him... them. Her lashes lifted slowly and she stared at the sight of Logan's dark, tanned skin against her paler flesh. His hands cupped the undersides of her breasts, and as she watched, his thumbs circled her nipples, drawing them tight. The dark shirt fell to the sides, but she didn't want its warmth now. A fine mist flushed her skin and she grew embarrassed when he lowered his head and nudged aside the shirt from her shoulder.

Kissing her, he whispered, "You taste like passion, Jessie. But there's so much more I want to taste from you." He frowned at the sudden tenseness of her body. "What's wrong? What have I said? Done?"

She turned her head away from him, unwilling to admit how much she regretted an end to all the sweet, gentle touches. She should have known. But Logan had lulled her, for he had let it go on so long and hadn't seemed to mind. She thought he was enjoying—

"Jessie, don't hide from me like this." He turned her with his arms, guiding her chin up, coaxing until she opened her eyes again. "Now, what's all this? If you don't tell me what pleases you, or what doesn't, how can you find pleasure?"

She searched for the lie, but all she found was concern in his gaze. "Do you really want to know? Harry never—"

"I'm not Harry." Logan bit off the words. If the man had hurt her, when he found Jessie the most responsive woman— He broke off his thoughts when she spoke.

"I can't tell you unless I do it in my own way. He grew angry with me when I asked him to kiss me a little longer or to touch me gently. He'd promise. He even tried. But then he'd get mad and tell me that most women didn't get any pleasure, so I shouldn't stop him from having his." Pensive, she drew her lower lip between her teeth.

"No," Logan said softly, using one finger to free her lip. "You've abused it enough. Bitten down real hard today. I told you," he murmured, bending his head to take her mouth with his, "let someone have a care with these lips. Someone who knows how to be gentle, Jess," he whispered, brushing his mouth against hers. "As gentle as you want, as gentle as you need.

"And Harry was wrong. That's a selfish man talking. Oh, honey," he said, caressing her back. "I learned never to be a selfish man. I know what's gonna happen on my side, Jess. Making you feel pleasure is the challenge for me."

She snuggled her head against his shoulder, and Logan cradled her head in one hand, keeping the long, sweeping strokes going over her spine with the other.

"Now, I don't want you takin' that the wrong way. For me, I like knowing that you're enjoying touching me as much as I like touching you. But if you don't tell me, then I won't know if the touches are the ones you want, or even how."

What he didn't say, couldn't say, was Conner's rule. Pleasure a woman the first time, and she'll invite you back to her bed. Logan had never faulted Conner's logic, and he never lacked for female company.

"Logan?"

"I'm listenin', Jess."

"What if a woman doesn't know?"

"Then she learns. Like you're gonna learn with me. You only need to trust me. Trust that I really want to give you pleasure, Jessie. If you can believe that, then you'll let me give you pleasure. Anything I do that you don't like, say so. But, please, pretty lady—"

"Tell you if I do," she finished for him, and pulled back to look at his face. Cupping his chin, she planted a kiss on his jaw, and smiled. "A kiss, then—"

His mouth closed over hers before she could say another word. He kissed her soundly, hungrily, rubbing his mouth against hers until her lips parted. His tongue slipped inside, and stayed until he had thoroughly sampled her, until her breaths were as ragged as his, and the pounding of his heart slamming against his chest reflected the thundering noise filling his ears.

He pulled back and grinned at her wet, rosy lips.

They both turned to stare at the door, realizing that the pounding they heard was not from passion, but was real.

"They're here. Jeez! Not now."

Before Jessie could gather her wits and question him, Logan was buttoning up her shirt. One finger flicked her chin. "Hold that smile and the rest of that kiss, lady. We're not finished."

Fear set in the moment he left her. All the terror she had held at bay rushed back. *They're here.* Logan's words meant only one thing. Those men he'd been with had come looking for him. With a sob, Jessie forced herself across the room to grab hold of the shotgun as Logan opened the door.

Kenny stood before the door, his brow beetled into a pronounced frown. He was as spruced up as Marty, whom he held by the hand. Slicked-back hair, clean shirts and pants, boots spit-polished to a shine. In his other hand he held two rabbits.

"You sure you want us here?" he asked Logan.

"I invited you both, didn't I?"

"Yeah. But we saw you hangin' all over her like she was honey and you the fly. Marty, here," he said with a jerk toward the smaller boy, "figures you'd have sticky fingers."

"Yeah. Do you? Huh? Do you?"

"Jessie's got a right large bar of lye soap she ain't had a chance to use yet. You boys take my meaning?"

They nodded, but Logan had to resist the urge to turn and look at Jessie. She was making awful choking noises, and he swore beneath his breath when he realized that he had completely forgotten to tell her that they were coming. He fixed a stern stare first on Kenny, then Marty, wishing he could say something that would lessen her embarrassment. Damn Kenny for having a mouth that didn't know when to quit.

Jessie, regaining control over herself, snatched the whiskey bottle off the table and shoved it on the bottom shelf of the cupboard. She straightened and smoothed her shirt, trying to muster some semblance of calm before she went to the door.

Sniffing loudly, Kenny peered around Logan. "Don't smell like much's cookin'." He held out the two rabbits. "My ma always said ya can't go visitin' folks without takin' 'em something to eat. By the looks of things, it's a good turn I did for all of us."

"What's that mean, Kenny?" Marty pressed closer to him as the widow woman came to stand behind Logan.

"Means that when big folks got a game of slap an' tickle on their minds, they ain't got room for thinkin' 'bout food, too."

"Jeez, boy, watch your mouth. Jessie's a lady. You owe her an apology."

"Sorry, ma'am." But he turned to Logan with one brow quirked, the grin spreading on his thin lips and a knowing look in his eyes. "What do you folks call it?"

"Call what, Kenny? What kind of game is it? Can we play?"

"Jeez!" Logan exploded.

"Jeez!" Kenny yelled.

Both Logan and Kenny looked at each other and burst out laughing. Marty shook his head much in the same manner as Jessie.

When the laughter died away, she came forward. "Why didn't your mother come with you?"

"Didn't ya tell her?" Kenny shot Logan an accusing look.

"I didn't get around to talking to Jessie. But I'll remedy that situation right now."

"Well..." Kenny heaved a long-suffering sort of sigh. "Seein' as how you gave us an invite for supper an' none's cookin', Marty an' me'll make it. You can walk out with him, ma'am, iffen that's all right with you. Might want to tend those horses."

Logan grabbed hold of Jessie's arm. "Excellent idea." He hustled her outside and away from the cabin before he took that boy over his knee.

Jessie's protests remained unspoken. First the pace had her stumbling, then the moment they reached the corral, Logan swung her into his arms.

"So I was all over you like a fly to honey?"

"That's what that impossible—"

"Yeah. But he was right." A quick, hard kiss settled the matter as far as he was concerned.

Jessie hadn't begun. The second he broke their kiss, she placed her fingertips over his mouth. "Do you really think it's a good idea to leave those two little boys in the cabin? I can't believe you agreed to let them cook for us. They're likely to burn my house down."

"Kenny has more savvy in his one hand than many men I know. Trust me, Jess. He'll have supper sittin' on the table by the time I'm done with the horses."

He saw her glance at the animals, and the way she looked away. Quickly, maybe too fast. He'd not forgotten about his unanswered questions. Wisely he decided to let them be for now.

Taking her by surprise, he lifted her up and swung her around so she could sit on the top rail of the corral.

"Logan! Your shoulder—"

"Won't ever get stronger unless I work it. You sit." A grin and the still-warm glitter of desire in his eyes softened the order. And as he worked, stripping off the gear and supplies, he told her what he had learned about the two sagebrush orphans.

"Why call them that, Logan?"

"Just a handle folks hung on little ones left without folks from an Indian raid, sickness, accidents. There's too much out here," he explained, gesturing toward the mountains, then at the flat below the cabin. "Man can die—"

"Don't talk about it. I don't want to remember that you were out there, left to die."

"That's all over, Jessie." Logan slung the saddle he removed from Adorabelle over the top rail, then went back and stripped down the brown horse Jessie had bought for him.

Jessie watched the fluid grace of his every move as he checked over the horse, until she had to stop imagining his hands stroking her in the same gentle manner. She closed her eyes, gripping the rail on either side of her hips. Logan's words replayed in her mind.

She started when she felt his hands cover her own. Opening her eyes, she looked down at him. "All done?"

"You picked a good horse, Jess."

She smiled. The words were simple. The praise behind them held a great deal more meaning to her. "I didn't have much of a choice. The other one Silas had was a showy paint. There was something very appealing about this one's stability."

"He'll get me where I need to go."

Jessie didn't answer. Thoughtful, she glanced over his head toward the shed where the two horses munched the hay Logan had forked out for them. She wished she could recover as easily and as quickly as Logan had appeared to from those passionate minutes they had shared before the boys arrived. Her body still ached, and a strange tension hummed through her.

"What's wrong?"

"Nothing. I . . . I was wondering what's to be done with those boys."

Logan had the grace to look away before he told her what he had in mind. "Ah, Jess, I sorta figured they could stay here with you."

"With me?"

He backed up a little and planted his hands on his hips in reaction to her snippety tone. "Don't get all het up before I explain."

"I'm listening. But let me tell you this first. I don't believe either you or I will make this decision. From one meeting with Kenny, I know that boy has a mind of his own. He won't take kindly to any plans you made."

"I did talk to him."

"You did what!" In her hurry to get down, Jessie's heel caught in her skirt hem. Only Logan's quick move forward to catch her stopped her from sprawling in the dirt.

With her hands braced on his shoulders, Jessie thanked him, suddenly wary of his grin. She squirmed, trying to get him to release her. Logan's arms tightened around her hips.

"Damn you, Logan. Put me down. Your shoulder—"

"Hurts like hell's own fire," he finished for her.

"Then why—" Jessie lost her breath. His lips closed over the tip of one breast. The warmth of his mouth penetrated the wool cloth. Heat and moisture and the gentle abrasion of his teeth gave her a pleasure so intense that she cried out.

"Stop. You must stop. The boys'll see."

Logan released her, unwilling to have her retreat again. "Wait here. I'll take the sack inside, then we'll go pick greens for supper." At the corral gate he turned. "And then you won't worry about anyone seeing us."

All through supper Jessie retained the flush she had obtained following Logan's version of picking greens. Kenny, she was grateful to see, had lost his smirk after a warning look from Logan.

To her surprise, the rabbit tasted every bit as good as her own cooking, and she was lavish with her praise to both boys.

Jessie couldn't help noticing how Marty directed all his questions to Kenny, who showed a great deal of patience in repeating them to either Logan or herself.

As the meal came to a close, Jessie grew very quiet. Once or twice Marty had stuttered, due to his excitement, Kenny explained. She found the trait endearing. And for the first time in a long time, she thought again of the family she had expected to be raising.

Without conscious thought her hand folded over her belly.

She remembered her disappointment in the weeks following one of Harry's trips home when she'd taken to her bed seized by cramps, aggravated by the tears she'd shed. The vividness of the memory shocked her.

When she looked up, the expression on Logan's face held her absolutely still. She saw the deep masculine curiosity and the restrained flicker of desire that invaded his compelling dark blue eyes. Every instinct she possessed came to life. The result was a chaos of emotion and mixed signals that left her feeling as if she would be easy prey for him.

She wrenched her attention from him and focused on the boys. "Kenny, I would be pleased if you and Marty want to stay with me. We can work out a fair exchange, but more importantly, I'd really enjoy the company. I just want you both to make the decision."

"Tell her, Kenny. Tell her."

"I was gettin' 'round to it, Marty. The way we figure it best is to sorta try it out. You ain't got young'uns an' we ain't got no folks tellin' us what to do. Bound to set up a heap of trouble if we was to jus' move in."

She couldn't help herself. Her gaze strayed to Logan. He was desperately trying not to smile. Well, he had warned her about how bright Kenny was. She was looking forward to the challenge. What's more, Jessie knew she needed these children. They would fill the lonely hours. She knew Logan would leave come morning. He had delayed only because of his concern for her.

The warmth inside expanded, and Jessie lowered her head. It would be so easy to fall in love with Logan. But how could she love a man who had secrets he refused to share with her? How could she trust him? She'd been asking herself that question too many times today, and always came up with the same answer. On every level that mattered, Logan had her complete trust.

"Ma'am. Ma'am," Kenny said a second time, louder, then repeated it once more. When Jessie looked up at him, he continued. "We left water heatin' for the dishes. 'Pologize that Marty an' me can't stay to help. But we got things to do back at our camp."

"Oh, you're not leaving. I thought, that is, I hoped that you both would stay the night. We can ride up to your camp tomorrow."

Kenny shot a look at Logan, who was toying with his fork, an act that required intense concentration, for he didn't look up or say a word.

"Don't seem like a good idea, ma'am. Com'on, Marty. We head back."

"Please call me Jessie," she asked as they started for the door.

"Wait for me outside," Logan said, rising. "I'll walk back—"

"Ain't a need—"

"Kenny, the first thing a man learns is that when someone bigger and older than him gives an order, obey it. I'll be with you in a few minutes."

The moment the door closed behind them, Jessie rounded on Logan. "There was no need for you to be so sharp with him. He's just a boy, for heaven's sake."

"Keep thinking that way and he'll have you wrapped around his finger in a day or so."

"What difference will it make to you? You won't be around to see." Jessie shoved back the table bench, but he moved so fast around to her side that she didn't have the chance to stand up. Settling for a heated glare took the edge off her temper.

"Oh, Jess, don't do this. If I could stay, I would. How could you think otherwise?"

She squeezed her eyes shut, fighting for the courage she needed to push him away. *Let me find the right words. Please, Lord. The right ones.*

Jessie suddenly remembered the two double eagles that were left from the money he had given her. She recalled the coins paid to Silas's Indian woman. Regret for the missing money disappeared with the memory of what had followed. When she arrived home she had taken off the small deerskin bag... where? Her eyes lit on the cupboard shelf.

"Excuse me, I need to get up."

He stepped aside, and she rose stiffly. *He's leaving. Just remember that he's leaving. No matter what you say, no matter what you do, Logan is going out of your life.*

She felt the heat of his stare following her every move. Jessie spilled the coins into the palm of her hand, then curled her fingers over them. *Courage.*

She turned, started to speak, shook her head and held out her hand, palm side up. "Your money."

"My—" He broke off, looking from the money to her eyes. Anger built slowly, but it threatened his control. "I don't understand, Jessie. I told you—"

"This is what's left from buying your horse and supplies." The lie wasn't an easy one for her. But the truth would reveal what she was determined to keep from him. "I'm taking your offer to share the food-stuffs I bought. But this belongs to you. Take it."

"Don't do this." His voice was flat, cold and hard.

"I need to," she answered as coldly.

"I said I didn't want it. The money is yours to keep, Jessie."

"Take it," she demanded again. "Since you don't understand, I'll make it plainer. Take your money, Logan. Take it because I don't want anything left here that belonged to you."

She witnessed the battle he waged with his temper. A trembling beset her and the coins spilled from her hand and landed on the table. For a few terrible moments she thought he would come right over the table at her.

Out of sheer desperation that he would lose his temper with her, Logan fled the cabin. The door slammed behind him.

And Jessie was once more alone.

But Logan would come back tonight.

That one inescapable fact kept returning as she cleaned the dishes, to tease and tug and cajole.

Chapter Twelve

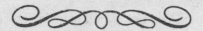

Logan was so blinded by rage that at first he didn't see the boys hiding near the corner.

"I told you to wait right here, didn't I?"

Kenny, shoving Marty behind him, stepped out. "Since you was pinchin' the starch out of her drawers, we got out of the way."

"Don't talk about Jessie like that," Logan snapped. He rubbed the back of his neck, willing himself to calm down. What devil had taken hold of her? Tossing the money at him like it was dirty? Hell, he didn't steal it. And if he had, he was only stealing it from himself. A mess of lies, fried up and served, and all he could do for now was eat it.

"You still set on walkin' back with us?"

"Yeah. We've got a few more things to talk about." Logan scooped up Marty and settled him on his shoulders, much to the little boy's delight. The shooting pain in his shoulder helped to take his mind off Jessie.

Marty placed his hands on either side of Logan's face, yelling for Kenny to see how tall he was, while Logan arranged the boy's feet beneath his arms. The laughter they shared had a silent, deeper meaning for both Logan and Kenny when the boy nodded with approval glowing in his eyes.

Logan reached out and drew Kenny beside him in a loose neck hold. "Still have doubts?"

"Nope. But I'm sure glad you ain't a mean mad."

"Pardon?"

"You come out like a bull snortin' an' ready to charge whatever moved," Kenny explained. "That's mean mad."

"Yep," Marty agreed. "So m-mean you'd hurt something."

"If I frightened you both, I'm sorry. I learned a long time ago never to hurt someone smaller than me unless my life was at stake. Or they were robbing my horse. That would rile me plenty."

"If you was awake," Kenny reminded him. "Like I said, I'm sure glad you ain't thinkin' on it. I'd need to protect Marty."

"From me?" Logan stopped in his tracks. He let Kenny squirm free.

All the laughter was gone from the boy's expression. "Only if you was hurtin' him, Logan. I ain't got a gun, but I got ways to hurt a man big as you."

All Logan had to guide him was his own childhood, and all the times he would challenge Conner or one of the hands so he could show off something new he'd learned. His voice was skeptical. "Tell me."

"I'd kick your shin 'cause you're so tall an' I'm only chest-high."

Logan started walking. "Yeah, you're little, all right. Little like a stick of dynamite is little."

Skipping alongside, Kenny smiled. "Yep. Kick a man in the shin an' the pain's worse than bein' snake-bit."

Kenny had more to say as they walked back to their camp. Jessie wasn't ignored by the boy. She was a subject that Kenny, in his forthright manner, had no qualms broaching despite Logan's attempts to stop him. Logan let him ramble on, till he expressed his final opinion that Logan was making a mistake to leave a woman like her.

"She's got land an' a cabin. Got a real nice little herd of cattle. You ain't dead, so you know she can take care of you. She's pretty, too," he added, kicking dust.

Logan agreed. But, he explained, a man sometimes didn't have a choice. He had to do what he had to do.

Kenny snapped back. "My pa usta say the same thing just before he whopped me for not obeyin'. Said it hurt him worse than me. Don't see how that stands to reason. Folks sure got funny ways of lookin' at things."

Logan left it at that.

He parted from the boys with Kenny promising that he'd stick closer to Jessie than a horseshoe to a hoof until Logan could send word. He didn't promise them he would return—he might not survive his next encounter with Monte and his bunch—but he'd make sure his brother knew about Jessie and the boys. Conner could be counted on to take care of them.

Personal feelings aside, he could do no less for the boys and woman who had saved his life.

He expected to find the cabin door bolted against him when he returned. Not only was the door unbolted, but Jessie had left a lantern burning outside to guide him. Wary of her uncertain temper, Logan took the precaution of making sure she hadn't tossed a quilt outside. He wouldn't put it past Jessie to leave that as a message he was no longer wanted here.

Jessie, lying quietly in the darkened cabin, listened to him moving around outside. After he had left her, she knew exactly what a piece of cloth felt like after she had heated her iron on the stove and applied it to the wet material. There was hiss and steam, but not a wrinkle remained to mar its surface. The cloth was soft and malleable, allowing the heavy flatiron to guide smoothly where she directed it.

Logan was exactly like that flatiron, wielded by a heavy hand with a deft touch. She was scorched, but she had little fight left in her.

The door opened and she stilled. He had shuttered the lantern so only a tiny stream of light spilled from the glass.

"Jessie? Are you awake?"

"No. I'm sound asleep, dreaming, I'll have you know, of those two little boys off goodness knows where, at the mercy—"

"All right. I got your point. You're awake and full of vinegar."

"No. I mean yes," she said very softly, "I'm awake, but the vinegar, as you call it, is all gone."

"Stop worrying about the boys. Kenny'll take better care of you an' Marty than anyone I know." Logan set the lantern on the table. He'd already figured out that Jessie had claimed her bed—the folded quilts on the floor just confirmed it.

"It's too much of a burden for a boy to bear, Logan."

"Kenny's already shouldered man-size burdens. He buried his folks and Marty's. Death has a way of turning a boy to a man overnight."

Jessie sat up, finding his shadowed form. "You say that as if you had been through the very same thing." She was doing exactly what she had sworn to herself she wouldn't—snatching up every scrap of information about him that she could keep and remember.

"I know." But Logan wasn't thinking so much about himself as he was his brother Conner. Like Kenny, Conner had been the eldest and, suited or not, had stepped into their father's boots when he died.

"Where will you go?"

He looked over at her, barely able to make out more than her shape sitting up with the blankets bunched up around her.

"Jessie, the less you know, the better it is."

The answer was no more than she had expected. Hope she hadn't realized that she harbored faded. He wasn't going to make any last-minute promises about coming back, if not for her, then for the boys.

She waited to hear him settling down on the quilts. Logan didn't move. The sense that he was waiting for her to say something more formed in her mind. The only subject Jessie felt safe talking about was the boys.

"I'm not sure that I'm the right one to take care of those two, Logan. I don't know anything about being a mother."

The underlying worry in her voice was all the excuse he needed to cross the room to her. He dropped down to his knees beside the bed, grabbing hold of the sideboard to keep from gathering her into his arms.

"Jessie, I think they need a friend more than anything else. Kenny, like I said, claims they're cousins and that they have no kinfolk back in Kansas. You know I can't take them with me. They like you. Told me so and, what's more, I believe they'll trust you."

Jessie's fingers curled over the edge of the blanket. She wanted to know why he couldn't trust her. But wasn't going to ask.

"I'm sorry for the way I stormed out of here."

"You had reason, Logan."

"Yeah, I guess." Her tone was cool and dismissing. He had no one but himself to blame that Jessie wasn't the passionate woman who had been so eager for his kisses this afternoon.

"You'd better get some sleep. Morning will be here before you know it. Good night, Logan."

"Jessie, I—"

"Good night." Jessie blessed the darkness that kept him from seeing her worry her lip. She lay back on her pillow and pulled the blanket up to her chin. For a few moments more he remained by her side, and she listened to his uneven breathing, fighting not to ask him to stay with her tonight.

She released her breath when he finally moved away. After a while, when only the night noises outside could be heard, Jessie felt her eyes drift closed, but sleep when it came was not restful.

Logan ignored the faint, muffled sounds of Jessie's restless turnings as long as he could. Twice he got up, and twice as he neared the bed, she seemed to quiet.

He was tempted to wake her and find out what was wrong, but stretched back out on the floor. The thick quilts cushioned his body, but his thoughts kept straying to the feel of Jessie in his arms.

When she cried out, his response was immediate. He didn't stop to think about it. He dived across the room and gathered Jessie against him. She was damp with sweat, her rigid body resisting, then limp in his arms.

She let go of the blanket she had been clutching and wrapped her arms around him. Logan didn't mind. He held her tight. He wasn't going to whisper words that made little of her bad dream. He'd always hated being told that it was nothing. Bad dreams were just that for the dreamer.

But he wondered why this night of all the nights he'd been there had brought bad dreams to Jessie.

He hadn't forgotten this afternoon and the unanswered questions he still had. Smoothing one hand over her tangled hair, he knew he wouldn't be asking them now.

She was trembling, but he sensed that the dream had ended. She snuggled against him, and Logan rocked her until the trembling subsided. Even then, Jessie made no effort to move away.

Her warm breaths slowed, touching his skin, and he could feel her nipples through the thin cloth of her nightgown pressing against his chest. He tried to ease back a little, but Jessie held him tight. Logan didn't think she knew what she was doing to him.

He wasn't about to fall on her like some ravening beast, but the ache that had begun this afternoon had only eased, not left him. And Jessie was the woman who aroused him just by being close.

He couldn't take advantage of her. But the scent of her was filling him with every breath he drew. He wasn't a saint, and had no wish to be.

One of them had to be sensible. Logan hadn't applied for the job—the Lord knew his good sense went out the door when he was near Jessie—but he quickly realized he was stuck with it.

"Jessie? Jessie, do you think you can get back to sleep now?" He attempted to disengage himself from her arms, but she burrowed closer.

"Can't sleep." Her voice was muffled. Her open mouth tasted his skin for the first time. Warm. A little salty. Intrigued, Jessie licked her lips and touched him again.

Heartbeat after slow, heavy heartbeat, she was warming him in all the wrong places in all the right ways. He was supposed to be comforting her, not putting himself on a rack. Jessie had made her decision very clear. But now...now, she was tempting him to forget all his good intentions.

"Jess, honey, stop. You don't know what you're—"

"Yes. Oh, yes, I do." She scattered tiny kisses over his shoulders, touching the edge of the bandage, then working her way back to the strong column of his neck. Her fingers kneaded the tense muscles across his back as she came fully awake.

Logan brought his hands around to cup her face. He released an exasperated breath. The last thing he wanted to do was refuse her, not when he ached to bury himself in her and never let go.

"Jess, listen to me. Listen real good, 'cause I don't know if I can say this again. If you don't stop, I'm going to kiss you, and kissing you sets a very short fuse on fire. I don't think I could stop, Jess.''

He felt her mouth slide into a slow smile. At that moment he wanted to see her face, but nothing could make him move away from her. Nothing but Jessie telling him to go.

''And if I want you to kiss me? If for once I didn't want to think about tomorrow, but only now, would you say no? If all I wanted was you...'' Her voice trailed off. She didn't know where the courage to speak had come from. Dreaming of what had happened in the store, and knowing the danger he faced, sharpened her focus on what mattered to her. Logan might want to come back; then again, he might not live to do it. The reasons went on, reasons that tore through all the wrongs of making love to a man she might never see again, and made them right.

His thumbs brushed the satiny skin of her cheeks. He hesitated a second, giving her one last chance to change her mind. Jessie didn't take it. His eyes drifted closed and he covered her mouth with his.

Her cool lips soon warmed, but never reached the heat of her mouth. She parted them and he slipped his tongue inside.

All the honeyed sweetness he'd dreamed of was there, his for the taking, and he took, chasing every rational thought from his mind.

His tongue delved deeper, stroking hers with gentle, consuming thrusts. He opened his mouth wider, silently asking her to do the same, and when she did, the warmth turned to heat. The slow, almost hesitant duel she began changed heat into a slow, burning flame.

Shimmering and potent, the incredible feelings filled Jessie. Logan assaulted her senses, and she held him tight, afraid she would melt away before she discovered where passion would lead her. The wave of desire welling up inside her stormed over her body and mind.

Logan groaned his pleasure. She lifted her hands to the slightly curly hair on the back of his neck, sliding her fingers through it as she captured his husky groan with her mouth. The sound echoed in her mind, igniting her passion with his. Jessie moved restlessly against him, wanting him closer, not knowing how to show him.

The change in her streaked through him. He resisted the temptation to fill his palm with her breast, for he didn't want her to stop what she was doing, those teasing forays of her tongue into his mouth. She felt so good in his arms, so perfect, and she seared him with every hesitant touch that built a fire in his loins. And it was all so effortless, so quick, that Jessie didn't know how close to the edge she pushed him. But when he went over it, she was going to be right there beside him.

He slanted his head, and the new angle deepened the kiss. Jessie never wanted the kisses to stop, never wanted him to stop. Logan stole her thoughts, her doubts, and replaced them with a languor that spread throughout her body.

He pulled back, allowing them both a chance to draw breath. "Jess, oh, Jess." He pulled her against him, seeking her lips as everything inside himself coalesced into one driving need. He wanted her now, to the point of no return. She gave so much. No teasing, no holding anything of herself back, and unlike any other woman he'd known, Jessie didn't ask for more than he could give her now.

"Jess. I want to see you. I want to feel your skin against mine." He breathed the words into her mouth, his fingers seeking the ribbon tie at the neck of her nightgown. He trailed a string of kisses across her jaw, his masculine laughter soft when she tilted her head to allow his lips to follow the curve of her bared neck. He didn't pause to taste the hollow of her throat where her pulse beat wildly. There was softer skin his lips longed to touch. Logan's hands caressed her upper arms and shoulders, sliding the cloth down, and once more he wished he could see her. The cloth caught on her nipples, and he lowered his head, using the edge of his teeth to drag the thin cotton free.

He loved the hungry little sounds she made as he took her into his mouth. Holding her breast in one hand, he lifted the satiny flesh, feeling the race of her heart that matched his own. With an outpouring of passion he hadn't expected, Jessie covered the back of his neck with kisses. Her hands guided his head, and Logan let her set the pace despite the intensity of need that built inside him.

Her lips and touch played havoc with the sensitive nape of his neck. Logan had never realized just how sensitive that part of his body was. But Jessie made him know, and made him want more.

Jessie tried to separate the sensations, to savor them, to cherish each one with her mind to be drawn out later, when he was gone. The heat of his mouth...the warm strength of his callused hand gently holding her...the heated silkiness of his skin and the hard muscles bunching in his back, even his ragged sigh as he eased her down on the bed became part of her memory. His hands spanned her rib cage, drawing the nightgown down, kissing the tips of her fingers when shyness had her move to stop him. He swept the nightgown and the blanket to the foot of the bed.

He made a light, sweeping caress of her legs on his return to pay homage to her other breast, noting the faint tenseness of her body.

"You don't have to be afraid with me, Jess. You know that, don't you? I wouldn't hurt you. Ever. Not here, not now when you're as vulnerable as I am."

"But you're not," she whispered. "You've still got your pants on."

"I'll take them off, Jess. When you're ready."

"When I'm—"

Her question was lost as she caught her breath before Logan took her mouth with his in a kiss that had her twisting against him, trying to draw him down on the bed with her.

But when he attempted to reclaim the prize he wanted, Jessie cupped his cheeks to stop him. She strung kisses down his throat, scattering them over his chest.

"Jess?"

"Please?"

Logan couldn't refuse her. He caught one hand in the long tangle of her hair, loving the feel of her warm breath sighing through his chest hair. She murmured approving sounds, then sank her teeth into the meaty muscle of his chest and took a love bite. Moaning, he clasped her head tighter. When her questing lips touched his nipple in the whorl of dark hair, they both froze for a second. Logan held his breath, waiting.

"Do men... I mean, would you feel what I did when you, ah..."

"Whatever pleases you, Jess, pleases me." He was so hard that even baring his teeth against the pleasure didn't work. He felt her smile against his skin before her lips gently closed over the nub of his flesh. Daintily her tongue flicked against it. He stroked the bare curve of her hip, burying his thumb in the crease of her thigh. With the hand entangled in her hair, he tried to lift her head, but she resisted, moving lower until the edge of the bed stopped her.

"Come up on the bed with me," she pleaded softly, giving in to his urge to lift her head. She scooted back toward the wall to make room for him.

"That's all the invitation I need, Jess."

Logan thought getting to his feet was an accomplishment considering the state he was in. Shucking his pants proved a sheer miracle between the tremor in his hands and the stubborn buttons. Well, he couldn't blame the buttons, only the flesh swollen beneath them.

Logan placed one knee on the bed when she reached up and touched him. "Jess!" he hissed. Desire formed a red mist before his eyes. Her boldness amazed him. Caught off guard, Logan remained as he was, for he suddenly realized how hesitant her touch was. Hesitant, questing, almost shy. He wanted to give himself over entirely to the pleasure of filling her hand with his flesh, but he was afraid to move, afraid that he would make her stop.

"I never knew a man could be so velvety soft and hard at the same time."

Logan thought he would strangle. *This* from his once-married Jessie? He wasn't going to ask the obvious question. He gritted his teeth until his jaw ached from not asking it. Her caresses grew bolder and his body responded until the merest thought disappeared and his attention focused on the gentle tugging motion of her hand.

The warmth of her breath fanning his flesh snapped him into moving. "Jess, wait. Not like this." Lord! Had he really said that? But he knew how little control he had left. She withdrew up against the wall, and he realized his mistake. Coming down on the bed, stretching out beside her, he gathered her against him.

"I was wrong to touch you, wasn't I?"

"No. I loved you touching me. I want you to touch me."

No trace of a lie was hidden in his voice. Jessie wished the lantern was lit. She would love to see his face. Reaching up with one hand, she traced his lips and smiled when he kissed her fingertips.

"If you loved it so much, then why did you stop me?"

"Because, sweet lady, a few seconds more and I'd be finished before we got you started. Pleasure, Jess. Remember what I said?"

"I remember. That's what made me so bold. Harry never let me—"

"Harry's dead. Harry," he whispered over her mouth, "is not going to be a ghost between us tonight. There's just you and me and a whole lot of lovin'."

"A whole lot? As in more than once?"

Logan's rich male laughter brought her own. She swore there was a choked agreement somewhere but she had buried her head against his chest until the laughter stopped.

And in a voice of needy desperation, Jessie whispered, "Logan, love me. Love me now."

And he heard the plea beneath the need, a plea he couldn't answer. But he wanted to, God, how he wanted to.

So he gave Jessie what he could, as much pleasure as she could stand, as much as he was capable of. He found her a generous lover, ready to return every touch, every kiss, boldly following his lead, then coming up with a few moves of her own that had him groaning.

Jessie welcomed the total assault on her senses. He wore her inhibitions away, taking her with him into a realm of sensation where the treasures of life were the heating of skin touching skin and the soft explosions he relayed to her body with each added pleasure. She was lost in the rocking motion of his body, sliding against him, beneath, always wanting more. Without a word he seemed to know what she wanted before she did.

She didn't know she was starved for praise until his dark voice whispered it.

When her flesh was damp and heated, and her chest hurt from the breath she couldn't take, Logan showed her another side of loving as he filled her body the same way he had filled her mind and her heart—completely.

"I'm going to be very, very careful with you, Jess," he murmured, his lips finding the wildly beating pulse in her throat, his hips grinding softly against her. "Loving you...shouldn't ever...be rushed." His voice matched the cadence of his body.

He'd gone to the edge and barely clung there, waiting for Jessie. He'd never had trouble waiting for a woman before, but Jessie, ah, Jessie, with her sweet heated touches and soft lips whispering...Jessie drove him crazy.

She cried out, her body trembling, and he knew the danger of wanting more. Just once more, he promised himself, driving her higher with the thrust of his body, taking her mouth, wanting everything she had.

The need was inescapable. Minutes later Jessie melted for him like sugar in the rain and he was shocked at the strength of will he exerted to withdraw. Her hands closed over his hips, stopping him.

"Think, Jess. Think what you're doing," he growled in a savage voice.

"I can't think. I only know I want you. Stay. Stay with me, Logan."

And once more the underlying plea for what he couldn't give her beyond tonight overcame any good sense he had.

He'd never spilled his seed inside a woman. He'd never wanted to. Never lost control of himself to forget that a man didn't leave a woman with a reminder nine months later of a night of pleasure.

But he couldn't deny Jessie. Wouldn't deny himself. He wanted it to last forever. Jessie tightened around him. And then there was no room for coherent thoughts or demands. The storm of their desire broke, leaving them drenched and shuddering.

It was a long time before Jessie opened her eyes. Logan was still sprawled on top of her, his weight crushing her into the bed. She smiled to herself, fingertips tracing small circles on his back. His mouth roamed up the side of her face, tenderly, gently. He rolled them to their sides, and held her close, kissing her until she lay quietly in his arms.

"Are you all right?" he asked, brushing the damp hair back from her face.

"Yes," she said softly, scattering kisses of her own wherever she could reach. She didn't realize her arms had tightened their hold on him until he spoke.

"Easy, sweet lady, I'm not going anywhere."

But you are! she wanted to protest. Jessie didn't know where she found the strength to tease him. "You can't leave yet. You promised me a whole night of—"

"Lovin', Jess," he finished for her. "Tonight I'm yours and you're mine."

"Yes, for tonight. Hours and hours and—"

This time he sealed his mouth to hers, silencing her, silencing the minutes mentally ticking away, knowing there weren't all that many left. Certainly not the time he wanted. That would take forever.

He gave her a night to remember, just as she had asked for, a night where she didn't know where she ended and he began.

A grayish light filled the cabin the last time she looked into his eyes. Her own drifted closed, carrying the image of the smile on his lips.

When she woke, Logan was gone.

Chapter Thirteen

A lone horseman studied the lay of the land from the small rise. He sat his horse in a thick stand of cottonwood trees, his gaze touching each spill of moonlight, each shadow that he knew from memory.

Logan judged the time somewhere past midnight. His three-day trek south to the Rocking K was at an end. To avoid a roving band of renegade Apache, he'd been forced to make a wide swing to the east, riding across mesa and butte, skirting the Casa Grande ruins where the ancient ones once dwelled.

But he was home.

Trouble was, he couldn't ride down, whooping and hollering as he'd done in the past. Announcing his homecoming would give the lie to his turning his back on his heritage to ride the outlaw trail. Unless his suspicions proved right.

The night was surprisingly cool. Logan jogged his memory and realized he'd been gone almost eight months. Fall had arrived without his noticing.

His one regret was that Jessie wasn't here with him. A foolish thought at best, since he couldn't keep up his charade and have her with him. And, he reminded himself, he'd just broken a promise made the moment he'd walked out of her cabin—he wasn't going to think about her.

The promise had served him well during the lonely hours of riding in a land where survival was the only law.

The leaves of the cottonwood stirred above him as they were wont to do in the slightest breeze. Below, the only movement came from the restless milling of a few horses in the far corral. Breeding stock was housed in the long barn.

Set out in the open country with a stream winding past, the big Spanish-style house was surrounded by trees that helped to keep the thick adobe walls and tiled roof cool. There was a dam across the stream, and a fair-sized pond had backed up behind it. He and his brothers had had their first swimming lessons under Santo's guidance there before they attempted the swiftly moving current of the river. Memories of those carefree, competitive days assaulted him. This, too, had to be put aside.

He studied the sprawl of the buildings, probing the shadows each cast. At the back of the main house an adobe wall encircled his mother's pride and joy, her garden. He'd climbed the thick wooden gates many a night, sneaking back into the house without her knowing, without Conner knowing, either. And it still seemed the best way for him to get into the house tonight.

There was a stillness about the place, a peaceful one that reached out to him. The windlass that pulled the water from the center courtyard well was silent, the low tower where a man stationed with a pair of field glasses could see the surrounding area for miles was empty.

Logan slid from the saddle, tying the reins to a low limb. The horse Jessie had bought for him had been a good mount, deserving of a well-earned rest and plenty of grain. Stripping off his gear, he set the saddle aside, then wiped the horse down with the reverse side of the blanket, knowing this was the best he could do for now.

He set off, keeping to the deepest shadows, being careful to avoid going anywhere near Santo and Sofia's small house. The old man—who became indignant when Logan or Ty referred to him as such—was a light sleeper. It pained him that the truth about his leaving had to be kept from them. But with the fiancé of their daughter, Rosanna, high on the list of suspects, he had agreed with Conner and his mother that they couldn't be told.

The one thing the Rocking K didn't have was dogs, due to his mother's fear of them. It served him well as he flattened himself against the adobe wall near the gates. The bedrooms were all at the back of the house and that made a climb necessary.

Rubbing his shoulder, Logan was thankful he'd been blessed with the good fortune to heal quickly. But he wasn't sure he could make the leap for the top of the high-set gates. Reminding himself that he should have taken that rope that Jessie had bought him didn't sit well with him.

Delaying the attempt wasn't going to make it happen. He jumped and promptly fell back. *Jeez! Why did something he'd done a hundred times as a kid seem so easy then, but now, as a man grown, was going to prove difficult?*

If he had another way of getting into the house... No, there wasn't any. He walked away and took a running start, this time clinging to the top of the gate. He heard the grate of his teeth when fire streaked down his body from his shoulder. The cry of pain stayed buried as he scrambled to keep his grip. He had to deny the pain and boost himself on top of the thick wood. He balanced in a crouch on the six-inch-wide gate and jumped down to the soft earth of the garden.

He landed on his feet, feeling the jar through his bones, and had to wait until he caged the pain.

Late-blooming roses scented the air. He made his way along one of the flagstone paths bordered with lemon trees, unable to stop images of playing here as a child with his brothers from coming to mind.

As he headed for the window to his room, the darkened house whispered to him of love and laughter within its walls.

One of the first things he intended to do was get into a pair of his own boots. He swore his toes were numb from being pinched in Harry's old ones.

Logan gave thanks that there hadn't been any recent rain. The window frame would have been swollen and given him a devil's time to get it open. As it was, the window slid silently open. He tossed his leg over the sill, ducked his head and swung inside.

"Come in, come all the way into the room and talk fast, mister. Tell me why I shouldn't blow a hole through you." Dixie Rawlins, soon to become Mrs. Tyrel Kincaid, placed the cold metal barrel of her gun against the intruder's neck. "I don't hear you talking, mister."

"Who the hell are you!" Logan was furious.

"I asked first. Since I hold the gun, that means I get answered first, too."

"Jeez, lady, get that gun off my neck. I'm not going to hurt you. For Almighty's sake, I—" Logan paused. He didn't know who she was. He couldn't tell her who he was, that he lived here, that this was his room, or had been until he had taken off. His only choice was to convince her to get Conner in here fast before she accidentally shot him.

"Why don't you go—"

Dixie rapped against the inside wall.

"What're you doing? That room's empty. Or it was. Look, lady, just get Conner in here."

The rough voice held command. That grabbed Dixie's attention. His telling her about the empty room, Ty's once-empty room, wiped the last vestige of sleep away. She repeated the three short raps against the wall. It was a signal that she and Ty had worked out to slip into each other's room when both became overwhelmed by the constant chaperoning Ty's mother insisted was proper until their wedding.

"Will you stop that!" Logan hissed. "You'll wake the whole damn house."

"Sounds like a fine idea to me," she returned. "I don't know what you hoped to steal, but mister, you picked the wrong place. You haven't seen possessive until you've met the Kincaids. And I'll warn you, I'm an excellent shot. But this close, it would take the turning of the hand of God to miss you."

"Dixie?"

"Ty, come in and light the lamp. I've caught us a polecat sneaking into my room."

"Ty?"

"Oh, hell!" Ty, hearing his brother's voice, rushed forward and slammed his bare foot into the edge of the bed board. Groans and swears filled the air.

"Damn and double damn! Lady, put the gun away."

"The hell you say. Ty? Ty, what's wrong? You sound as if you're in pain."

"I am. Dixie, that's my brother. That's Logan."

"Logan?"

"Yeah. I'm Logan. Put up the gun, honey."

"Don't call me that. But now I know where Ty picked it up from." Ty struck the match and lit the lamp, and she had her first look at the missing Kincaid brother. She was grateful that Ty grabbed him in a bear hug that left Logan facing her. She set the gun down on the dresser and grabbed her shawl from the back of the rocking chair. She wrapped it around her, watching the two men.

The similarities were there for anyone to see. The same rugged good looks, although Dixie thought Ty the handsomer by far. Both had the same dark blue eyes, similar shapes to their noses and brows. Logan was a mite taller than Ty. Where Ty's hair had a slight curl and was black, Logan's was dark brown. Logan was heavier in build, and his lips were thinner than her love's. Ty's brother appeared not only older but harder, as if time had not been kind to him.

Dixie admonished herself. If the whispers were true that she and Ty heard—despite the effort of Conner and their mother, Macaria, to stop the talk among the hands—Logan hadn't just left the Rocking K, he'd become an outlaw. More than once in the past two months Ty had left her to track down some rumor that Logan had been seen. She ached for her love when he'd return, filled with more confusion at the path his missing brother had chosen. And now Logan had come home.

Ty stepped back from his brother. Both had their hands resting on the other's shoulders. When he saw Logan wince, he dropped his hands. "You've been hurt."

"Just a flesh wound. Nothing to worry about. You know how fast I heal."

The far-off look in Logan's eyes warned Ty that his brother was thinking some serious thoughts. He swallowed question after question, unwilling to push Logan until he was ready to talk.

"Don't look so worried, Ty. I had a real pretty lady nurse me."

The same wolfish grin on Logan's lips creased Ty's mouth and brought a loud throat-clearing from Dixie.

"Ty is no longer in the market for pretty ladies. And while you two are undeniably brothers, and closer than two peas in a pod, I can't help wondering if there's something significant in the fact that you were both wounded in the same shoulder."

"If you're thinking what I'm thinking, Dixie," Ty said, breaking into a short laugh, and sobering quickly, "then my brother should be heading for the altar."

"Never mind. What happened to you, boy?"

"Can't call me that anymore." Ty looked into his brother's eyes and all he saw was Logan, ready to take on the world if need be to right any wrong done to his little brother. There was a wealth of love and no shame in the bear hug he gave Logan, whispering that he was thankful he was here, alive and, for the most part, well.

Breaking away, Logan glanced from his brother's smiling face to Dixie's studied expression directed at him. "That really true? You're gonna give up your roaming ways to settle down?"

"Yep. Gonna be a married man next week."

"You? Married?" Logan wasn't sure he could handle more. First the shock of finding a woman in his room—a woman who appeared capable of using the gun she had held on him. Then finding out that Ty was home after years of drifting all over the territory, and swearing he'd never be back as long as Conner ran the Rocking K. And now this, his little brother, who wasn't quite the lean, cocky kid who had walked away five years ago. The few times Ty had returned, Logan had seen the subtle changes, but they hit him hard now.

His brother had seen his share of trouble and had survived. Sometimes a man couldn't ask for more.

"Who knows you're back?" Ty asked.

"No one. I came over the fence."

"Wait till Conner sees you. I didn't believe what they were saying, Logan. I know how arrogant our brother can be, and Lord knows, he ran me off with his set ways, but I know you. You'd never take to riding with outlaws. But I'll admit, if it wasn't for Dixie, I wouldn't have come home. Com'ere honey, let me introduce you to my brother properly."

Ty made the introductions. He heaped praise on his brother until Logan warned him to stop. Ty laughed, then said, "Almost all of my bad habits can be blamed on Logan's example." When he told him who Dixie was, all he added was, "the lady I love."

Shaking his head, Logan said, "I still can't believe it. You swore you'd never wear any woman's brand, Ty." Looking at Dixie, he finished, "Not that I blame him. You're a beautiful woman. And a smart one if you got your rope around him."

"That's not exactly what happened," Dixie began.

"Dixie," Ty interrupted, "was hunting her father's killer when I rescued her from a mob of angry miners getting ready to lynch her."

"You didn't so much rescue me, Ty," Dixie corrected, "as stick yourself right in the middle of my problems for devious reasons of your own."

Ty's grin was sheer sin. "Yeah. Real devious reasons. I had a hankerin' so bad for her that I took a knife in my shoulder, stole horses an' nearly ended up getting Greg Rutland and his family killed." He put his arm around Dixie and pulled her closer to his side. "But I almost lost my lady, which is why I came home. She took a bullet meant for me."

"But that only happened because you were so sure we were safe in the gully. If that storm— Oh," Dixie said, shuddering with the memory of them both battling the storm and men intent on killing them, "don't talk about it now. We're safe, and I only hope that the man behind my father's death will someday pay for what he did."

"So you see, Logan, it was a good thing I happened along. Otherwise, my lady here would have ended up a set of bleached bones in the mountains.'' Planting a kiss on Dixie's cheek, he smiled. ''Right, honey?''

''I'll honey you. I wasn't exactly some helpless female—''

''That ain't what you told me last week. Called me your hero, didn't you?''

''Ty!''

''Only teasing.'' And to Logan, ''She means more than anything to me. I did find the man who killed her father and almost took her life, too. But I haven't discovered who ordered his death. We went back to Aztec to find out who filed on her father's land after she lost it. Some company with a dead trail owns the place.''

''Aztec? That's west of here.'' Logan frowned. He'd heard something from Monte.... Whatever it was escaped him.

''Yeah,'' Ty answered. ''The other side of Gila Bend. I hope you'll welcome Dixie into the family, Logan. Just remember she's mine.''

Logan's expression became serious as he studied the woman who obviously had captured his brother's love. With her dark brown hair pulled back to fall in a single braid to her waist, there was nothing to obscure her features. What he saw was a lovely young woman both strong enough to be a match for Ty and soft enough to hold him. He sensed she'd had her share of troubles, but he liked the way her gaze remained direct and level with his. He smiled when he assured himself there were no secrets in her eyes.

"Dixie, you take care of my brother, and you'll have me as a friend for life. And now, if the little brother won't mind, I'd sure like to kiss the coming bride."

She felt shy with Logan as she hadn't felt with Conner. She stepped away from Ty, laughing at his low teasing to remember that she was promised to him. For a moment she hesitated, then slipped her arms around Logan and kissed his dark, stubbled cheek. "Welcome home." Then she murmured softly into his ear so that Ty couldn't hear, "He's missed you. He's worried, too."

Logan caught her chin with his fingertips as she pulled back. "Not so fast, pretty one." He saw the surprise in her eyes and thought he knew what she was expecting him to do. But Logan didn't kiss her lips; he touched his mouth to her forehead. "Make him happy and keep him home. He loves this place, an' if he gives half that love to you, Dixie, you're a lucky woman." He hugged her tight, meeting his brother's gaze over her shoulder. Logan beamed approval before he let her go.

Ty welcomed her to his side. Looking at the two of them, seeing for himself the love in their eyes, Logan was overwhelmed by a wave of loneliness.

He tried to block out the image of Jessie that came to mind. He might as well have tried to stop breathing. He hadn't known he could miss anyone this much, so that the ache was raw and painful.

Ty grew alarmed to see Logan close his eyes, his lips taut, his fingers curling into fists at his sides. "What's wrong?" he demanded of his brother, letting Dixie go and stepping nearer Logan. "Com'on, sit down." He reinforced his words with a gentle nudge that landed Logan on the bed.

Shaking his head, Logan opened his eyes and looked around. "Hell of a place for a reunion, Ty."

"Hell is about where I figured I'd meet up with you again. Dixie, get some whiskey. But don't wake anyone yet, honey. I want to talk to my brother alone."

"No. Dixie, get Conner. I never expected you to be here, Ty. But now that you are, there are things you need to know. I'm not up to tellin' the story twice."

Dixie looked at Ty.

"Do it, honey. Seems like there's a few secrets been kept."

"Don't get all het up about it, Ty. No one knew where you were. You haven't exactly been a regular visitor here in the past few years." Logan didn't say anything about the curt nod Ty gave Dixie. He waited until she slipped quietly out of the door and closed it.

"Hell of a woman you picked for yourself, boy. I had a feeling if she didn't like my answers I'd've had a mighty close and personal acquaintance with her gun."

"Believe it, Logan. Dixie knows which end of a gun is for business."

Once more Logan was assailed by the memory of Jessie the night she'd run out to scare off the egg thief. He had to stop this, but his focus blurred and he saw her in his mind's eye, soft and warm, tawny hair tangled and those wide golden brown eyes . . . No!

His fingers clenched with the need to touch her, and he was tormented by the guilt of leaving her without saying goodbye. Logan glanced at the floor, scrubbing his fingertips over his forehead.

When he finally looked up, he saw compassion in his younger brother's gaze.

"I have a feeling I looked a lot like you some nights, Logan. Mostly when I was troubled about Dixie. You fall prey to some woman, too?"

"Is that what this is?"

"Got an ache that won't quit?"

"I don't believe this. My little brother is gonna tell me about feelings for a woman."

"Believe it, big brother," Ty said, then laughed. "Guess when it comes to falling in love, I beat you and Conner all to pieces. For the first time, I'm the one to be first—"

"First in what?" Conner demanded from the doorway.

Chapter Fourteen

Dixie followed Conner into her bedroom carrying a tray of glasses and a heavy cut-glass decanter of whiskey.

"Before anyone else says a word, I want to make a toast to my brother and his bride." Logan, finding one of Conner's questioning blue-gray stares directed at him, shrugged and added, "How was I to know she had my room? Cat's out of the bag now, so make the best of it."

"Damn it! You two better start explaining to me. I've a right to know what's been going on. You," Ty said, rounding on Conner, "told me he just took off, that you didn't know where he was, or what he was doing. You had to know we'd find out about the whispers going around that Logan's turned outlaw. Yet you did nothing, said nothing to stop them."

"Ty." Dixie brought him a glass of whiskey. "Give your brother a chance to explain." Handing a nearly full glass of liquor to Logan, Dixie then shot Conner a furious look. "And you both will explain, won't you?" she asked in a too-sweet voice.

"Oh, do I detect a little vinegar with all that sugar?" Logan laughed when Ty nodded and Dixie was quick to elbow his side. "Gonna get your gun out again, little lady, and make me?"

Sliding her arm around Ty's waist and resting her head on his shoulder, Dixie gave Logan a smug look. "If that's what it takes. Ty's been very worried about you. When he worries, I worry. So make your toast, Logan, and then, please, end the suspense for all of us."

Conner, barefoot and shirtless, poured a small amount of whiskey for himself. Taking up a leaning position against the door, he lifted his glass as a gesture for Logan to get on with it.

"Back off, Conner. The little I have to tell you will keep. Ain't every day that a man comes home to find out his little brother's getting hitched." Logan's voice roughened with emotion. "The first toast is to the bride—lovely, smart and skilled enough to rope and brand one of the best men I know."

The glasses were raised and emptied. Dixie did the honors of filling them again, spilling only a little into Conner's glass.

"And to you, Ty," Logan continued. "The best brother a man could have, the most ornery, too. I offer my best wishes to the first of the Kincaids to wed, and may all your troubles be little ones."

"Corny, Logan. Real corny," Conner said. "That the best you can come up with?"

"Traveling three days to get here, and all I find is abuse. But that's all I can think of now."

"Drink to the sentiment, if not the words," Ty added, and tossed his drink down. He frowned when

Logan held out his glass to Dixie for a refill. "Don't you want to eat something, Logan?"

"Nope. And I'm glad to see how much you've grown, Ty. There was a time when you would've been all over me demanding that I tell you what's been going on. Yep, the lady is good for you."

Dixie joined in their hushed laughter, and took it upon herself to replace the glass stopper in the decanter. She wouldn't say anything now, but she wondered if Ty or Conner had picked up the underlying note of sadness in Logan's voice. She had a strange feeling that he was missing someone, missing them badly. For a moment her gaze locked with Logan's and she sensed that he knew what she was thinking.

"Would you mind if I make use of the bed?" Logan asked Dixie. "I must be gettin' old. Feeling every ache there is. Wouldn't mind another drink to loosen the last of the road dust. Best make it quick," he told Dixie as she propped the cushion from the rocker behind his pillow. "I don't start talkin' fast, old Conner's gonna have apoplexy. Just let me shuck these damned boots before my feet forget they belong to me."

"They're not yours?" Dixie asked, bringing him the decanter. She refilled his glass and left the decanter on the table beside the bed. She realized how foolish she was to think that Logan couldn't hold his liquor.

Conner kept to his leaning stance against the door, but Ty took the rocking chair and pulled Dixie down to his lap.

Logan began. "When Conner and I ran up against stone walls everywhere we turned trying to find out who's behind the rustling and the mine robberies, we came up with a plan."

"I finally heard the truth from Hazer about the fight you two had."

"Don't you believe it, Ty. 'Course, those punches Conner threw at the end of it sure added truth to his ordering me off the ranch. But it took me months before I hooked up with the right bunch." Rubbing his jaw, Logan looked at Conner. "I was in on the last four mine robberies at the Silver Belt. Real sorry about those men getting killed."

"You couldn't have stopped them, Logan. If you had, you would have blown your cover and we would have had to come up with another way to find the bastard behind this."

"Conner, your understanding doesn't lessen my guilt. But that's when I got shot, too."

"No! The remaining guards didn't say anything about hitting one of the outlaws," Conner protested.

"I don't know if the bullet that hit me came from them or the men I was riding with. All I know is I lit out, and somewhere south of the mine I got knocked off my horse, had my outfit stolen and was left for dead."

"Obviously," Dixie said, "you didn't die. Is that when your pretty lady found you?"

Sipping his drink, Logan stared at her. Sharp lady to have remembered what he'd said to her and Ty. "Not exactly. Two sagebrush orphans were about to bury me—"

"Good Lord, Logan, what the hell were you doing?"

"Hold on, Conner. I'm here, ain't I? The boys thought they were doing a good deed. Anyway, when they saw their mistake, they wrapped me up in a quilt and delivered me to a widow's door."

Dixie snuggled closer to Ty. To lighten the tension in the room pouring from all three brothers, she tried teasing Logan.

"Bet she thought you were an early Christmas present?"

"No way, Dixie. That widow, Jessie, couldn't—"

"Jessie?" Ty cut in. "I forgot about Jessie!"

"Ty, you promised Greg you'd check on her."

"I know I did. But I forgot. Clean forgot to go up there and check like I promised."

"Would you two mind explaining what the hell you're deviling about?" Logan demanded, attacked by a sudden queasy feeling that he tried to shrug off.

"You don't know her, Logan. A few years ago Greg Rutland bought stock from us. I ran them up to his place and stayed a while. His sister, Jessie, had just come to live with him. Their aunt died and she had no place else to go. Livia, that's Greg's wife, sort of tried to do a little matchmaking, but Jessie was such a quiet little thing that I backed off. 'Sides, I wasn't looking to get tangled up with calico."

"Good thing, too," Dixie reminded him. She folded her arms over Ty's, which were wrapped around her waist. "Ty told you how we met up. What he didn't tell you was that we were running from the men whose horses we stole the night he got knifed trying to rescue me. We went to Greg's ranch, never realizing that we'd been followed. But while we were there, Greg told us that his sister had married a man he didn't like, didn't trust and didn't know one end of a steer from another. He was worried that he hadn't heard from her. Ty said he would try and stop by and find out what he could. I don't remember where he said their place was."

"Near the Superstitions, around Apache Junction. Only I never did. Damn!'

"Stop it, Ty. It's not your fault," Dixie assured him. "I got shot—"

"You nearly died," Ty interjected.

"But you brought me here, and Sofia and your mother nursed me. But this is pointless. It couldn't be the same woman. You said that she's a widow, didn't you, Logan?"

"Yeah. My Jessie's a widow." *Of a man who wouldn't know one end of a steer from the other, since he was too busy hunting gold.*

Logan held up his glass and watched the lamp's light play in the rich, amber-colored liquor. They were all watching him, waiting, he was sure, for him to confirm or deny that his Jessie and their Jessie were one and the same. *His Jessie.* He liked the way the words came together so naturally. What he didn't like was the speculation in his brother's eyes. A quick glance at Dixie showed him that she had already reached her own conclusions.

"What I really want to know," Ty said in a soft, very soft, voice, "is why you couldn't tell me the truth, Conner?"

"When? When you brought her home nearly dead with a raging fever that wouldn't quit? Or those weeks you were consumed with finding where her father's killer was hiding?" Low voiced and furious at being questioned, Conner, who rarely drank, tossed down the last of his liquor. The glass hit the top of the dresser with a thud. "I couldn't tell you. No one but Ma knows about what Logan's doing."

"Conner," Logan said, sitting up and quietly putting his glass down on the bedside table. "Tell Ty. He's got a right to know."

"It makes me sick to say it."

"Say what? What are the two of you hiding from me?"

"Someone," Logan explained when he saw that Conner didn't want to, "real close to our brother here, is working with the outlaws. I saw it up close. Even the times and days being changed for payroll or ore shipments didn't help. They knew."

"Are you telling me that a Kincaid hand is giving out information that will ruin us?"

Conner and Logan exchanged looks, looks that set Ty's temper on fire. "Who?" he demanded. "And don't put me off."

Dixie was glad she was sitting on Ty's lap. It was all that prevented him from bolting out of the chair. "Honey, can't you see that whoever it is, thinking about it, much less saying the name, is hurting your brothers?"

"Wait a minute. You just told me that Ma is the only one who knows about Logan besides you, Conner. That means Santo and Sofia don't know? You can't think he's involved? Damn it, not Santo!"

"Keep your voice down. All we need is Ma in here." Conner took a deep breath and released it. "No one said we thought it's Santo. But the man Rosanna's going to marry, Enrique, tops both my list and Logan's. How could we tell them that we suspected the man they love like a son? A man Rafael already calls his brother? You know how prideful the old man is. It would kill him to find out. That's why we kept it secret. The less anyone knew, the better chance Logan had."

Logan raked his hands through his hair and heaved a tired sigh. "By the look of you, Ty, you're still mad. You've got no right to be. You weren't around, little brother. We didn't know where you were. Would you expect Conner to send out word that I'd taken to riding with outlaws? Would you want to risk my neck that the wrong people found out? That's why we made it appear that Conner, in his greed to control all the Kincaid holdings, forced me out after he got rid of you. Boy, I hate saying this, but you never did want the responsibility to help manage the ranch or the mines.

"I can see that marrying Dixie is making changes in you. Conner won't shoulder the burden alone anymore. But direct your anger where it belongs—to the bastard who's trying to destroy us."

"All right," Ty said after a few minutes, and Dixie's whispered urging. "You couldn't tell me. And I do understand about Santo. The way he feels about this place and Ma, he'd kill Enrique without a qualm regardless of his daughter's or his son's feelings about him."

"You should know," Conner said, drawing their attention, "that the rustlings escalated after Rafael asked that we give Enrique a job here. Not long after that, the mines started getting robbed. Damn thing is, I let no one know about the changed time, or the days of payroll. How could he find out? How does he get word to them?''

''All I know is that we'd camp out. Next morning Monte'd have the information of where we'd hit next. A few times I heard him muttering about someone called Old Charlie getting paid back someday. But none of the others seemed to know who Monte was talking about. Only once did I manage to follow him. Sly fox that Monte is, he met his contact out in the open where I couldn't get close enough to see or hear them.''

Logan started drawing circles on the sheet. ''The Silver Belt is here,'' he said, almost to himself as he plucked up the top sheet to form peaks. ''Northeast of Florence. That's where I finally linked up with them. We hit that mine four times, and we know they hit the Reunion mine north of Phoenix twice, which forms a half circle. Come southwest to the Buckeye mine off of Robbins Butte, and close the circle by ending up at the Rocking K stealing cattle.

''If we're right about Enrique feeding information, then we need to look within this circle for the man behind the robberies. I know it isn't Leo Vesta or Joe Rawson. They're the only two ranchers with an ax to grind and the money to hire men like Monte and his gang.'' Logan looked up to find them crowded around the bed where he had drawn his imaginary map. ''Any ideas of who's within this circle that wants us gone?''

''I'd cast my vote for Riverton,'' Dixie said without a second's hesitation.

Conner shot her a surprised look. ''Yeah. Riverton's worked his way to the top of my list.''

"Who the devil is Riverton?" Logan asked, reaching back and pouring himself a drink.

"Charles Riverton," Conner answered. "But I never heard anyone call him old Charlie. He's more trouble that arrived since you left, Logan. Our new neighbor on the Circle R beat me out of the beef contract at the reservation. Man's building a spread that puts this place to shame. Claimed his land under the Desert Act, then got his men to file. But it's all Circle R land no matter whose name is on the deeds."

Conner looked at Dixie. "How come you thought of him right off?"

"When he sent the invitation to the fiesta to meet his neighbors and you and Ty refused to go, I couldn't let your mother go alone. The man's a braggart. He went on and on about his leading the fight to keep the territory capital in Tucson. And he insulted your mother when she pointed out that he had lost his fight, too. They have moved the capital to Prescott. He also claims that he's going to support John Fremont in his bid for the governor's chair. But I think he's after that himself."

Ty hugged Dixie. "I picked the smartest woman. Dixie and me have done a little looking around on our own. When I went after her father's killer, I had a passing visitor at my campfire. He mentioned you, Logan."

"You knew?" Conner asked. "All this time and you knew?"

"He told me that word was out that Logan was seen with a bad bunch of hombres. I didn't want to believe him. I couldn't tell you or Ma, Conner. Hell, I had to protect her. I feel like a fool now."

"Don't, Ty. I'm sure your brothers don't think that about you. You did what was right."

"Spoken like a woman in love," Logan said. He grinned at Dixie, and her soft laughter, with her cheeks flushed pink, lightened their mood. Unfortunately, he knew it couldn't last.

"Look, I can't risk either Sofia or Santo discovering me here. You really suspect this Riverton, Dixie?"

She felt a warm rush of gratitude for Logan's total acceptance of her into their family circle. And she reached down to squeeze his hand, silently thanking him with a look.

"My answer is yes. But I'm not as sold as you are about Enrique. I've been here two months. I've had a chance to know him. He's very much in love with Rosanna, and she's as devoted as her mother to this family. I don't understand why it couldn't be any one of a number of hands that work here."

"No!" the three brothers chorused at once. They shared sheepish grins.

Conner explained. "Most of these men have been working on this ranch since before I was born. You know that most of them are older than me. I'd trust my life to any one of them. Enrique is the only newcomer I've hired to work on the ranch. And we are agreed that it is someone right here who's passing information along."

"I see that I have lost my place as the head of this family," Macaria announced from the doorway.

Four pairs of guilty eyes focused on her as she entered the room and closed the door behind her. But her gaze was for Logan alone. "My son returns and does not see fit to tell me?"

The others backed away from the bed to allow Logan to rise. He wiped his mouth with the back of his hand, but she'd smell the whiskey on his breath when he kissed her.

Macaria opened her arms to this middle son who most resembled his father. She forced a smile despite seeing the new lines that had formed on his beloved face.

"*Madre.*" Logan held her tight. They'd never needed words. She smelled faintly of sweet mountain lilacs, and he caught sight of a bit more gray in the two long braids that fell to her hips. He couldn't remember the last time he had seen her with her braids down. Usually she wore them pinned in a crown that gave her a regal air.

"Is it done? Have you come home to stay?" she asked him.

Logan pulled back, kissing her cheeks, then framing her slender face within his hands. "No." His gaze held hers, silently begging that she not question him. He had no worry that Ty or Conner would tell her that he'd been wounded. He could only hope that Dixie didn't.

"If it is not over, then you have come to tell us who is behind the stealing?"

"No, *madre*. I lost my outfit and horse and my boots and came home to replace them."

Macaria gracefully slipped from his hold and looked at the others. "Why did you not come and wake me to tell me that Logan was home?"

He caught hold of her slender hands, bringing her attention once more to him. "*Madre,* I asked them not to wake you. I'm not staying. Before the first light I will leave."

"No!"

"*Sí, madre.* Now," he said, standing back and holding her hands out, "let me see if you are still as supple as the willow and as strong as the hickory."

"Strong, yes, a mother must be strong when she has sons such as you and your brothers. Tell me, my son, have you eaten?"

Logan threw back his head and glanced at the thick cedar beams overhead. "I have come home to tell my brother that I have failed, and you want to feed me."

Freeing her hands, Macaria smiled because it was what Logan wanted. She tightened the tie of her bright red wool robe and beckoned Dixie to her side. "Go and speak with your brothers. Your soon-to-be sister will help me in the kitchen."

Dixie cast a helpless look at Ty. He shrugged in response, and she followed Macaria out of the room.

"She's aged since I left," Logan remarked.

"She worries that all her chicks are not around her," Conner replied. "Since you can't stay, Logan, I suggest we get back to the problem at hand. I want to tell you that I don't think it's a good idea for you to try and join up with Wheeler again. Suppose they know who you are and meant to kill you?"

"I've already been over that ground. I don't think that's it."

Logan hoped that Conner accepted his dismissive tone. If Conner knew that he had voiced the very thought that Logan harbored, Conner would use any means to stop him from going back. Despite the risk,

Logan had to go back. He had a score to settle and he refused to fail to protect his family's holdings.

"This kid Billy Jack had a hankering for my horse. I was wounded and don't remember much, but he was riding close enough at one time that he could have knocked me out." Logan paused and stared at the wooden cross over the bed.

The memory of searching out the wood for the cross with Santo returned with a sharp poignancy. It shelved itself in with the ache that had grown watching Dixie and Ty together. He missed Jessie. She was a woman his brothers would like, strong in a different way from Dixie, soft, too. And he worried how she was making out with the boys.

"Logan?" Conner called, seeing the distracted look on his brother's face. "What's wrong?"

"He's been drifting off like that since I came in here," Ty answered. Coming closer, he snapped his fingers in front of Logan's face. With a jerk of his head, Logan glared at him. "Whatever's got you moon-eyed—"

"Nothing. It was nothing. Tell me more about this Riverton. Where'd he come from?"

"No one's really sure. He's got hands from Texas working his cattle. A damn fine-looking herd, too. With the losses we've had," Conner said with anger riding his voice, "I would've been hard-pressed to meet the need for beef at all the reservations."

"Well, I tried to get a closer look at his cattle, and was warned off. Real polite-like, you understand," Ty added. "But there was no mistake that the order went out that Mr. Riverton don't like strange folk poking around his cattle."

Ty stretched and yawned. "Damn," he said, shaking his head. "Been a while since I've stayed up half the night." He started for the bed, intending to throw himself across it, when he suddenly stopped.

"I just remembered something funny that Dixie said to me. You remember that mossback old longhorn, the one whose left horn got broke?"

"The one Blue Dalton tried to rope that plumb near took his thumb off?" Logan laughed, although there hadn't been anything funny at the time. "Blue was always trying to sneak up and get a rope on him. Why?"

"Well, I'd told Dixie the story and, if I remember correctly, she thought she saw that old longhorn."

"Ty, what the hell has this got to do with Riverton? That old mossback shows up now an' again." Conner shook his head. "Go to bed. You're too tired to think."

"Ain't so. And it has plenty to do with Riverton. That's where Dixie thought she saw him."

Conner, in the act of rubbing his neck, jerked his head up. "When? Where?"

"The day we rode up there for his party. Ma had insisted we take the carriage," he explained for Logan's benefit. "Like you, I'd lost everything I left here with, too. I'd finally picked out a sorrel for myself and we were still working out who was giving orders. I rode him out a ways to get rid of some of the pepper. When I got back, Dixie gives me this funny look and tells me about the mossback. I figured she was wrong. But what if she isn't? What if our new neighbor is running our cattle with his?"

"The only way to know for sure is find a Rocking K brand on his stock."

"Whose stock?" Dixie asked, coming inside the room with a basket that she set on the bed. Macaria followed her with another basket. As Dixie smoothed out the top sheet and blanket, she waited for an answer.

"Well?" she prompted. "Who were you talking about?"

"Our new neighbor and his sleek, fat cattle."

"Conner! This cannot be." Macaria left the basket she had been emptying and went to stand in front of her oldest son. She stared up at him, sorrow rising for the son who had been forced to become a man before he'd had a chance to be a boy. Anger roiled within the blue-gray depths of his eyes.

"Conner, you will not speak disrespectfully of Charles. Not in my home."

Mother and son ignored the sharp gasps from the others. But both were aware what had caused them. Macaria had never, not once, reminded her sons that this was her land, her home first.

"Charles?" Conner tried to control his temper, but having his mother defend the best suspect they had was intolerable. "Since when, *madre,* did the man become *Charles* to you?"

"Since he courted me at the same time your father did."

Chapter Fifteen

"The hell you say!" Conner exploded.

For moments there was a shocked, hushed silence in the room as Macaria, satisfied that she had made her point, calmly returned to the bedside and removed bread and cheese from the basket.

"Conner!" Logan warned.

"Stay out of this," Conner snapped.

"Like hell I will. You apologize. Now." The look of disbelief that Conner shot him sent Logan lunging for his brother. Ty grabbed hold of his arm, yanking it hard to stop him. Logan cried out in agony when pain raced up to his shoulder. "For Almighty's sake! Watch what the devil you're doing to me."

"Conner?" Ty prompted as he released Logan's arm.

"Do it," Logan added, cradling his arm against his body. He shook his head when he saw his mother start toward him. "Nothing," he whispered. "I swear it's nothing."

"More secrets kept from me?" Macaria asked, but without expectations of an answer. She knew she would be told by her sons, and Dixie, only what they wanted her to know.

"Madre," Conner said softly. "I do apologize for losing my temper with you. But you can't just drop that fact into the conversation and not expect me to react. I can't believe you kept this secret."

"You cannot? How strange. Is there one of you in this room that does not have a secret? A secret that will not be shared until you deem the time perfect?" Her dark, piercing eyes searched each face in turn.

Ty, unable to meet her gaze, stared down at his bare feet. He believed no one knew of his continuing search for information about the man who had ordered Dixie's father's death.

Logan, too, could not bear her gaze, and turned toward the window. Macaria caught the set of his mouth and knew he was in pain. So, he had been wounded and thought to keep it from her? But there was more within the dark blue eyes of this son. Memories that troubled him. What would he hide from them? Always Logan had a woman. But there was an older secret this middle son kept. He'd never once challenged Conner's place, but he longed to take the reins of leader into his hands. This, too, no one knew.

Macaria smiled a little when she saw that Dixie found polishing the apples with the end of her shawl a refuge from her gaze. Her secret was one of joy for them all. She remembered well those first months and the need to hold tight a little while longer to the woman soon to be a wife before the biggest change in her life would be shared with the family. Her poor son did not know, and she had no intention of telling him.

For Conner, he hid his dream. Never once in the years that he had worn the boots of his father had this oldest son retreated from doing what he must. But she judged the time coming soon for Conner to walk the path he longed for, and one more secret had to be kept.

"I believe," Macaria said softly, "that this matter of secrets is done."

"No, *madre*."

"Conner?" she queried.

"I want to know why you didn't tell me. Forget that I'm your son. I'm the ramrod of this outfit. That position gives me the right to know."

Her short laugh caught them by surprise. "You did not ask me if I knew him," she stated calmly. "I recall you took an instant dislike to Charles when he came to invite us to his fiesta. As you did, Dixie."

"He's very attractive, but there's something about him that makes me uncomfortable," Dixie offered in her defense.

"Don't forget me," Ty muttered. "I didn't exactly want him for a dance partner."

"I am very well aware of your feelings, too. It is because of this open dislike you have rudely displayed that I have not returned his kind invitation and asked him to dine with us. Now that the matter has been discussed and you are all aware of *my feelings,* I shall hasten to remedy—"

"*Madre*." Calm and soft, but commanding, Logan's voice brought his mother's instant attention, and silence from the others. "We are talking about the possibility that this man may be the one behind the rustlings and the mine robberies. You can't expect us, your sons," he reminded her, "to ignore the facts we have put together. And I know that you are also aware to the penny of how much we have lost. Would you reconsider and allow us time to confirm or put the lie to his involvement?"

"Such sweet reasoning, Logan. But you are wrong, my son. All of you are wrong. Charles Riverton has no need to steal from us. He was already a very wealthy man when he first courted me." Macaria's tone grew impassioned as she stated her reasons. "I loved your father, and begged my own to choose him for my husband. Charles was a gentleman when he understood that my heart and mind were filled with love for Justin.

"If your brothers had behaved as I raised them, and not spoiled children, when he invited us to see the grand hacienda he is building, they would know that he has purchased large tracts of land to the west of our holdings in hope of convincing the owners of the Southern Pacific Railroad to route their track closer to Sweetwater. And think, my children, what that would mean to all of the ranches. We would be able to ship our cattle while they are fat, not herd them for miles with terrible losses of weight."

She allowed them a few minutes, then added, "Now, tell why such a man of wealth, a man who carries the same vision as your father once had for the growth of this land, would have a need to steal from us?"

"I don't know. But I'm going to find out."

"Conner! Have you not heard a word that I have said?"

"I heard you, *madre*. I just don't believe it."

Logan, more exhausted than he dared to admit in front of his mother, grabbed hold of Conner's announcement and used it for himself. "I'm for letting you all sort this out. I'm starved and when I'm done eating, I need to leave. Conner can investigate from this end, and I'll make Monte Wheeler talk or die trying."

"Do not say such words!" Crossing herself, Macaria cast Logan an angry look. "You will bring ill luck upon yourself. I never wanted you to ride with these men. I ask you not to go back."

"*Madre,* I love you. But this is best left to us. I don't think you're looking at this with the eyes of Macaria Kincaid."

"And who, then, am I if not your mother?"

"Forgive me for making you angry again. But you are perhaps a young woman thinking of long-ago nights and the handsome caballero who paid you court?"

"You insult me, and you insult the memory of your father to believe I would ever forget my place and put at risk what your father lost his life to build. Eat, then, I will see to clean clothing and boots, so that you, too, do not forget your place."

Her exit brought a shared disbelieving look among the brothers. Dixie shook her head and began slicing cheese and dried spicy sausage.

Logan thanked her when she handed him the first plate, but before he ate, he asked Conner how he'd made out with the sheriff.

"About what we had expected. Verl Jenison tells me to bring him proof."

"Then we should have gone with the first plan," Logan reminded him. "We could've set a trap and captured Monte and his gang."

"I vetoed the idea then and still do. I want the man behind them. The more I mull over what we discussed tonight, the more Charles Riverton bears watching. The information Ma gave us about him encouraging the owners of the railroad to set track near Sweetwater is worth looking into. Bribes take a lot of cash. So does that place he's building. I haven't seen anything mentioned in the newspapers, but they're bound to keep it quiet.

"I recall that old miner...Crazy Judah, I think he's called. Well, he tried to get me to put up money when he took a notion to buy into the Central Pacific after they were almost busted. Those mountains in California cost them too much to blast and lay track. But he did mention that he and his partners were looking at the Southern Pacific, too. Claimed it had an imposing name and a charter just waiting for someone to pick up to build into southern California, but they had no track laid."

"Well, I can't see Ma being fooled by the man."

"Ty!" Dixie, who had been quiet till now, rounded on him. "How can you say that? Your mother, in case you've forgotten, is still a lovely woman. She's been widowed almost sixteen years. My goodness, that's how old she was when she married your father. How can you all be so selfish to deny her whatever pleasure she has in his company?"

"Now, honey—"

"Don't honey me! It's true and you know...you all know it," she stated with a sweeping look that touched

Conner and Logan. "Maybe he is behind this. But you'll have no more information from her about him. What's more, I believe that if you stubborn males dig in your heels about her seeing him, she'll do it out of spite."

"All that may be true, Dixie," Conner said with an infuriating calm. "But my mother—our mother—is a rich woman. Allowing Riverton to get anywhere near her—"

"I can't believe I'm hearing this from you, Conner!" Dixie closed her eyes and fought to calm herself. She took a deep breath, then released it. She opened her eyes to find Ty's worried eyes upon her. She forced a smile. "All right. I am yelling. I'm sorry for that. But I think you insult your mother when you question where her loyalty lies. She would never do anything to hurt you or the Rocking K."

Sensing another buildup of tension, Dixie turned to Logan. "You said that two boys had found you. What happened to them?"

While Logan told them about Marty and Kenny, Macaria remained outside in the hallway. She had gone to her sewing room where she had stored all of Logan's clothing in a large chest lined with fragrant cedar. Holding the clean clothing and the boots she had taken out for her son, Macaria half listened to his tale about the boys. But memories rose and she leaned against the wall, thinking back.

When she had lost the last child, a stillborn daughter, the midwife sent by her parents had said there would be no more children. She had cried for the daughter she would never have. Her love, her Justin, had reminded her then that as each of their sons married, they would bring her daughters.

She had accepted Dixie from the first, and loved her for herself, not just for bringing her lost maverick son back to her. But coming to her defense, reminding her sons that she was a woman as well as their mother, had endeared Dixie to her even more.

Coming back to hear the low rumble of Logan's and Conner's voices, Macaria glanced upward and wondered about the women they would bring to the Kincaid family.

She understood the fears her sons raised, but they did not understand the loneliness that filled her days and her nights now that they were grown men.

She would do nothing to endanger their future. But they could not dictate to her. Her family could be traced back to the soldiers who had ventured first from Spain with Diego Velázquez to claim the island of Cuba, then traveled with Hernán Cortés when he was sent to conquer Mexico.

The same passionate spirit that flowed in their blood was hers. And it still ruled her. She had come here, a bride of sixteen, and helped Justin carve out a home from a wild, raw land that had earned her love.

Yet she could not ignore that, for the first time, her three sons stood in agreement against her.

Rousing herself, Macaria walked into the room and gave the clothing and boots to Logan. She hushed Dixie when she asked if they should put off the wedding.

"There is no need. Would you give rise to talk that we wait for him to return? That would put Logan's life in danger."

"Madre—"

Macaria placed her fingertips against Logan's lips. She stood on tiptoe to kiss his beard-stubbled cheek. "Go with God, my son," she whispered, then left them.

Dixie, too, came to him to say goodbye. "I'll curl up on Ty's bed, so stay here as long as you can." Then she, too, kissed his cheek and left the room.

Ty closed his eyes, and Conner motioned to Logan to let him be. "He's been run ragged about the wedding and Dixie's strange moods these last weeks. I'll get you a new rifle to replace the one you lost."

Logan shucked his travel-stained clothes and made use of the pitcher of water on the dresser. It wasn't as good as a real bath—one of the things he kept promising himself he'd have when this matter was done—but he felt better once he was dressed in his own clean clothing. He tucked the nut brown chambray shirt into a well-worn pair of denims and, ever mindful of his shoulder, slipped on a brown leather vest. His mother had chosen comfortable clothing, with enough wear on them so as not to arouse suspicion. The boots brought a sigh of bliss from him as he stomped the low heel against the floor.

Conner returned with a Springfield .45-70 side hammer trapdoor model just like the one that had been stolen from Logan. The Springfields had been made by the firm's master armorer, Erskine Allin, and were treasured possessions.

"This is yours, Conner. I can't take it."

"Not mine. It's Pa's. You'll need it. Only I'm warning you fair, lose this one and I'll take it out of your hide." He shoved a box of ammunition into Logan's vest pocket. From his own shirt pocket Conner removed five double eagles. "I figure you lost your money, too. Just promise me that you won't take any unnecessary risks. I don't want to lose you, Logan."

"You won't." Logan pocketed the money. "I want you to arrange for another payroll shipment at the Silver Belt. Give me five days to find Monte. Put the word out that you're shipping ore, too."

"What are you planning?"

Logan told him while he packed food in one of the wide linen napkins.

"Simple plan," Conner remarked.

"Let's hope it works." Logan gently nudged the rocking chair, and Ty jerked awake. "Hey, little brother, I've got a date that won't wait. You take care of that little lady."

"Logan, I wish...."

For a moment regret filled Logan's eyes as he looked at his brother. "Yeah. I wish I could be here, too, and dance at your wedding. Maybe you'll dance at mine."

He was out the window before Ty came fully awake and realized what he'd said. "Conner, tell me you heard him, too." He spun around. "Conner?" Shaking his head, Ty told himself he'd made a mistake and began cleaning up the food left on the bed.

In her room, lit by two small candles, Macaria knelt at the elaborately carved wooden prayer bench she had brought with her from Mexico. Clutching her rosary, she offered prayers for her son's safe return.

From his darkened room's window, Conner searched the garden's shadows for a sign of his brother. He caught sight of him as Logan went over the gate. "Go with God," he whispered, echoing his mother's earlier words.

As he stood there, a nagging thought rose in his mind. He'd meant to ask Logan...no! Not Logan, but his mother.

Conner ran down the hall and burst into Macaria's room. "Did Riverton question you about Logan?"

"Calm yourself—"

"Never mind me. Did he ask you about Logan? He had to hear the whispers about him. Everyone else has. Did you tell—?"

"You go too far!" She rose from the bench and faced her irate son. "No, Charles asked me nothing about Logan."

"That's it! Damn it, that's it. He knows." Conner tunneled the fingers of both hands through his thick hair.

"You are not making any sense, Conner. How could Charles know about him? Yes, there are whispers, but if what you believe about him is true, why would he know that Logan—"

"It's the only reason why they dumped him. They know he's a Kincaid." Pacing the tiled floor, he sorted everything that Logan had told him, and revealed his reasoning to his mother.

"He—Charles—didn't ask you about the rumors that one of your sons was riding with outlaws. Didn't that strike you as odd?"

"No. A gentleman would not remind me of something so shameful."

"Wrong, *madre*. He didn't ask because he knew. And he'd already sent word to have Logan killed before he could follow a trail back to him." He stopped and faced her. "I know you don't want to believe me, but this is the only thing that makes sense. And Logan—" He broke off and started to leave.

"Conner! Conner, come back here." Macaria ran after him. "Where are you going?"

"After my brother before he gets himself killed."

"What the hell are you talking about?" Ty demanded, grabbing hold of Conner's arm to stop him.

"Logan's gonna find Monte and tell him he's got word that we're shipping ore and a payroll next week."

"He won't believe him after all the losses we've had."

"That's just it. Logan's to tell him that we figure the very same thing, that no one would expect us to do it, so the setup is perfect for them to rob us again. And they won't have time to check it out with Riverton, if he's behind it."

"I hate to tell you this, Conner, but I find a big hole in this plan you two put together. Where did Logan get this information?"

"There's ten, maybe fifteen small mining camps close to where they left him. Close enough that someone could have found him. You know how talk spreads. Whiskey's loosened a lot of tongues. It all would have worked, too, with us being in place to trap them, but if Riverton knows that he's a Kincaid, Logan's life is worth less than the spit to say it."

"I'm coming with you."

"No. Someone's got to stay here and keep an eye—"

"I'm coming. An' while we stand here, Logan's getting a lead on us."

Macaria pleaded with both of them as they hurried to dress. All Conner did was fire orders about how many men he wanted ready to ride at a moment's notice if he couldn't find Logan and stop him from setting the plan into action.

Conner stifled his impatience while Ty went to kiss Dixie goodbye without waking her. There was going to be hell to pay in the morning when she found out he was gone. Leaving her to his mother's care, he ran with Conner to saddle their horses.

Chapter Sixteen

"Miz Jessie, you lookin' for him again?"

Turning around, Jessie grinned at Kenny. "Caught me. I can't seem to help myself from looking. Hope, I've discovered, dies a hard, slow death." Climbing down from the jutting rock shelf that gave her a view of the flat below, Jessie looked around. "Where's the little one?"

"Marty's still down by the creek. He didn't finish cleanin' the fish we caught." Digging the toe of his boot into the dirt, Kenny hunched his thin shoulders. "Logan's been gone nigh on a week now. Don't recall him makin' any promises 'bout when he'll come back."

"I don't recall him making any promises at all."

"Now you got that sad look in your eyes again. Didn't mean to hurt you."

She reached out and tousled his hair. "You didn't. What say we go join Marty? I'll fix a picnic lunch for us. We couldn't ask for a more beautiful fall day." Jessie glanced up to find the sky a blue bowl overhead with thick white clouds that looked like puffs of clean picked cotton. But when she started to walk back to the cabin, she saw that Kenny stayed behind.

"What's wrong?" she asked him.

"Me an' Marty've been talkin', ya know, 'bout what's gonna happen to us."

"Happen to you? Nothing is going to happen to you. Not while I have a breath in my body." Jessie felt a little alarmed at the way Kenny avoided looking at her. The boy was always so direct, with his words, his manner and sometimes disconcerting gaze. "Have you held back telling me something I should know?"

"No. No," he repeated. "It's jus' like I said. Me an' Marty are cousins. We ain't got no kinfolk back home."

"Then what is the problem, Kenny? I guess I assumed that the two of you would live here with me. If that's not what you want, tell me."

Kenny glanced beyond Jessie toward the cabin where they had made their home this past week. For the first time in months he did not have the total responsibility for himself and Marty. But he didn't trust that they could just go on as they were. Fears built at night, and they weren't leaving him during the day.

"Ain't folks gonna talk 'bout you havin' us?"

"Why should they, Kenny? I'm a widow, that's true, but I am a grown woman perfectly capable of taking care of you and Marty." Jessie gnawed her lower lip for the lie. Until she found a way to sell her cattle, she had forty dollars between the three of them and losing it all.

"But what if someone comes an' tries to take us away?"

Frowning, Jessie walked to his side. He barely tolerated her hugging, but he appeared in need of more than verbal assurances. Dropping to her knees, she drew him close. "Honey, I won't let anyone take you and Marty away from me. I know how hard it's been for you, but I think of you two as mine. Family, Kenny. The three of us make our own family."

She held him, closing her eyes when he accepted her by wrapping his arms around her neck. *And Logan,* a little voice whispered in her mind, *would complete the circle perfectly.* Jessie, too, closed her eyes for a moment. She dreamed of him, and tried hard to banish the dreams upon waking. She was unable to stop them, the way she couldn't stop searching the land for a sign of a lone rider returning.

Jessie roused herself. She was determined not to allow her longings to sour the day. And that's all she had left for Logan, she told herself as she released Kenny and stood, foolish longings for a traveling kind of man.

"You and I," she said, touching the tip of her finger to his nose, "have a picnic to get ready."

His smile was all she hoped for, and if her own was a little less than genuine, Kenny didn't know as he ran for the cabin.

She followed him, but at a slower pace, looking over her shoulder once. *Wherever you are, Logan, I hope you're safe. And I hope that you miss me just a little. Just enough to draw you back to me so I can put a name to the feelings you awakened.*

"Jessie!"

"I'm coming, Kenny."

* * *

Logan guided his horse around the saguaro cacti that rose in contorted shapes from the valley floor. Some had the form of massive candelabra that beckoned a rider's eyes to follow their height to the tops and view the majestic and haunting mass of rock known as Superstition Mountain. But he wasn't heading for Apache Junction; his goal was the mining camp at Florence. The place where he'd first linked up with Monte Wheeler and the others.

He remained aware that when men desired to hide in this broken land of desert and mountains, the Apache were about the only ones who could find them. But he was determined to hunt them down. His family's holdings were at stake.

And he never forgot the personal score he intended to settle with whoever had stolen his gear and left him for dead.

Doggedly trying to keep his mind focused on what he had to do, Logan didn't have much success in keeping Jessie out of his thoughts. At odd moments he would remember her smile, or hear the tartness of her voice, or the wondering whisper of his name when she had trembled in his arms.

Last night, when he'd made camp in a dry wash, a cactus wren defending her nest of grasses and twigs high up in the thorny branches of a cholla cactus had caught his eye. Jessie was like that, all tawny shades, defending herself and all she claimed with the same single-minded devotion.

A man could do worse than to have a woman like Jessie at his side.

An ache he'd never quite subdued since he had left her began to grow. How could she have worked herself so deeply into his mind in such a short time?

Women had come and gone and he never let his thoughts dwell on them. Why Jessie?

He attempted to shrug it off, but the question remained. And all he could do was blame its lingering on seeing his younger brother, who had previously desired no shackles, suddenly ready to settle down.

He couldn't make any plans. But if he did...

Sensing the turn of his thoughts, Logan drew back mentally from the subject of Jessie. To distract himself, he considered Conner's report that Riverton had his men file on the land and then deed it back to him. It was by no means an uncommon practice. Most of the larger ranchers used this method to hold on to more land after the government began passing land acts.

Funny how someone else's doing it riled Conner, when Logan remembered Santo telling him once that their father had done the very same thing to claim land where there was water.

Any man who controlled water in the territory was the man who controlled the range.

He rode up a loose scree slope of a dry wash, keeping the horse down to a plodding walk.

This was Apache country, and if a man intended to survive he took his time to study the land before him. Logan had found places of incredible beauty, and others so barren it was hard to believe that life managed to exist there.

Shaded in rusts, copper and dusty gray flecked with the green of cacti and brush, it was a rough, broken country. Water was priceless, for every predator needed it to live.

He had pushed himself and his horse these past few days. Logan dismounted, ready to share the warm water in his canteen with his animal.

And the horse had to drink first, for without him, a man could die.

No land held death so close, waiting for a careless mistake, as the one he called home.

He led the horse toward a large rockfall, hoping to find a *tinaja*. Rainwater collected in these small pools in the rocks, but there hadn't been rain for weeks. Far to the west he spotted the circled flight of buzzards and a chill walked up his spine. *There but for those two boys and Jessie went I.*

As he leaned close to peer down into the crack between the rocks, his hand accidentally brushed against the stone. Logan jerked his hand back. The rock was as hot as a branding iron from the sun's baking heat.

Taking the canteen off his saddle horn, he poured some water into his hat and gave the horse his drink. All the while, his gaze moved in a steady searching pattern, ever alert to danger.

When the animal finished, Logan replaced his hat on his head, enjoying the coolness of the wet felt, then sipped the warm canteen water to quench his own thirst.

He had to push on if he was going to reach Florence by nightfall. The desert came alive when the sun went down, with predators in need of water, in need of food. It was one reason a smart man didn't make his camp close to a watering hole. The other had to do with allowing nature's cycle to play out its methods of ensuring survival of the fittest. If a man's scent kept the thirsty animals away from life-giving water, he broke the circle.

Yet he was reluctant to mount, despite the need that drove him.

Once more he sent a searching gaze over the land. Nothing moved but a heated breeze. He canted his hat brim low and slung the canvas strap of the canteen back over the horn. Gathering the reins in his hand, he started to mount.

The horse sidestepped toward the rock. Logan's curse died as his foot slipped from the stirrup.

Four Apache warriors were crossing the dry wash about three hundred yards ahead of where he stood. Although he'd just satisfied his thirst, his mouth was suddenly parched.

He saw the jerky fall of the horses' hooves, telling him the animals were tired. His gaze focused on the knife slashes that had forced the horses to lengthen their stride.

He ran one hand over the brown's muzzle, silently thanking him. If he had moved out they would have seen him.

Logan slid his rifle from the leather scabbard that protected it from trail dust. He waited, rifle ready, standing very still.

If those Apaches spotted him, he wouldn't take any bets on what his life would be worth.

His breathing was shallow. He didn't look directly at the Indians. There were some who said that an Apache could feel a white man's eyes upon him.

Logan wasn't about to test the truth of it.

They disappeared in the juniper and ocotillo that grew on a slope up ahead of him. Logan blew out the breath he'd been holding.

"Snakes in purgatory!" he hissed, feeling the coil of tension that gripped him. "Damn if that didn't shave a year off my life, horse."

Sliding his hand up and down the animal's neck, Logan praised him. "You done good, boy, real good. 'Course, I realize you were protecting your hide as much as my own. We could've ended up over those Apaches' campfire, you for supper and me providing the entertainment."

The horse flicked his ear, and Logan quickly scratched the area directly behind it.

"Jessie picked a winner when she chose you to buy. Didn't flick an ear when you saw them, did you? When this is over, I've a mind to find more stock like you, but your brand's been worked over so many times that it's hard to tell what it ever was."

As he lifted the corner of the saddle blanket, Logan thought he might have been army stock. Using one finger, he traced the burned hide.

"Lazy three, or running *M*, a boxed *M* or a boxed three," he murmured, then paused. A deep frown creased his forehead. "Damn! Hot damn! That's it!'

He swung away from the horse and dropped to his knees. Switching the rifle to his left hand, Logan marked the Rocking K brand in the dirt with his fingertip. The capital initial *K* had a half circle beneath it to indicate the rocking letter. If the *K* had been tilted slightly, it would have been a tumbling *K*.

It took him only seconds to close up the top of the *K* and form an *R*. More slowly, he finished drawing a closed circle around the new letter.

He stared at the new brand he'd just drawn. "From Rocking K to Circle R and none the wiser."

Including him. He might be wiser about how it was done, but it didn't end his problem. Without proof, the law wouldn't touch Riverton. Even with proof, they might not if the man had the money and political power behind him. But Logan had one solid clue that pointed to the man being the one behind the robberies and the rustlings.

And the only way to justify a necktie party would be to catch him with his crooked brand heating over a fire and a hog-tied animal wearing the Rocking K brand beside him.

Men like Riverton wouldn't soil their hands with working over another's brand to claim the cattle as his own. He had the money to hire men to do the dirty work for him. And he could always claim that he didn't know.

Once again, Logan reasoned, who would stand and call him a liar? His own mother had defended him by reminding her sons that he didn't need the money or the cattle.

But appearances were so deceiving. He had arrived with a large herd of cattle for his ranch. How could they prove he'd stolen the cattle from them, had had men hole up in any one of a hundred blind canyons, change the brands, smudge them with dirt and run the cattle on his newly claimed land?

The choice was to catch someone in the act, or get someone to talk who had actually done the deed.

Logan rose and wiped out his scratchings in the dirt with the toe of his boot. After another sweeping gaze over the land, he mounted.

"Horse, you just earned yourself all the shiny red apples you can eat."

Five hours later Logan rode into Florence with his rifle across the saddle in front of him. The town was old, almost eight years in the making, and might last for another eight. A huddle of shacks and tents gave way to the weathered wood buildings.

He'd kept his pace easy, as much to save the horse as himself. He rode in the middle of the dirt street, having his choice of three saloons. He was thankful it was a weeknight and most of the miners would still be at their diggings. If this were Friday or Saturday night, he'd have his work cut out searching out Monte or any of the others.

Neck-reining the horse toward the hitching post, he dismounted in front of Jager's Muleshoe, the name of the owner, saloon and the rotgut swill he passed as whiskey. Taking his rifle with him, he pushed open the door.

The place wasn't crowded. His arrival caused a few heads to turn, and cool eyes took his measure. He returned the looks of the men seated around the tables, and they quickly returned to their card games. Logan hid his disappointment that the faces he most wanted to see weren't numbered among these men.

But there was always the barkeep. After ordering a whiskey, he sipped from the none-too-clean glass and engaged the man in small talk. Information was passed along from the stage-line drivers, miners and those passing through, and served as the most reliable source.

When Logan finally got around to asking the questions he wanted, he didn't get the exact answers that he needed.

There had been no sign of Wheeler, or the men that rode with him, for almost a week. Logan left without finishing his drink and before the talk turned to why he was looking for him.

The second place he tried earned him more of the same, until a lone man, a down-and-out cardsharp by the cut of his fancy duds, stopped Logan as he headed for the door.

"Game, mister?"

"Ain't got the time," Logan answered.

"Right. You're lookin' in the wrong place for any man that's got money burning a hole in his pocket."

"That so?" Although anxious to leave, Logan hesitated. He knew if the man had information, he'd have to wait until he was ready to name his price or tell it in his own way.

"Nice-lookin' rifle," the gambler commented.

"An' I'm looking for a man with one just like it." Logan pulled out a chair and held up two fingers to the barkeep. He half listened as the gambler remarked about the lack of a good game in Florence, then he paid for the drinks that were served and waited impatiently for the man to say his piece.

"Like I was tellin' you, if a man has money he's gone over to Haskel's place. He's got a woman working his back room."

The word stirred Logan into a frown. Then he smiled. Billy Jack had a fondness for women, and he had money to spend.

"Much obliged." Logan shoved back his chair. He took a twenty-dollar gold piece from his shirt pocket. "For drinks or a stake," he said, laying the coin on the scarred tabletop. "The information is worth that much."

He left the horse tied and walked along the street until he reached the end and saw Haskel's, which stood alone from the other buildings.

Logan went inside with the hammer cocked on his rifle and his finger on the trigger.

"Monte been around?" he asked, approaching the bar.

The barkeep's eye went from the rifle to Logan's face. "We don't want no trouble in here."

"Ain't gonna be any if you give me the right answers. If Monte ain't here, then one of his men is."

"You the law?"

"No." Watching the man, Logan didn't miss his darting glance toward the back of the nearly empty saloon. The woman he had was either a dried-up old whore or someone had bought her time for the night, because no one was lined up and waiting.

"Who's back there?"

" Billy Jack. An' he's in a mean temper."

Logan started walking.

"Hey! Wait up, mister! You can't just go barging—"

"Watch me," Logan returned in a cool, deadly voice.

Chapter Seventeen

Logan kicked open the door on a dingy room no bigger than a birthing stall. Two candles cast flickering light over the rough wood walls. He ignored the scream from the woman bolting from the bed to cower in the corner.

Billy Jack, stripped down to his sweat-stained union suit, was on the bed, his back to the wall, his legs sprawled open. He blinked, rubbed his eyes with one hand and lifted the bottle to his lips with his other hand.

Suddenly he choked and spewed the liquor all over himself and the bed, shaking his head like a maddened bull.

Logan angled the barrel of the rifle up so that there was no doubt that his target was Billy Jack's flaccid flesh.

"It would give me the greatest pleasure if you moved, Billy Jack."

"You're a bad dream, *sí?*"

"You're gonna wish that's all I am by the time I'm finished with you." Then Logan said to the cowering woman, "Get your clothes and leave. My amigo and I are going to be busy."

"He didn't pay me," she returned in a sullen voice, hitching up the falling shoulder strap of her soiled chemise.

"Then take his pants with you and keep whatever's in the pockets." Logan shot a quick look at the pants hanging off the footboard. "But leave the belt," he added. "That's mine."

"Amigo, have a drink. We are friends, *sí?* This is a way to share—"

"No sharing, Billy Jack. I'm still deciding if I want to kill you now for leaving me to die, or wait until you answer a few questions for me."

A sly smile lit the outlaw's face. "If you kill me, you have no answers."

"But I'll have pleasure, boy, a great deal of it."

Logan heard the woman scurrying around behind him and watched her carefully as she came forward and took the pants from the footboard. Under his watchful gaze she stripped the belt off and replaced it over the board. Logan backed up behind the door as she ran from the room, then slammed it closed. To ensure it stayed that way, he grabbed hold of the straight-backed chair from the far corner and wedged its back beneath the door latch.

His smile was chilling as he caught the darting look Billy Jack made at his holstered gun that lay on the floor near the bed.

"Be my guest and go for it, Billy Jack."

"What ya want?"

"Let's start small. And to make it easy, all you have to do is nod. See, amigo, I won't take no as any answer. Understood?"

"*Sí.* The rifle—"

"Stays right where it is, just like you're going to while we talk. We all know how fond you are of the ladies, Billy Jack. You move and you'll disappoint them all."

Billy Jack took a long swallow from the bottle and Logan allowed it. He knew it was calculated as a gesture of disdain for his threat, and perhaps a little boost of false courage.

"Now," Logan began when Billy Jack lowered the bottle and hugged it to his side. "Who gave the order to leave me to die?"

Billy Jack took his measure. He'd faced his share of men and knew when one would kill and when he would not. Despite the fog induced by liquor, he stared long and hard at Logan. Every man would kill when pushed far enough. He didn't know how far Logan had been pushed. He wasn't paid enough to lose his life, or end up maimed so that he would wish for death himself.

"It was Zach," he said at last. "Not an order. He wanted the rifle. You would not trade him."

"He left me to die over a rifle," Logan repeated, fixing him with a hard stare.

"And I wanted your horse," Billy Jack admitted with a shrug. "You were bleeding badly, amigo. We did not think you'd live."

"I had a flesh wound, Billy Jack. It wasn't life threatening at all."

"Then it is good you found help."

"Did I say that? Not that it matters. I'm here now and I want to know where Monte is."

"He comes an' he goes."

Logan stroked his left hand along the barrel. "I'm gettin' mighty tired of holding this. And a man gets real careless when he's tired. A hair trigger on such a fine rifle, well . . ." He paused, then smiled. "You get the drift, don't you?"

"Monte goes up to an old line shack he found. The others, they wait for him there."

"More," Logan demanded.

"Monte, he is angry. He don't hear from—" Billy Jack lifted the bottle and swallowed until it was empty. For a moment he held Logan's steely gaze and thought of flinging the bottle at his head. He weighed his chances.

Logan didn't move.

Billy Jack grinned and placed the bottle on the floor where the temptation of his gun waited. With a curse he flung himself upright on the bed.

"I'm waiting," Logan prompted.

"It's my life you ask me to risk."

"It's your life if you don't finish."

"The boss man. Monte don't hear from him. He worries there is no more jobs. Zach an' Tallyman get angry with him. He sends word for them to wait."

"And Monte rode off to see the boss man?"

"*Sí.* This is all I know. I swear by my mother's—"

"Billy Jack, you could swear up one end of this territory and down the other and I'd still have to make the choice of whether or not to believe you."

"You have the gun. I tell you the truth. To show you I am still your amigo, I tell you your fine horse, he is out back. I will come with you. I show where the shack is." He swung his legs off the bed, ready to stand.

"Hold it." Logan had to think fast. He couldn't leave Billy Jack here, not on the loose. Tying him up wouldn't give him more than an hour's start if he was lucky. He didn't want to kill him, and that meant Logan had to take Billy Jack with him. With a gun in his back the breed would be careful not to cross him.

"Put on your boots, but that's all."

"You make a joke, *sí?*"

"Do I look like a man in a joking mood?" Logan kicked the chair away from the door. "Let's go."

"You cannot mean to do this to me. I will kill you before—"

"I warned you. You want to live, you march out of here just as you are."

Billy Jack reached for his boots and stomped into them. He buttoned up his fly and, with fury lighting his eyes, proceeded out into the saloon.

Logan grabbed hold of his precious belt, slung it over his shoulder and followed him out.

Spying the woman, Logan spoke to her. "You get enough out of his pockets?"

"Yeah, I did."

"Good. Then for the price of whatever his gear in the room will bring, go out back and get the horse he left there. Bring it around in front for me and I'll toss in twenty dollars more."

Logan had no doubt that she would do it. The offer was more than she would make in a week. He prodded Billy Jack outside.

Thinking about Zach looking for him had questions burning on Logan's tongue. But he couldn't ask

Billy Jack without giving away that he knew. Billy Jack might be smart enough to figure out where Logan had been, and he didn't dare endanger Jessie. Yet the more he thought about it, the more he needed to know if Zach had ever gone back to her place.

As if his thoughts had somehow reached the breed, Billy Jack shot him a look over his shoulder. "You do not say where it was you stayed. Zach, he go looking for you. But he tells Monte there is no sign. Me, I figure the buzzards got you."

"I guess you figured wrong."

"But it puzzles me. You come here, so far from where we left you. And you have another horse. I ask myself, where does this horse come from? Where does another fine rifle come from? A man must have much money to buy these things."

Logan didn't answer him. He worked loose the knot in his neckerchief, then pulled the bandanna free.

"So I think long and hard about this, amigo. And I remember the *señorita*."

The woman came around the corner of the saloon just then, leading Logan's horse, the one Billy Jack had taken.

"What do you want me to do with him?"

"Just wrap his reins over the post and go inside. My friend suffers his embarrassment poorly." Logan was not about to wait for her to leave. "Get down on your knees," he ordered Billy Jack.

"Amigo—"

"Cut the amigo. I'd rather have the devil call me his friend. Just do it and put your hands together over your head." Logan kicked his knees apart, making it harder for Billy Jack to attempt to rise. "Now lean out and grab hold of that hitching post with your left hand. Stretch,'' he added when he saw the man hesitate. ''Now bring your right arm down and behind you.''

Moves and timing had to be perfect. Logan knew he had seconds to tie Billy Jack's hands behind his back, and he couldn't hold the rifle on him. Cradling the rifle so that the barrel rested in the small of Billy Jack's back, he looped and twisted the neckerchief around one wrist, then ordered him to bring his left arm back. He could almost feel Billy Jack weighing his chances once more, and the tension hummed through him until he grabbed the breed's left wrist and finished tying his hands together.

Logan felt the leash he held on his control begin to fray. The rage inside him was building and he had to struggle not to let it free. He kept thinking about the men who had lost their lives doing their job to protect the payroll, all because of this man's taunting. He thought of the losses to his family.

But it was the moments of stomach-lurching fear that had gripped him when Billy Jack mentioned a *señorita*. It had all come together then for Logan. That day Jessie went to Apache Junction to buy him a horse. Something had happened to her, something she had refused to tell him.

And he knew Billy Jack's fondness for anything in skirts.

''You bastard!'' Logan moved before he even thought about it. Using the rifle barrel, he swung low and hard at Billy Jack's lower back, doubling him over with a cry of pain.

"Tell me about this *señorita*. And while you're talking, start walking." Logan saw him through a red haze of rage. He didn't know what stopped him from shooting the breed right then and there. Jerking him to his feet, he shoved Billy Jack into the street. "Move."

Billy Jack fell to one knee, and by the time he staggered upright, Logan was mounted on his own horse and had tied, to the saddle horn, the reins to the one Jessie had bought him.

Logan had to prod him as he rode back the way he had come. He ignored Billy Jack's whining that he was heading the wrong way. Logan felt as if he'd been in a fog and it had suddenly cleared.

He blamed the thought of Jessie occupying his mind when he should have been concentrating on business.

But he'd make it right. He had to. If anything happened to Jessie or those boys because of him, he'd never forgive himself.

Yet it was Jessie in his thoughts as he led the breed out into the broken land. Jessie telling him about an abandoned line shack. It had to be the same one that Billy Jack claimed the outlaws were waiting in for Monte.

"You need me!" Billy Jack cried out. "I will show you the way."

Logan ignored him and rode on. It wasn't the punishment he wanted to give Billy Jack, but something held him back from killing him. So he kept riding out into land where the bushes rustled with sounds of the night predators hunting.

And when the moon rode high, casting its light on the thorny heights of the cholla cacti, Logan, despite the danger of calling attention to himself, began firing his gun into the dirt at Billy Jack's feet, ordering him to run.

"I will die!"

"That's the idea." Logan emptied the chamber and saw that he was backing away.

"You cannot leave me without water. Without a weapon. At least cut me free."

"I've got a whole cartridge belt full of bullets here. I could get careless with my aim. The way I figure, I'm giving you a fighting chance, and that's a hell of a lot more than you've ever given any man."

"It is the woman, *sí?* I did not touch her. Monte stopp—" He caught himself, quickly saying, "It was Zach. He went after her."

Logan's hands shook as he reloaded his gun. His Jessie. His sweet, sassy-mouthed Jessie had been terrorized by this animal. As he slid each bullet into the chamber, he thought of where on Billy Jack's body he would fire it, and he talked.

"I've heard of the men you left staked in the desert for the ants. Ugly way for a man to die. But then, you're not a man, are you? A man never enjoys hurting things that are smaller than him." It was with some wonder that Logan heard his calm voice when rage was erupting inside.

But when he looked up, Billy Jack was gone.

And Logan rode for the line shack where he would come face-to-face with Monte and the others.

Two hours after Logan pulled out of Florence, Ty and Conner rode in. They fought off the bone-deep weariness that came from just failing to overtake their brother since they had set out to follow him.

They split up, and Ty went to Jager's Muleshoe, where the gambler excused himself from the card table to approach Ty where he stood at the bar.

"You've the look of a man who did me a good turn for a few words."

"My brother," Ty answered. "He's been here, then?"

"Not long ago. He was looking for a man, and I directed him to Haskel's at the end of town. He's got a woman there. That interested your brother."

Ty added the price of another drink to the coins on the bar. "Obliged. Have one on me." He went to find Conner.

"There's only one saloon left," Conner said as Ty approached him coming out of the second saloon.

"And that's where Logan is. Man said he was interested in hearing that Haskel has a woman there. I know my brother, it wasn't the woman he was interested in, but maybe one of Monte's men might be there."

"You can't go barging in and give him away if he's with them," Conner warned.

"Then what do you suggest? We stand here till sunup?"

"Give me a minute, Ty. I don't want to do anything that will get Logan killed."

"I thought that was why we came after him in the first place." Ty thumbed back his hat. "For all we know he could be dead already."

"No. We'd know if there'd been a killing here. It's all they'd be talking about. One of us has to go inside. One of us has the reputation to go inside Haskel's place and ask questions.''

"The one of us being me. What the hell are we standing here jawing about, then? Let's go."

"Ty—"

He glanced at his older brother and slipped the thong on his holster. Settling the belt a little lower, Ty then canted his hat brim forward. "This is one time I'm gonna enjoy this unwanted reputation."

Conner followed him, and despite his worry about Logan, he noticed the change in Ty's walk, the way his brother carried himself. When Ty paused before the bat-wing doors and Conner saw his face in the spilling light from the saloon, he had the strangest feeling that he didn't know him at all. What Conner did know was that he didn't want to be the man who crossed Ty's path right now.

It frustrated him all to hell to be the one who waited outside. Waited with his gun drawn, ready to roll through the door firing if need be.

But the minutes ticked by, and there was no alarm, no shots. Conner could feel his muscles tensing with every passing moment. What the devil was Ty doing?

But more importantly, was Logan inside?

When his nerves were stretched to breaking, Conner fought the temptation to walk inside. It was a good thing, too, as Ty walked out, grabbed his arm and hustled back down the street.

"He was there, all right. We missed him. But he left with a mixed breed named Billy Jack. According to the woman, they headed west out of town."

"West? Why would Logan—"

"I don't know, Conner. That's all she knew. That and the fact that he made the breed walk. Seems he recovered his own horse from the man, tied his hands behind his back, left him in his boots and union suit and took him out of town."

Conner shoved his hat back and slumped against the wall of the building. "There's nothing out there."

"He's alive. Logan's nobody's fool. He wouldn't ride out blindly. My guess is that he knows where he's going. Taking this Billy Jack with him was just insurance."

"That leaves us to sit here and wait and give him time to get set up. Then we'll ride up to the Silver Belt. I've got my own kind of welcoming party in mind for the next robbery."

"You sit and wait here. Me, I'm gonna keep a promise. We're not that far from Apache Junction. I can ride up and back in a day. I've got to at least try to find Greg's sister. I've never broken my word to a friend before."

"I won't wait here, Ty. Com'on, we'll make camp and ride out first light. I wouldn't be any good waiting."

"None of us are," Ty said, walking alongside his brother to their horses.

Mounted, they rode north, silent but having parallel thoughts each refused to voice so as not to add to the worry of the other.

Where was Logan?

Chapter Eighteen

Jessie, plagued with a restlessness that did not abate but only increased as the moon disappeared behind a bank of clouds, slipped outside where her pacing would not disturb the sleeping boys.

She wrapped her shawl around her and huddled on the bench with her bare feet tucked beneath the hem of her nightgown.

All day her thoughts had been fixed on Logan, which was not unusual, but there was an added edge of tension that refused to leave her. She longed to have someone that she could talk to about her feelings for him. She had believed the desire to see him, hear him, touch and kiss him again would lessen as the days passed. She needed to believe it.

But tonight she had come to terms with her feelings.

Logan had asked for her trust.

Jessie had given that to him and more. Logan wasn't going to leave her thoughts and give her any peace. He had made a place for himself in her heart.

Every argument that she marshaled against him, all the suspicions she harbored, paled against the blazing intensity of her need to be with him.

There was an old proverb that kept running through her thoughts: what is woven by reason is by passion undone.

But she knew, despite every effort she made to deny it, that there was more than passion involved.

Yet she feared to name it.

To give name to what she felt would allow the more sensible side of herself to ridicule the idea that she could have these strong feelings for a man she barely knew.

She denied that part. She knew Logan. She knew what he made her feel—pretty and strong and young, so very foolishly young.

She remembered his whisper in the dark that night that he had shown her the woman she could be. How many times had he asked to feel her smile against his lips? Teasing her when she understood it was a game and played coy. Telling her he loved her smile, while she yearned to hear him murmur that he loved her.

There, she had silently said the word. Love. It was totally impossible. You couldn't love someone so suddenly, so deeply.

But a picture came to mind of herself reading a letter from her brother when Greg had written that he had met the woman who would be his wife, the only one he would ever love. Two weeks later Greg and Livia had been married. Jessie recalled her hastily written advice begging her brother to wait, to be sure.

And she didn't know any two people who were more in love with each other than those two.

So much for her practical nature and beliefs.

As memory stirred, an older one came to mind, that of her parents. They had met at a church social, and following an intense courtship that set tongues wagging, they, too, had married within weeks of meeting.

Where had her dreams of finding such a love gone? *Buried beneath the lost youth, and the folly of marrying in haste to the wrong man.*

Giving herself a mental shake to rid herself of the nagging little voice, Jessie rose and paced the hard-packed earth in front of her cabin. So, what good did it do to name what she felt for Logan? She had no way of finding him. And even if she did, he might not return her feelings.

Adorabelle snorted and Jessie stopped her pacing, turned, then lifted her head. The moon, with a pearl-like luminance, broke from behind the dark bank of clouds and revealed the mare poking her head over the pole fence of the corral. Her whinny had a strange effect on Jessie. She thought it sounded lonely, as lonely as she felt.

Jessie dismissed the tiny ripple of fear that streaked down her back. It was only some animal, and not a dangerous one or Adorabelle wouldn't be repeating a sound as if she were calling whatever was out there.

But Jessie couldn't remember her mare ever doing this. *And you've never been out in the middle of the night, either.*

When the noise was returned, Jessie stood stock-still. Her heartbeat was suddenly faster, and a small heat raced through her body. She was afraid to turn around, afraid that her need would make her see what wasn't there, what couldn't possibly be there.

From the darkness came his whisper. "Jessie?"

And she didn't dare deny her heart's desire. She turned and ran toward the rider coming down the slope, heedless of the stones beneath her bare feet, heedless of any danger as she rushed, the way her blood rushed through her, to the lover the night had returned to her.

Seeing him draped in light and shadow, Jessie stopped her headlong flight. The doubts fled the moment she beheld him and heard her name whispered from his lips. She knew if he came to her a hundred times out of the darkness she would welcome him, for she felt alive again. Like a wild, raging current, emotions swept over her, then she was moving toward him.

Logan caught her up in his powerful arms, his lips finding hers in a hungry kiss as he settled her across his thighs. The added weight sent the horse into a side-stepping dance, but a hard press of his knees stilled the animal.

One hand caught in the loose single braid of her hair to hold her head, the other cradled the small of her back as he lost himself in a kiss that was more than her lips parting and hungering against his mouth. It was all of her, coming up tight against him, generous with her total response, until he felt enveloped with the sweet, heated press of Jessie's body.

It wasn't enough. This would never be enough.

Jessie's fingers clung to his leather-clad shoulders, knowing the ache of her own buried hunger. His teeth and tongue played over her mouth, making her cry out, utterly defenseless against the need he called from her.

Hammer blows of desire thudded inside him. The tiny hungry sounds she made snapped whatever control he had left. His mouth took all she offered with an almost savage intensity. With a muffled groan, he felt the force of his kiss bend her back over his arm, and she held him tight, the supple molding of her body to his sending fire licking his insides.

She trembled against him like a leaf caught in a windstorm. Her kiss more than matched the passion unleashed in his. Jessie felt as if she were drowning in a swirl of fevered darkness and Logan was the only one who could save her.

With a vicious curse, Logan tore his lips from hers as the restive moves of the horse threatened to topple them to the ground.

He drew her up against his chest, burying his face against the soft warmth of her neck. "Jess, I swear, I feel like I found a part of me that's been missing."

Jessie was too overcome to speak. She wrapped her arms around him, her fingers tunneling through his thick, silky hair. He'd lost his hat in the first few moments, and if she had ever thought to keep claim on her heart, Jessie realized she had lost that, as well.

"I need to set you down," he murmured, trailing kisses along the curve of her neck until he found the softer prey of her earlobe. He smiled, recalling how sensitive Jessie was, and teased her with his lips and teeth and tongue while he teased himself as well, for as the fever spread inside her, it ensnared him.

"Jess," he whispered. "Jess, this is crazy. I shouldn't have come here now."

"I thought I was dreaming—"

"I was going crazy missing you. Crazy with thinking that you wouldn't want me to come back, that you couldn't forgive me for leaving you the way I did." He lifted his head. He touched her cheeks with his fingertips. "Mostly I couldn't believe that you might feel what I do for you."

His look was challenging. His voice held a low-pitched timbre of sensuality that stroked her. "Yes." Her lips curved into an uncertain smile while she battled the tears that burned her eyes. "Yes, all that and more."

Logan gathered her close, feeling a peace the like of which he had never known steal through him.

"I dreamed of you," Jessie confessed in a soft voice. "I prayed that you would come back to me."

"Is that what you're doing out here in the middle of the night?"

She jerked back from him, and the horse, having had enough, started to rear. Logan quickly controlled the animal and, with a short laugh, set Jessie down on the ground, then dismounted.

The moonlight caught on the silver buckle of his belt and Jessie stared at it for a moment, then backed away. She had seen that buckle or one just like it on the man called Billy Jack in Silas's store.

But she didn't question him about the buckle. "The horse tied to the saddle, that's the one I bought for you, isn't it?"

"Yeah. A fine horse, Jessie. I wouldn't mind having stock like—"

"And this other one?" she asked, gesturing to the horse he had ridden. "It's yours, isn't it? This is the one that was stolen from you?"

There was an edge to her voice that hadn't been there before, and he had noted the distance she put between them. Alert to the direction of her questions, Logan tensed.

"The horse is mine, Jessie. I raised him from birth. I don't part easily with anything that I claim as mine, unless I want to give it away." He dropped the reins he held, ground tying the horse.

From the corral came Adorabelle's whinny. Logan slapped his horse's rump. "Go on, boy. Pay the little lady some attention."

"She's too old—"

"He's a gelding, Jess. And I don't know of any animal that won't seek its own kind."

"Perhaps when the urge to mate comes, then the male usually takes off."

"Is that why you think I've come back here?"

"No. I didn't mean—" She broke off, pulling her shawl tight around her.

"Jess, I swear it must be a trick of the moonlight, but you're blushing."

"I don't blush."

"Coloring up as pink as a desert flower—"

"Stay right where you are, Logan. I won't let you distract me. I refuse to allow it. If you got your horse back, then you found the men who left you to die."

"One of them." His hands curled at his sides. He took a deep breath, then released it. "Don't be afraid of me, Jessie. I couldn't stand the thought that you are. I would never hurt you. And I didn't kill him. I sure as hell wanted—"

"I didn't ask."

A cynical smile curved his lips. "It's about the only thing that you didn't ask me."

"That's not true. I haven't asked you where you've been." *Or a hundred other questions that have plagued me. Did you miss me? Did you get hurt facing him? Are you staying?* That one she wanted to ask, wanted an answer to.

"Jess?" He took a step toward her, and when she stood her ground, almost as if she challenged him to come to her, Logan wasted no time in coming to stand before her. But he didn't touch her. He didn't trust himself not to brush her very real concerns aside by sweeping her up into his arms and kissing her senseless, back into the heated welcome he had received.

"I want you to know that you can ask me anything you want."

She studied his chiseled features, imagining that she could see how tired he was. The lock of hair that fell over his forehead tempted her hand. Jessie resisted the urge and the need to touch him.

"Anything?"

"Whatever it is that's keeping you away from me."

"Who are you, Logan?"

There was truth, and then there was truth. "I'm the man who came back looking for the other half of himself. The other half that matters, the one who's full of hope and love and a smile that turns my middle to something close to jelly."

"Logan—"

"No. You asked, and I'm answering. I'm the man who still needs to ask for your trust a while longer. Then, and only then, will I finish answering your question."

"I see," she murmured, looking off to the side. "I have a feeling there was something missing. A few words about when I come back—"

"Jess—"

"No. I do see."

"Do you, Jess? Do you really understand?"

The earnest plea in his voice invited her to look at him again. There was something different about him, more than the clothing that, while not new, wasn't the same as he had worn.

"You may have a little mule in you, Logan. I'm not running, am I?"

It had been so much to hope for that her answer sank in very slowly. But when it did, a deep smile of sheer masculine satisfaction creased his lips.

"Oh, Jess. My sweet, sassy Jessie. You may wish you had run while you still had the chance."

Jessie gave him back a smile that was every bit as satisfied, and danced away from him. "I've regretted a few things in my life, Logan, but not one moment that I've spent with you."

He went after her with laughter, and caught her close, stealing the joy of her smile with his lips.

From inside the cabin Marty, who no matter how hard he strained to see above the sill couldn't, demanded an accounting from Kenny, who easily reached it.

"What's he doing? Com'on, Kenny, tell me. Tell me."

"Keep your voice down. Do ya want them to hear? They're kissin'. What else?" Twisting away from the window, Kenny pulled Marty into the other room, where their whispers wouldn't be overheard. "I swear, he comes ridin' in this late an' I figured for sure we'd see some real excitement, an' all he can do is kiss her."

"Maybe he brought us a present, Kenny. Do ya think so?"

"I don't know 'bout us. But Miz Jessie's sure actin' like he brung her one. Bet they wouldn't be smoochin' so much if they knew what we did."

"I told you we shoulda told Miz Jessie. She won't like finding out those men are up there. We shoulda told, Kenny. We shoulda—"

"Tell you what. Let's get dressed. We'll fix up the beddin' jus' like we were still sleepin' an' go up there. If they're still in the shack, we'll run down an' get Logan. He'll know what to do."

"We'll get caught."

"You can stay." Kenny stripped off the nightshirt that Jessie insisted he wear like a proper young man and grabbed up his clothes.

"Baby," he taunted Marty.

"Ain't."

"Are too." Kenny shoved his shirt into his pants.

Marty scrambled to pull off his nightshirt and get dressed. "Wait for me. Miz Jessie's sure to tan me if she finds you gone."

"Com'on, slowpoke." Kenny went to the window again and saw that Logan had taken the saddles from his horses and turned the animals into the corral. He didn't see them at first, but a closer look showed them standing together just inside the shed.

"Hurry up. We can get out the door without them seein' us."

"You sure about this, Kenny? Miz Jessie—"

"If you're scared, stay here. Be lookin' like a fool iffen I tell them to go up there an' there ain't no one around." But for all his brave talk, Kenny climbed up on the chair and took down his father's shotgun and the box of shells that Jessie had put there for safe-keeping.

Marty, not to be outdone, shoved his slingshot into his back pocket and checked the front pants pocket for his collection of small round stones that he was never without.

Kenny opened the door just wide enough for them to slip out. He took hold of Marty's hand, leading him away from the shed and into the brush that would bring them out well beyond the cabin and the hen-house. He didn't want the old rooster squawking. The bright moonlight made finding their way easier, and while Kenny wouldn't admit it to Marty, also made him feel braver.

And bravery was the very subject that Logan managed to work into the talk he was attempting to have with Jessie. The woman made it difficult, what with her lips getting in the way for the most pleasurable kisses.

"That day you went to the Junction. Why didn't you tell me what happened in the store? I know Billy Jack was there. I know that Zach and Monte were there, too. Jess, if I'd known, I would never have left here—"

"Let me tell you what I dreamed about you from the night you left," she whispered, snuggled against his side on his blanket while he rested his back against a bale of hay. To make sure she had his attention, she drew his head down to meet her waiting lips. His kiss was sweet, but far too short for her.

"My brave lady," he murmured, lifting his head to finish, despite her offered temptations. "For what he did to you I would have killed him, if I'd known. Why didn't you tell me, Jessie? You had to have some idea that I was connected with them."

Jessie closed her eyes and sighed. She had done her best to avoid this, but Logan wouldn't let it be.

"I wasn't brave. I was scared. But all they did was frighten me." For a moment she saw again the image of herself cringing beneath Billy Jack's touch, and she couldn't stop the shudder that ripped through her. "No, don't, I'm all right," she protested when he held her tighter. "And I couldn't tell you. I was...I wanted, no, I needed to forget it."

"The whiskey—"

"False courage, I discovered, and it made me sick."

"Damn it, Jess. You shouldn't have gone through that. I just don't understand why no one stopped them."

"Silas? He wouldn't. They were spending money and I'm not a very good customer. His Indian woman was paid to...well, I can't judge another. And David—"

"David? That guy that's been courting you? He was there? He—"

Jessie covered his mouth with her hand, silently cursing herself for letting that slip. She rose to her knees and leaned over him. "I want you to listen to me. I am my own woman. I didn't ask for David's help that day because I knew those men would hurt him. It's over, Logan. I don't want to talk about it."

Logan settled his hands on her hips, slid down until he was supine and urged Jessie to stretch out on top of him. "Comfy?"

"Actually—"

"You're delighted to be in charge," he said with underlying laughter that lulled her. "I want to ask one more question, Jess. Just one more, all right?"

"Only one?" She heard the strain in her voice, and knew he had, too, for his hands stroked over her back as if to calm and reassure at the same time.

"I want to know the reason why you didn't tell me. And don't tell me it was to protect me, Jess. I already know that part."

Jessie lowered her head to his chest and listened to the strong, steady beat of his heart. She wished he hadn't asked her, wished she could stay like this forever, safe and warm in his arms with no thoughts of his leaving her again circling through her mind. Silently she blessed him for his patience and for the touch of his hands gently telling her how much he cared.

The moments stretched into minutes, and with them grew a fear in Logan that more, so much more, had happened to her that he was hurting her by asking that she tell him.

"Jess—"

"Logan—"

The apologies were quick, but Logan told her to speak first. He needed to know if he had to go back and hunt down Billy Jack, and this time he'd make sure that animal never hurt anyone again.

"I don't know if I can explain this to you," she began. "But I felt helpless that day. Helpless to stop them. Helpless to punish them. And I felt so dirty. Dirty and a-ashamed," she finished, sniffing as tears gathered.

But she was very aware of the tension gathering in his body and knew, even without a word from him, what he was going to do.

"I told you the truth. Now I want a promise from you. I—"

This time Logan slipped his hand gently over her mouth. "Don't ask that of me. You're mine. You know that, Jess. I don't want you to ever fear anyone. And you need to understand that you're not alone anymore."

He removed his hand and stroked her cheek, gritting his teeth when he felt her tears. "Come up here, sweet lady. I need to kiss you."

"It doesn't matter to you, does it?"

"Jess, how can you ask me that? You matter to me more than anything. Well, those two boys can't be forgotten." He liked the way she wiggled her way upward until her mouth hovered over his. Logan liked it so much he was fair to bursting his britches.

"I want very much to make love with you," she whispered, glad of the dark that allowed her to be bold.

"The boys?"

"Are soundly asleep after the day we spent—"

"Later, Jess." He rubbed his mouth against hers. "Later you can tell me all about them."

Jessie dipped her head and kissed the corners of his mouth. "Will you promise you won't leave without waking me?"

Logan cupped the back of her head as hunger would no longer be denied. "Don't ask that, Jess. Don't ever ask me to say goodbye to you."

And he took her mouth with a kiss that slowly deepened, stroking her tongue with his until she was trembling. He couldn't taste enough, couldn't touch enough of this woman who had come into his life and left her mark on his mind and his heart. His lips slanted across her face, wooing and greedy. Jessie made those hungry little sounds that he loved to hear, running her hands over his chest and arms, whispering encouragement when he arched his body upward for more.

And his pleasure increased when she overcame her shyness to murmur what she wanted, then grew bolder still when he demanded that she show him.

There was laughter as he blocked what tomorrow would bring from his mind, and cherished these loving moments with the woman he wanted beside him forever.

Wildness and fire came together until they were one in flesh, body and mind and the shimmering pleasure that awaited them once again.

He hated leaving her, hated it and knew he had no choice. When he eased himself from her sleeping form, Logan wished he could carry her inside the cabin, but fear of waking the boys stopped him. He left her wrapped in his blanket with the silent promise in his mind that he would come back for her.

Chapter Nineteen

Jessie drifted awake slowly, then bolted upright. She knew she was alone. For a moment she sat there, clutching the blanket that was filled with the scent of their lovemaking, her loose hair falling around her.

She kept the promise she had made to herself that there would be no regrets this morning. She pushed her hair back. From the open shed she could see the lighter shades of gray in the sky. Her shawl lay across the blanket, and she took hold of it as she stood. Wrapping the shawl around her against the slight morning chill, she went to the doorway to watch the dawn chase the last vestige of night, wondering where Logan was, and if he, too, watched the coming day.

The light brightened in seconds, and long shafts of color began to appear, a yellow glow lifting the shadows from the land. Lavender streaks suddenly blended with the yellow, then pink and pale orange showed for a few moments. Abruptly, it was sunrise.

Knowing that the boys might also be waking up, she took a few minutes to finger comb her hair and plait it into a single braid. Bits of straw fell as she worked, and each one was a reminder of the night past. She refused to cry, just as she refused to linger a moment longer.

She hurried across the yard to the cabin and eased open the door. The room was filled with a soft, shadowed light, but she breathed a sigh of relief when she saw that the boys were still asleep. Tiptoeing to her bed, she gathered up her clothes and slipped behind the blanket strung on a rope in the corner to afford her some privacy.

The water was barely warm even though it had sat in the pitcher all night. Jessie hurriedly washed, feeling a strange sense of urgency that she could not explain or find the source of. Donning her chemise, she fumbled tying the ribbons closed. Impatience with herself only made matters worse as she knotted the drawstring on her petticoat. By the time she had slipped on her skirt and shirt and buttoned the last button, she was in a sweat. Picking up her boots, Jessie pushed aside the blanket. Sitting on her bed, she pulled on her boots. The light was brighter now inside the cabin. Bright enough for her to stare at the still forms on the floor. Marty always kicked off his quilt during the night. She hadn't woken up one morning since they'd been staying with her and not found him huddled into a tight little ball.

Not only did he appear covered with his quilt, but it had been pulled up over his head.

Could he have woken up and heard her with Logan? Jessie felt heat rise in her cheeks. She closed her eyes for a few seconds, praying that had not happened. And if it had...

Her inexperience in dealing with young boys and their incessant questions rushed over her. But she had never been one to shirk her obligations. Although she never thought of Marty and Kenny as such. They had given her so much these past days. And she believed that she had given them something they needed in return. Love and someone to count on being there no matter what happened.

"All right, sleepyheads," she called out softly, thinking to tease them awake, "time to rise." Jessie stood and crossed over to Kenny.

Leaning over, she eased the edge of the quilt down.

A rolled-up pillow met her disbelieving eyes. She flung the quilt aside and saw his clothing bunched on the bottom quilt.

"And where Kenny goes..." She knew Marty wasn't there, but, pulling the quilt away from his place and clutching it to her chest, all Jessie could do was stare.

It took minutes of arguing with herself that there was no reason to panic for panic to take hold and override every reason she thought of to explain their disappearance.

She had promised they would go up to the wagons today with Adorabelle and bring back whatever they could load on the horse and carry. It was something that Kenny had suggested, and she had agreed to, thinking they would enjoy having things from their homes around them.

Kenny wouldn't have gone without her. He had made her a promise that he wouldn't go off without telling her.

But what had made them leave? And when? Guilt hit her so forcefully that she staggered back until the edge of the table stopped her.

Had they awakened and needed her? Had Marty had one of his bad dreams again? She would have heard him cry out.

Would you? Lost as you were in your lover's arms, would you have heard anything but the murmur of his voice?

"I would have. I swear I would have," she insisted. Jessie threw the quilt down and grabbed her hat and shotgun. She ran from the cabin to the corral.

The sight of the brown horse she had bought for Logan stopped her for a moment. But even as she ran for the saddle and bridle he'd left hanging on the pole fence, she knew it was a blessing. Adorabelle was not the horse she needed now.

She talked as she worked the bit between his teeth, desperate to keep the panic at bay. "Blessing is going to be your name. That's what you are. And if you're half as good as Logan thinks, you'll help me bring my boys home."

The animal's quiet steadiness enabled Jessie to work quickly. Logan's saddle was heavier than her own, and she saw that he'd left his rifle behind. She wouldn't allow the question to rise of where he'd gotten such a finely made rifle. Engraved silver plates were worked into the gleaming wood of the stock.

The sound of men's voices arrested Jessie. She froze with her hand touching the rifle. The horse stood between her and the fence and she slipped the rifle from the scabbard, crouching down as the sound of a hoof striking stone joined their voices.

"I'm telling you, they've got to be one and the same. I can't believe he listened to me go on and never said a word."

"Maybe," Conner returned, "he didn't want us to know." Topping the slope, he drew rein and cast a searching gaze over the yard, noting the open door of the cabin and the meanness of the place. "Not exactly a thriving concern, is it?"

"Remember what I told you. Greg—"

"Just hold up right where you are." Jessie stepped out and away from behind the horse, aiming the rifle at them. "State your business. And make it fast. I'm in a hurry."

Jessie prayed the stomach-churning fear wouldn't betray her. She made quick judgments of both the men and their horses. The sleek hides, despite a coating of dust, told her these horses weren't range fed but had been grained recently and regularly. The riders were covered with the same dust, indicating a long, hard ride. Dark stubble on their faces lent a dangerous air to both men. She tried to avoid the gaze of the younger one, who was studying her with the same intensity.

"Talk," she prompted. What would she do if they were after Logan? Without her being aware, her hand slid over the hammer and cocked the rifle.

"Hold on. Don't this beat all," Ty said, thumbing back his hat. This woman wasn't the mousey Jessie that he remembered. That one wouldn't know which end of a rifle to aim at a man. But he couldn't deny that she had not only the same lush figure of Greg's sister but, from what he could see of the braid hanging over her shoulder, the same color hair. The pieces all fit. They had to fit, or he'd come on a wild-goose chase and taken Conner with him.

Ty held his arms out and away from his body. "You don't remember me?"

"Should I?" Jessie frowned. There was something about that cocky grin that nagged the back of her mind.

"Ty Kincaid," he prompted with a small edge of annoyance in his voice. "I met you up on your brother's place. You are Jessie, aren't you? Greg's sister," he added when she still showed no sign of recognizing him. "I'm the one Livia tried to match—"

"Ty?" Jessie shook her head. "What are you doing here? Did something happen to my brother?" She started to shake, and fought to control it.

"Greg and his family were fine when I left them."

Jessie's gaze went from Ty to the other man. His very stillness and waiting air alarmed her. If Ty hadn't come because of her brother, then her suspicions were right. They had come after Logan.

"I've no time to visit. Make yourself and your quiet friend here at home. I've got to find my boys."

"Boys?" Ty spurred his horse to cover the short distance to the corral, where he quickly dismounted. "What are you talking about? Greg never said anything about you having any children."

"My brother hasn't bothered to keep in touch with me since I married."

"You can't put all the blame on him," Ty said in defense of his friend. "Greg worries about you. I know he didn't care much for the man you married and I'm sorry to say it to you. But what really bothered him was you're living so far away. Greg'll come around." Ty's thoughts raced. If this was the woman Logan had been with, she had lied to his brother. He grew uncomfortable with the thought that Logan didn't care that she was another man's wife.

"Greg doesn't need to worry anymore. Harry's dead. And the boys aren't exactly mine. Please, Ty, it's a long and complicated story. When I woke up the boys were gone, and I've got to find them."

Jessie's matter of fact tone stopped Ty from murmuring words of sorrow for Harry's death. He hid his relief that she was a widow and not a liar. He hopped the fence and went to her. "Jessie, take it from me, boys love to get up early and take off, especially if there are chores waiting." Seeing that she was shaken, despite his attempt to reassure her, Ty proceeded to finish saddling the horse.

Jessie slipped the rifle back into the scabbard, trying to sort through her worry about Logan and her need to make Ty understand about the boys.

Neither of them noticed that Conner had dismounted and stood holding the reins to his horse and Ty's outside the fence, until he spoke.

"Ty? Did you notice the rifle?"

Jessie looked up. She was instantly leery, her fear rising for Logan and what these men wanted with him. She stepped around the horse to block this stranger's view, sorry she had been so quick to set the rifle aside.

"What about *my* rifle, mister?"

Eyeing the challenge flaring in her brown eyes, Conner answered her in a soft, controlled voice. "I'm Ty's older brother, Conner. That rifle you claim as yours belongs—"

"No!" Jessie didn't want to hear that Logan had stolen it. She turned, yanked the rifle free and tossed it over the fence at Conner. Her nerves were strung so tight she couldn't seem to think straight.

"You've got the rifle," she said to him, then rounded on Ty. "I don't know what's got you chuckling, but I've no time for this." She hated stepping closer to the fence where Conner stood, but she intended to untie the reins to her horse and leave.

"Jessie, you don't understand," Ty said. A glance at Conner's furious expression should have stopped him from grinning. But it was so rare that Conner appeared buffaloed, Ty couldn't help himself.

Conner, hanging on to his temper by a hair, ignored Ty's grin. He tried once more to explain. "You took my asking about the rifle the wrong way, Jessie. It is all right if I call you that?"

"Fine. Just hurry up."

"I gave that rifle to my brother. And it's not something that he would give away." Despite his effort, the last was spoken in an angry voice. He'd been riding all night, worrying about Logan, his mother's involvement with Riverton and a hundred other smaller problems. Now he had to put up with a woman who simply glared at him as if he had lied to her.

"Now, Conner—"

"If you know what's good for you, little brother, you'll shut up."

"You're telling me," Jessie asked Conner, "that this rifle belonged to your brother?"

"That's what I said." The hair holding his temper frayed. She had to make up her mind quickly or she was going to witness what few people ever saw then talked about—Conner Kincaid losing his temper.

Jessie turned to study Ty, the suspicion forming, but she was afraid to voice it. If it was true...

"Ty, who is your brother?"

His grin disappeared. With serious regard he answered her. "My brother is the man two boys found and brought to a widow."

"His name?" Jessie's voice was a bare thread of sound. She could hardly swallow past the sudden dryness in her mouth and throat. "Tell me."

"His name's Logan." Conner answered before Ty did. He watched her carefully, judging her reaction as she grabbed hold of the fence and stared at him.

"It's obvious he was here, and just as obvious that he's gone," Conner added. When she looked up at him, his whole manner changed. She had taken the news hard.

"I thought he was an outlaw," Jessie said, more to herself.

"He's... Like your story about the boys, this, too, is long and complicated. Do you know where he went?"

"No. Conner, he's—" Confused, Jessie rubbed her forehead. "I don't know when he left, sometime during the night," she said after a few seconds. "Please, I've got to find the boys. They never do this. Kenny would not break his promise to me."

"You're real sure Logan didn't say anything about where he was heading?"

"I said as much, didn't I?" Jessie heard the shrill note in her voice. "Give me a moment, please. I know he had found one of the men that left him for dead. He didn't kill him," she added quickly before Conner could interrupt. "But he did take back his horse. The one that was stolen from him." Jessie shot Ty a helpless look. "He went after the others, didn't he? And he could be in trouble?"

"We don't know, Jessie. Conner has an idea that the reason they left Logan to die was because they found out who he was." Seeing the confusion fill her eyes, he added, "It's just like Conner told you. Long and very complicated. I had promised Greg I would look in on you and see how you were doing. Despite your differences, he does care about you. We're scheduled to meet Logan in a few days. When he came home—"

"Home?" Jessie looked from Ty to Conner. "You're right. This is too much for me to take in now. I've got to find the boys. I have an idea where they are, so you are both welcome to stay here and wait."

Adorabelle came trotting up to Jessie when she saw the gate open. "No, girl. You stay here." She gently pushed the mare's nose and led the brown horse through. Ty was right behind her.

Jessie mounted and Ty held a quick, whispered conversation with Conner, then announced to her that they would go with her.

"Just in case the boys aren't where you expect, Jessie, Conner is an excellent tracker."

Jessie rode out and the Kincaid brothers followed.

A blue-gray finger of smoke finally led Logan to the line shack. He remained hidden behind the bare upthrust of rock about a hundred yards away. There were only three horses in the newly erected corral. One of the men was missing, and he figured Monte as the likely choice.

The smell of frying bacon sent his stomach growling and he thought of the jerky and water that he'd eaten a few hours ago.

While he'd been searching for this place he'd thought of Jessie, and of the plans he'd made with Conner.

Logan didn't want to wait to catch this gang in the midst of robbing another shipment and payroll from their mine. He wanted justice now. But he knew his kind of justice had to wait until all the suspicions and facts were confirmed and he had the name of the man behind the robberies. Conner wouldn't have it any other way.

Three to one weren't the best odds a man wanted, but they weren't impossible ones.

Tallyman appeared in the doorway, scratching his belly. His suspenders were looped on either side of his hips, his union-suit sleeves had been ripped off and he wore blue army-issue pants with the yellow stripes. Logan cupped his hand over his horse's muzzle. Tallyman looked around, stretched and yawned, then disappeared around the corner of the cabin.

The opportunity to lessen his odds was too good to pass up. Logan moved out, keeping to whatever brush and rock cover he could find to circle around the back of the line shack.

The shouts and yells were so unexpected that at first Logan made no sense of what he was hearing. The impossibility of Kenny yelling for Marty to run was cut off by a roar of fury coming from Tallyman.

A shotgun blast split the air. Logan felt his blood freeze. No longer keeping to cover, he came around the back of the line shack at a dead run, half dreading what he'd find.

The scene before him was a nightmare come to life. Kenny took a blow from Tallyman's fist and sprawled in the dirt. Held in Tallyman's other hand by the back of his shirt, Marty swung wildly as another roar erupted. Kenny rolled and made a grab for his shotgun, but Logan, who hadn't realized that he'd drawn his gun, couldn't shoot for fear of hitting either of the boys.

He shouted for Kenny to get out of the way. Logan went after Tallyman, who spun around and dropped Marty to the ground. The man outweighed Logan by a good fifty pounds, but he didn't have rage boiling inside him. And Logan knew he'd have to take him fast before the other two showed up.

Frustrated at not finding the boys at their former camp, Jessie had led the way to the hidden valley where she kept her cattle, growing frightened when Conner had confirmed what she knew. There was no recent sign that Kenny and Marty had come this way.

It was Ty who halted them as the faint echo of a shot filled the air. Ty who shared a worried glance with Conner, then attempted to reassure her.

"It's likely those boys went hunting."

Jessie didn't answer him. She relied on her own instincts. They weren't telling her to be calm, they were screaming at her to find those boys.

And then she remembered Logan questioning her and her telling him about the abandoned line shack. Had the boys discovered it, too?

"Ty," she called, urging her horse around, "a little while ago you said you came to see me because you were heading up this way to go to your mine."

"That's right. I told you we've been plagued with robberies."

"Would it be north of here?"

The bright glitter in her eyes, the desperate edge of her voice alarmed him. "Yes."

"There's an abandoned line shack north of here. I just remembered that Logan asked me about it. No," she said quickly before he cut in, "not because of those men—it had to do with the boys. I told him I hadn't been up there since the first time I found it, but what if—" Jessie stopped and closed her eyes. *Dear Lord, please let me be wrong. Please let me be making a terrible mistake.*

"Jessie?" Conner called. "What's wrong?"

"No more questions. Just come with me." She set her heels into the horse's sides. "If you two have any prayers, say them. Pray we get there in time."

Chapter Twenty

Marty was scared. More scared than the night he'd helped Kenny bury their folks. He didn't want to cry. Kenny would tease him if he cried. But Kenny wasn't here to see him.

He'd run when Logan had yelled at him to, but he hadn't gone far. Logan was fighting the man who had grabbed him and Kenny. He'd kept calling for Kenny to come with him, but Kenny had gone for his shotgun.

Only he'd never reached it. Two other men had come running from the shack. One of them had hit Kenny, and he didn't get up. Then they'd pulled Logan off the big man and held his arms while the black man had punched and punched Logan. There'd been no one to tease him when he'd covered his ears and squeezed his eyes closed.

They were all inside the shack now and he didn't know what to do. If he ran home to get Jessie, they could leave and take Logan and Kenny with them. Then he wouldn't know where they were. He knew they might come out looking for him again.

He'd have to be brave and think of what Kenny would do.

Inside the shack, Kenny wasn't feeling very brave. He hurt all over from trying to stop these men when they had beaten up Logan. At least he was awake. Logan lay beside him out cold. One of the men sat on a crate near the door. It was the only way out. The one called Tallyman sat near the table, nursing his cut lip, saying over and over that he'd thought he had seen a ghost when he found himself facing Logan.

He guessed they didn't think Logan was any threat, for after taking his gun, they hadn't bothered to tie him up. Even if he could rouse Logan, they would have a hard time whispering to make a plan without anyone hearing or seeing them.

Kenny sat with his back against the rough wood wall. Logan lay with his back to the others. More to reassure himself, Kenny wiggled closer to Logan and took hold of his hand. He ducked his head to hide his surprise when Logan squeezed his fingers.

It was nothing compared to the shock he felt at the poke in his back through the crack in the wall. Marty! It had to be him. But how was he going to tell him that Logan was all right?

"What ya wanna do with these two?" Tallyman asked.

"Shoulda killed him when I wanted to," Zach answered, shooting a murderous look at Logan.

From the doorway, Blackleg warned, "You'd better wait for Monte. Still don't understand why the hell he went after you. Or where these kids came from."

"That one," Zach said, pointing at Kenny, "is the kid from the ranch. Remember I told you he said he ain't seen no strangers. Lying little—"

'That's enough, Zach. He's just a kid." Blackleg sipped his coffee but once more sent a searching gaze over the front area of the shack. He had a funny feeling about Logan showing up like this. "One of you better go out and find his horse."

"You go, if you're so worried," Zach snapped. "An' while you're out there, find the other little brat."

Kenny tried to whistle the two short notes of a bob-white's call, a signal he'd been trying to teach to Marty. He couldn't find enough spit to wet his lips. He grew desperate when he saw the man at the door rise and finish his coffee. Marty'd get caught for sure.

"Hey, mister," he called out. "Let me go with you. You'll spend all day trying to find my little brother. My ma's gonna tan my bottom for getting into trouble."

"You're gonna have more than trouble or a tannin' to worry about, boy," Zach warned.

"Hold on there, Zach. I ain't killing no kids."

"You telling me what to do, Blackleg?"

"I'm telling you I ain't killing no kids. Com'on boy, you come with me."

Zach pulled his gun. "Stay right where you are, boy. As for you, Blackleg, you go find his horse."

He eyed the gun and then let his gaze rise to meet Zach's eyes. Shaking his head Blackleg left the shack.

Kenny slumped down against the wall. He hoped that Marty had heard every word and had run like hell. As the minutes passed and there were no shouts, he began to think Marty was safe.

It was Conner who spotted the lone rider down below them. He didn't want to risk the sun's reflection off his field glasses giving them away, so he left them in his saddlebag. Since there wasn't enough cover for the three of them, he turned his horse back toward the dry wash they had just ridden out of.

"Keep the horses quiet," he ordered, glancing at Jessie. She was pale and silent. He wished he could offer her some reassurances that those boys were all right, but every passing minute made him believe that they were in trouble.

Ty brought his horse up alongside his brother's. They were far enough into the wash that a whisper wouldn't carry. Still, Ty leaned close. "Logan?"

"Too far to tell."

"No more shots," Ty said.

"It shouldn't, but it worries me."

They both looked at Jessie, who sat perfectly still, her eyes closed and her hands folded together.

"Hell of a woman," Conner murmured, more to himself than to Ty.

Ty didn't answer. The sounds of the steady plod of a horse reached them. Both men did no more than pat the necks of their horses to keep them still. Jessie had already forced her horse's head around and was stroking his muzzle to keep him quiet. The minutes they waited passed with an agonizing slowness before Conner signaled them to ride out.

* * *

Logan found it unfortunate that he was becoming aware of the individual pains in his body. For a little while he thought of himself as one massive hurt, but he couldn't allow the pain to rule him. He had to get Kenny out of here.

Squeezing the boy's hand was all the warning that Logan could give him. With a loud groan he rolled over and came up on his knees. The groan was real—Tallyman's fists seemed to have pushed his stomach somewhere in the middle of his back. But Zach reacted as he'd expected, rushing over to kick him back down.

Only Logan was ready for him. He grabbed hold of Zach's extended foot, twisting it sharply in a move that almost cost him his breath. But there was enough to yell at Kenny to get out.

Zach went down flat on his back with a thud, his hand scrambling to draw his gun. Logan lunged and landed on top of him.

Kenny, instead of obeying, jumped up and lowered his head, charging Tallyman before he could get to Logan. He hit the man's side, grabbed hold of his leg and let fly with the hardest kick to the shin that he could. Tallyman let him go, screaming as Kenny landed another kick to the same leg, then darted around to repeat his damage to the other one. If he hadn't been so scared he would have laughed to see the big man's eyes bulge in disbelief while he tried to rub first one leg then the other.

Once more he came after him and Kenny shoved the table between them. Tallyman couldn't stop his forward lunge, and went crashing to the floor over the broken wood.

Logan had his hands full trying to get Zach to let go of his gun. He lay sprawled on top of Zach, fighting the dizzying waves of agony that rolled up from Zach's fist pounding his side. Both his hands were wrapped around Zach's and the gun, banging it repeatedly against the floor. He had no breath to answer one of Zach's muttered curses.

He could feel Zach gathering himself to attempt a full body heave. The crashing sounds behind him were all the distraction that Zach needed to make good his move. He dislodged Logan halfway. Logan refused to let go of his gun hand despite the added shove from Zach's free hand that forced him closer to the floor.

With another heave, Zach rolled Logan over. The position allowed him to land a solid blow to Logan's jaw. Scrambling a few inches higher, he had both of his hands around Logan's and managed to rip one of Logan's free from the gun. Before Logan could recover, Zach had the gun between them.

Logan didn't know where the strength came from; he was only glad that he had enough to pull the trigger.

The shot was muffled. Zach stared at him. Logan shoved him away just in time to see Kenny swing a piece of the broken table and knock Tallyman out cold.

"You bastard. You gut-shot me."

Logan didn't answer. It was all he could do to crawl over to the wall and stagger upright. Kenny started for him, but he gave a quick shake of his head. Wiping the back of his hand across his mouth, every breath sending pain shafting through his battered body, Logan worked his way along the wall toward the door.

"G-get going," he told Kenny.

"But—"

"Move." Once again he wiped blood from his split lip. He tried to put some anger in his gaze when Kenny handed him his gun. Logan drew the gun from the holster and let the belt fall. He couldn't spare the strength to wrap the belt around him.

"Go."

"But there's still one more."

As if his words had conjured him up, Blackleg stood in the doorway.

He took one look at the bodies on the floor, then looked at Logan. "How the hell did you manage this?"

"You're s-smart not . . . to go for . . . your gun."

"I told them I wouldn't kill no kids. Put the gun down. I didn't have nothing to do with them leaving you. Didn't take one thing of yours. You ain't got no cause to shoot me, Lucky."

"No." But Logan didn't explain that it was the name he denied, and only that. He knew he had to get Blackleg out of the way. He couldn't let him go.

"Where's Marty, mister? What'd ya do to him?"

"I told you to get out."

"You're hurt, Logan. I can't leave you here. Suppose there's more of 'em? Who's gonna help you if I go?"

"Logan?" Blackleg repeated.

"Yeah. That's his name, mister. An' he's gonna be all over you like—"

"Kenny!"

"Well, I know you'll take care of him jus' as soon as you get a second wind."

For a moment Logan didn't know if he wanted to curse the boy's stubbornness or give thanks for his courage. And he couldn't deny that Kenny was right. He still didn't know how he was standing.

"Go find something to tie him with," he ordered the boy, motioning Blackleg inside.

Kenny ran for the pile of gear in the far corner and in minutes returned with a wicked-looking blade and a blanket. He didn't wait for Logan's order to cut strips. And when he had enough, he went first to Tallyman and bound his hands behind his back, then tied his feet. He avoided looking at the man still groaning on the floor. Logan ordered Blackleg facedown on the floor. Holding the gun on him, Logan waited until Kenny was finished tying him up. "Now, you get out of here."

"But—"

"No. I'm proud of you, boy. So proud I can't even tell you right now. Find Marty. Get back to Jessie."

Kenny's face took on a look of sheer mule-thick stubbornness. Logan briefly closed his eyes and prayed for patience.

"Listen. You nearly got killed, Kenny. You think I could face Jessie if anything happens to either one of you boys? Go. I need to know that you're all safe and together."

Kenny turned and almost made it out the door. Monte Wheeler blocked his way. A sweeping glance took in the wreckage and the bodies, along with the gun that Logan aimed at him.

Monte started to throw up his hands and back out of the door.

"Don't move," Logan yelled.

But Monte's move had been a ploy. His arm snaked out and he snatched Kenny up against him. Holding the boy in front of him, Monte drew his gun. Kenny stopped struggling the moment the gun barrel touched him.

"I'll give you three seconds to throw down your gun and start talking before I shoot."

Logan dropped the gun. Slowly he brought his arms up and out from his body. Any man who claimed there was nothing that he feared was a liar. Logan wasn't one. He thought he had experienced the kind of stomach-lurching fear that brought a man to his knees earlier. He found out it came back, in a stronger, bitter dose.

"Let the boy go. This is between you and me, Monte."

"I heard the kid call you Logan. You're a Kincaid."

He wasn't asking, but Logan answered him. "That's right. But you already knew that, didn't you?" Logan voiced his suspicion. If he had not been watching Monte, he would have missed the barely formed frown and the slight tightening of his mouth. Excitement filled him at having his suspicion confirmed. And if Monte knew that he was a Kincaid...

"It's why you left me to die. And if you know about me, you know there isn't a crack in a rock where you can hide if you kill me. My brothers'll tear this territory apart to find you."

"Big talk for a man who's about to die. Get over in the corner. I ain't standing here with my back open."

"Afraid, Monte? Someone on your tail? Someone see you meet with Riverton?" It was another shot in the dark, but a damn lucky one. Logan caught the fractional narrowing of Monte's eyes. "You didn't think we knew?"

"I told you to move or I'll shoot the kid."

"Sure, Monte, sure. Anything for the man with the gun." A cold, deadly calm settled over Logan. He didn't know how he'd do it, but he'd kill this bastard for the fear that he made Kenny feel. The boy's head hung down as if he had no hope left. Logan wasn't sure he had any to spare.

He moved slowly in a half circle, avoiding the bodies on the floor behind him, and not really going deeper into the cabin. It seemed to satisfy Monte, for he inched his way inside and stopped when he felt the wall at his back. Logan noticed that Kenny's body appeared to sag almost as if he had passed out. If he had, his deadweight was straining Monte's arm. Kenny wiggled his fingers.

That's it, boy, play opossum. Get him to set you down, thinking you're no longer any threat.

Logan forced himself not to react when Monte did just that. He lowered Kenny's body, then let it slide to the floor.

Immediately Logan started talking to keep Monte from looking at the boy. "We figured out the whole operation, from the stealing of our cattle to the way you managed to change our brands. The money from the mine robberies goes to pay Riverton's way for land—"

"Who the hell told you? None of them knew. I'm the only one he had contact with."

Logan smiled.

Monte realized his mistake. "You son of a bitch! You tricked me!"

Logan made a rolling dive for his gun.

Monte's shot sent chips of wood flying. "It ain't gonna do you any good to know. You'll be dead."

Kenny crawled out the door and took off running.

Monte fired again. His bullet splintered the corner of the crate that Logan flung at him.

There was no time to take aim. Logan started to return Monte's fire. His shot went wide. The second sent Monte's gun flying as he screamed, grabbed his wrist and bolted for the door.

Firing from a prone position, Logan aimed his gun over his head in warning. A simultaneous shot sent Monte staggering back inside, where he fell.

For a moment the silence was absolute.

Logan stared in disbelief. Monte lay dead. The one man he needed to link Riverton to the rustlings and the robberies was dead. And he couldn't say a word to Kenny for shooting him.

Only it wasn't Kenny's voice that shouted his name.

It was Conner.

Logan dragged himself to his feet. "Hold your fire, I'm coming out, Conner."

It was over.

The moment he stepped outside, the two boys flung themselves at him, clinging to him. Logan dropped his gun. He cradled the boys against him, but his gaze locked on the woman running toward him, throwing aside her rifle.

"Jessie!"

It was a good thing that the boys were clinging to him, bracing his legs with their own bodies, because she cried out and flung herself into his arms.

"Oh, my Lord, what have they done to you?"

"It's all right, Jess. It's all right."

"No. No. I thought they killed you. The boys... Oh, my love, I wanted to die, too."

He rocked her, burying his face against her shoulder, too spent to talk.

Conner slipped around them and went inside the shack. Ty coaxed Marty to let go and held the little boy while he beckoned Kenny to his side. He took them off a little way to give his brother some privacy. Seeing Conner come back out, Ty waved him over.

It wouldn't have mattered. Logan had eyes for no one but Jessie. Her tears soaked his shirt, but her whispers were less frantic now. And still he held her until the shudders running through both of them stopped.

Very gently he cupped her chin and lifted her head so he could see her face. Wiping the tears with his fingertips, he brought them to his lips.

"I never want to see you cry again," he whispered.

She tried to stem the flow, truly tried, but the tears kept coming as she gazed at his battered face. She longed to touch him, and was afraid to.

"Ah, Jess, what am I gonna do with a woman who won't obey me?"

"I don't know."

He angled his throbbing head and brushed his swollen mouth against hers.

"Guess that's all you're getting in the way of a kiss for now. But I've the rest of the answer to your question, Jessie. Remember last night? You asked who I am. Logan Kincaid of the Rocking K ranch and the man who wants to marry you. Come home with me, Jess."

From the hope that blended with the love glowing in her eyes to her trembling mouth, she was too much of a temptation for him to resist. He needed to bring his lips to hers, needed the sweet, glorious taste of love to chase the moments of death away.

When she broke the kiss to answer yes, he looked up and found a grinning audience of males.

"My brothers, Jess—"

"We've obviously met. The boys—"

"Are ours, no question about that." But he looked at her. "You want them, don't you?"

"I don't think I'm the one to ask. I want the choice to be theirs, Logan."

He wrapped one arm around her waist and walked over to where the group stood. If either of his brothers was impatient to hear what had happened, they hid it well. Logan directed his attention to the boys.

"Jessie has agreed—"

"To marry you. Figures. With all the kissin' you two do. Now she won't be mopin'—"

"Kenny!" Jessie protested.

All bright-eyed innocence, he looked up at her. "Didn't you want him to know how much you missed him?"

"He already knows, thank you."

Logan ignored every pain in his body and hunkered down to talk to the boys. "Before I ask you two a very important question, I need to thank you."

"See? See, I told you, Kenny. I told you he wasn't gonna whop us."

Logan tousled Marty's hair. "For being disobedient you deserve a tanning that won't let you sit for a week. I bet Jessie's gonna find gray hairs come morning for all the worry you caused her. Not to mention that I'm likely to turn white for the scare I've been through. But all that aside, I'm proud of you. Your folks must be watching from heaven and smiling to put the sun to shame to know how you're turning out. There's not a man walking this land that wouldn't be honored if you carried his name."

Marty leaned into him, and Logan hugged him tight. Kenny, however, stood silent, his eyes watching and weighing.

"You're troubled, Kenny?"

"Yeah. Sounds a lot like you're goin' off with Miz Jessie."

"Not just her. That's the important question I've come, no, we've come to ask you and Marty. We want you both to come home with us, to be part of our family."

"You mean that? You'd just take us in—"

"Not just take you in, boy, we want you to be family. Our spread—"

"Guess Marty an' me be acceptin' your offer." Kenny stuck out his hand. "You ain't jus' doin' this 'cause I helped you?"

"No," Logan answered, shaking his hand. "That's a debt I'll never be able to repay. You're a boy full of man-size courage whom I'm proud to call my friend."

Conner cleared his throat and drew Logan's attention.

"Ty'll ride back with you. I'll clean up here. Figure to bring them in to the sheriff."

"Monte confirmed that Riverton's the one who's given him his orders. But with him dead, my word is all we've got."

"And we still don't know who has fed information to him," Ty added.

"Maybe not, but let me show you what I discovered." Logan shifted Marty so he could scratch their brand in the dirt. "Rocking K, right? Now watch how easy it is to make this a Circle R brand."

Logan rose. "One step closer to nailing his hide to the wall. We either catch his men doing it, find the brand or spread the word to anyone that buys from him to—"

"You must have already figured out that Riverton will deny having anything to do with it. He'll say his men acted on their own. There's one sure way of getting him." Conner paused and took a deep breath. This wasn't the way or the place he would have chosen to tell his brothers his plans now that they had come home to stay.

To their credit, they heard him out. Even the boys quietly listened as he told them they would run the ranch without him.

"This is something I've wanted to do and couldn't until you both were ready to assume your rightful places. I never wanted to take over. I never was given a choice."

"But a sheriff, Conner?" There wasn't so much demand in Ty's voice as there was a plea to understand his brother's decision.

"I believe in the law. I've been studying. And I know that if this territory is going to be civilized to where a man can raise his family and keep what is rightfully his, then we need to work within the law. Without it, we'll have more gangs like this one running wild unless there are men willing to uphold the law."

Logan and Ty shared a long, thoughtful look. They had seen their oldest brother in the role of ramrod, protector and law on the Rocking K, but never as a man who had shared his dream with them.

There was a moment of confusion as Ty and Logan acted as one and both offered their hands to Conner, pledging support. Laughter eased the seriousness of the moment, then Logan turned to Jessie.

"How would you feel having a sheriff for a brother-in-law?"

"Logan, please. Let me get used to the idea of having you for a husband before you ask."

"Are you gonna have a badge?" Marty asked, tugging on Conner's pants. "Can I have one, too? Can I?"

Conner scooped him up and held him. "You get the first deputy badge. But first we go home so I can win the election."

"Oh, boy! Kenny, did you hear? Did you? I'm gonna be a dep-uty!"

"Home first," Conner instructed, handing him over to Ty. "And when I pin that badge on, I'll show how to skin a polecat named Riverton and nail his hide to the gate of his Circle R spread."

"Sounds like we got more trouble ahead," Kenny said. "Guess you'll really need me around, won't you?" He looked up at Logan and shyly clasped his hand.

"No guessing about it, son. I'll need you right there. Jess?" He held out his hand to her, and as she took it, he thought of the months he'd ridden the outlaw trail.

"There'll be whispers about me," he told her. "To make it real, I rode with them and stole—"

Her fingertips silenced him. "I love the man I trusted, be he rancher or outlaw."

"That simple?"

"Love, I have recently learned, often is."

Once Jessie had mounted, Ty handed Marty up to her while Kenny settled himself in front of Logan. "Go on. I'll help Conner. We'll meet you down at Jessie's place."

Logan leaned over his saddle and held Ty's gaze with a hard, level one of his own. "Tell Conner that you found the man who ordered Dixie's father's death. Word spreads, Ty. I know you've been looking for a man named Charles who hired a vicious killer who died in Ajo. Word was, a fast gun put him to rest and a kid named Cobie with him.

"You were a maverick, Ty, and Dixie put a brand on you, so you're ready to settle down. Me, I'll look over my shoulder for years to come after riding the outlaw trail with these men. I'd hang up my gun in a minute for the chance to love my Jessie and live in peace.

"You've had your differences with Conner, and Lord knows he can be a hard man. But be fair with him. Let him know how the deck is stacked against him, and who's sitting on his side of the table."

Logan shook his head when Ty started to speak, and touched his heels to the horse's sides, anxious to catch up with Jessie, anxious to leave death behind him.

"How come you didn't tell Jessie that you loved her?"

Logan was caught by surprise at Kenny's question. The boy missed nothing, yet didn't ask about what he'd said to Ty. "You know, son," he said, the word slipping easily off his tongue, "you have the makings of a fine man." He caught sight of Jessie up ahead and called to her.

"Jessie! Our boy Kenny just reminded me that I forgot to say I love you."

"Can't hear you, Logan," she shouted back, laughing as she bent her head and cuddled Marty.

"I said I love you!" he yelled.

"Know something, outlaw? I love you, too!"

*   *   *   *   *